Praise for *Meeti*

"Oft-quoted American scholar and eternal optimist, William Arthur Ward once said, 'The mediocre teacher tells. The good teacher explains. The superior teacher demonstrates. The great teacher inspires.' We have found in *Meetings at the Metaphor Café* a great teacher, Mr. Buscotti. The descriptions of Mr. B's and Ms. Anderson's curriculum is enough to make anyone want to go back to school, re-read old favorites like *To Kill A Mockingbird* or at the very least, listen to some Bruce Springsteen! Every student deserves at least one teacher like this; a teacher who is passionate about the world we live in and determined to light a fire in each child. This debut novel rings with authenticity. This book is a must for anyone looking for a little meaning and a lot of inspiration, whether you are a new teacher or a lifelong student."

-BaBette Davidson, Vice President,
Programming for Public Television –PBS

"If you are an English teacher--particularly American literature--you would want to read this novel right along with your students. *Meetings at the Metaphor Café will* challenge the minds and hearts of teenagers everywhere"

-Bruce Gevirtzman, author of *An Intimate*
Understanding of America's Teenagers

"*Meetings at the Metaphor Cafe* reads like an invitation...an invitation to sit down amongst its characters and relive your youth. With the turn of every page, you are transported back to a time when the world was new to you, sitting among friends, sipping a latte, discussing love and the meaning of things, and discovering life all over again like it was the first time. Along with the characters, the readers are sent on a journey toward rediscovering themselves and reconnecting with what really matters at the heart of who they are. All the while, the book reads like a who's who and what's what of the 20th century. As a teacher, I can say that this book is a MUST read for any high school English or history class. *Meetings at the Metaphor Cafe* should be in the hands of every teenager in America, and those of anyone who once was one!"

-Danielle Galluccio, Trinity Montessori School,
Adolescent Academy Director

"I thoroughly enjoyed this book. Mr. Pacilio inspires the reader to be a better person and gives us faith in our new generation of youth. The take-home messages, however, engage a much wider audience and offer life lessons that build resilience and encourage a positive outlook on life, encouraging both youth and adults to make a difference in our society. This book is a must read for students, educators, and all the people who believe in positive change."

-Michele Einspar, Director, Transformative
Inquiry Design for Effective Schools

Praise for *Midnight Comes to the Metaphor Café*

"Wonderful! "Midnight Comes to the Metaphor Café" was every bit as enjoyable as Robert Pacilio's first work, "Meetings at the Metaphor Café." Robert Pacilio further develops his characters as Maddie, Mickey, Rhia and Pari prepare to face life after high school. It is a sensitive account of the issues, hopes, and fears of young adults preparing to enter the world"

-Debbie Szamus, Class of '85

"The way the book immerses you into the minds of students about to make a tough decision as to what path they will take that will lead them to their future as they make the first decision that is really on their own in terms of going to college."

-Zack Markowitz, Class of '09,
Serving in the Coast Guard

"I read, and re-read, Mr. Pacilio's *Meetings at the Metaphor Café*, so I was ecstatic when I discovered that he had written a sequel. I see so much of myself in each of the main characters in the story that, in a way, their story has become my own. As Mr. Buscotti encouraged our quartet of protagonists to find and follow their North Star, he encouraged me to do the same."

-Caela Provost, University of Limerick, Ireland

"*Midnight Comes to the Metaphor Cafe* is a testament to the possibilities of great teaching and the bounty in mind and spirit it can generate in young people. It is chicken soup for the teacher's soul."

- Mark McWilliams, Michigan Special
Needs Advocate and Law Professor

Praise for *The Restoration*

"Robert Pacilio's aptly named third book, *The Restoration*, does as it says. Set in the romance of the Art Deco styled Village Theater on historical Coronado Island, its characters emerge from the devastation of loss and the hopelessness left by the Vietnam War to new beginnings, unexpectedly. The warmth of the Southern California sun and the strength of the human spirit make it a nourishing and satisfying read."

-Sandra Gonnerman, San Diego County/
Humboldt County Schools Librarian, Retired

Meet Me at Moonlight Beach

Robert Pacilio

This is a work of fiction. All the characters and events portrayed in the novel are either the products of the author's imagination or are used fictitiously with the exception of the actual settings in Encinitas, California: the Pannikin Coffee and Tea, Alfonso's of La Jolla, Las Olas Mexican Cantina, and Vigilucci's Italian Cuisine, the various locals at Mammoth Lakes, and naturally Moonlight Beach.

Pre-publishing technical assistance provided by Michelle Lovi (www.OdysseyPublishing.com.au)

Photography and cover design by Robert Bjorkquist.

ISBN 978-1725702158

Other Works by Robert Pacilio

<u>Novels</u>

Meetings at the Metaphor Café

Midnight Comes to the Metaphor Café

The Restoration

"The Secrets of Generation NeXt": *Listen Magazine*

Whitewash, a readers theater

Seventeen, a play

"La Petite Café at Midnight New Years Eve": *Creative Communications* Top Ten Poems by American Teachers

Dedicated to the memory of Chris Saunders:
He not only reported the truth, he enlightened us all.
He fought for justice for those who needed an advocate.
He was the first person to introduce me as "an author."
To me, he was truly "the Guitar Man."
His legacy as a husband, father, and friend lives on.

Part One

"The only thing worse than being blind is having sight but no vision."

—Helen Keller

Chapter One: 1998

4:00 p.m. The office of Amos Adler, M.D.

Dr. Amos Adler is on the phone with his wife, May. In general, he hates being on the phone, but this is a conversation which especially annoys him. He knows his wife's mantra: *Make yourself clear, Amos. They will understand. And don't leave any doubts, Amos. And remember what you told me you would do. Don't back off on it, Amos. If you do, you will regret it, and I will never hear the end of it.*

"Yes, May. Yes. Yes, I know that, May. I will. Okay. Okay, May. Now, I might be home just a little late. Why? Because like I told you, this is very unorthodox, what I am doin', honey. I am not sure they will agree…Look, I have to go. I'll call before I leave, May. Yes…Yes, I love you. I know it's for the best. Bye."

He disconnects. He takes a deep breath. It is January 20. He is seeing his last two patients. They have been his favorite ones, and they have been the two for whom he has held back on retirement. He feels like he is abandoning them. They have come so far but still have a ways to go. He has asked Lewis Bennett if he can stay after his session while he meets with another patient Noelani Kekoa because of special circumstances; two extraordinary clients who never saw it coming. Not for a second.

Four years ago, Lewis and Noelani came into his office glassy-eyed. The description *shell-shocked* is apropos, even if an anachronism, PTSD being the diagnosis de jour. As a psychiatrist, Dr. Amos Adler thought he had seen it all in his nearly fifty years sitting across from troubled souls. Now he hopes that what he is about to do to these two stubborn, heartbroken people is so unconventional that he is quite certain he would be decried by colleagues. But on this his final day, well, he just doesn't give a damn.

As he sits in his well worn chair, he stares at the two envelopes before him. Then his eyes revert to the gallery of framed pictures of his wife, their children, and his treasured grandchildren. He leans back and clasps his hands behind his head and lets out a sigh. How does one end a career? How does one just separate from the lives he has served for years? How does he retire from his passion, a calling he has followed since graduating from the University of San Francisco in 1955?

Dr. Amos Adler laughs out loud alone in his office at the thought that maybe *he* will have to see a psychiatrist after today.

Chapter Two: 1994

4:15 p.m. The waiting room of Amos Adler, M.D.

Embarrassed, Lewis approaches the window. *Funny, why do we call it a window when there is no outside to the inside?* A young woman in her early twenties with blonde hair that has dark black roots maneuvers her computer's mouse frantically as she bites her lower lip. She squints into the screen. Lewis attempts to speak, despite the fact that the "window" appears shut. He realizes the futility. The young woman applies her burgundy fingernail to the sliding glass—then suddenly, as if she has had a Eureka moment, she holds the finger up. It is a stop sign. Lewis freezes.

The finger tells him simply, "I see you. Now wait." He obeys. Lewis is out of his element. He doesn't want to glance around the waiting room...so he waits. He hopes he is invisible, at least to the people sitting patiently in banal grayish chairs behind him. There are no indications that Christmas is two weeks away. There is no holiday music playing. Lewis realizes that there is no music at all.

Then the burgundy fingernail moves to the crack between the window and the wall and silently glides the glass to the left. The young woman looks up, even as her eyes seem to dart back to the computer screen.

"Can I help you?"

"I have a 4:15 appointment to see Dr. Adler."

"Wait." She rolls her eyes as the phone flashes. She rapidly recites, "This is Dr. Adler's office. Can you hold?" It isn't really a question.

"I'm sorry, it's always busy before Christmas—who are you?"

"Lewis. L-e-w-i-s. Lewis Bennett...I have a 4:00..."

"Okay, sir. I need your insurance card and driver's license. You're here for the first time, right?"

"Um, right."

She scoops up the documents, rolls her chair backward, slaps the documents on the Xerox machine, and pushes herself back to Lewis. She has done this routine hundreds if not thousands of times before.

"There's a ten-dollar copay, Mr. Lewis."

"Bennett. Lewis is my first name."

"Sorry. Lydia, do you have change for a twenty?" The girl working behind her turns, pulls out a drawer, and hands her a ten.

"Dr. Alder's running a little late. He'll call you in." The burgundy fingernail makes contact with the edge of the window, and the glide begins, signaling closure.

Lewis finds a seat, then immediately gets back up to look at the assortment of magazines. None of them interests him. They are silly, gossip magazines. Except for the one *Psychiatry Today.* Lewis worries that picking up that magazine would clearly identify him as a patient as opposed to someone merely waiting for their loved one to be treated by the psychiatrist. He grabs an *Us Weekly* instead. Kris Jenner is on the cover, which blares, "Kris Jenner was simply a mother to the Kardashian-Jenner family." *As opposed to what?* Lewis thinks. "See her shocking story!"

A striking woman enters the waiting room and walks toward the window, her flip-flops *snap, snap, snapping* with each step. Lewis cannot help himself; he peers over the top of the magazine. The woman is wearing black leggings that accentuate her finely toned calves. A gypsyish, long-sleeved, cream-colored top cascades over her shoulders. The top has a jagged hemline that swishes around her thighs. Exotic in appearance, Lewis finds the woman startling in a room in which so much is understated. A large, yellow, cloth bag with bamboo hoops is balanced on her shoulder, serving as her purse, he assumes, although it seems like it has been inflated with something other than the regular accoutrements that women deem necessary. *A workout bag, possibly?* Her jet-black hair is pulled into a tight ponytail. While waiting for the young woman with the burgundy nails to acknowledge her, she turns and glances backward at Lewis. Clothes may make a certain impression of one's age, but Lewis realizes when she sees him that she is older than he expects. *Perhaps mid-thirties,* he thinks. She scans the available seats, then looks back at Lewis and appears to claim the empty seat next to his. Then the window glides open, and the young woman with the burgundy nails starts the check-in routine with her.

Time moves slowly. A UPS man wearing a Santa hat brings in a box. An older woman and a teenage girl emerge from the door that must lead to the back offices. They wordlessly hustle out. It's now 4:30.

The door opens again. A slightly stooped, but extremely tall, black man wearing reading glasses on top of his head smiles and looks right at Lewis. He says softly, "Lewis? Come on back." Lewis delays a moment. Putting the magazine down, he checks his pockets, then slowly strides toward the gentleman he assumes is Dr. Amos Adler. He walks behind the woman waiting at the window, who turns to Dr. Amos Adler and says, "Hi, Doctor. I see you are running a little late. I'm your 5:00. Should I come back at 5:30?"

Dr. Amos Adler smiles reassuringly but seems to whisper, as if all that happens in the waiting room is top secret, "Of course, of course. I'm sorry, Noelani. Yes, 5:30 is fine. I apologize. But you're my last appointment, so we can talk at length. Will that be alright?"

"Okay, great, Doctor." She smiles as she hitches up her overstuffed purse. She pauses, looks at Lewis, and flashes an apologetic smile. "I'm sorry for holding you up."

Lewis breathes a sign of relief. "No, no worries." He returns her smile, and they hold that pose just a few seconds longer than what would be typical. Their eyes ask, *Do we know each other?* Then it breaks off. They both look down. Lewis offers, "If you need to see Dr. Adler now, I can wait. I'm not in any hurry, really."

The woman whom Dr. Adler has referred to as Noelani shakes her head. "No. No. I have—of course not. That's nice of you to offer, but no. I've got a gift to pick up—last minute Christmas stuff, you know."

Lewis volleys, "You sure?"

She nods. She heads to the door, but glances back at him. "But thank you for the offer."

Dr. Adler takes notice. He makes the decision to remain silent through this exchange.

"Please come in, Lewis." As Lewis enters the hallway, with Dr. Adler holding the door open, Lewis cannot help but note that the woman is still rearranging herself before leaving. Lewis mentally takes a picture of her face. He is not sure why. *Her name…Noelani. How unusual.*

* * *

Dr. Amos Adler reminds Lewis of an old grandfather with his gray-white hair and matching goatee, yet he towers over Lewis. A warm handshake. A knowing smile. A twinkle in his eye that seems to say, *Relax. Just sit awhile and tell me what's troubling you.*

Lewis Bennett does exactly that. Nervous and unsure of how to start, he blurts out, "Doctor, I have to say…you are the tallest doctor I've ever met."

Dr. Adler smiles, "I've heard that my whole life, Lewis. My whole life." He then glances over his shoulder to the photo on the wall. "Russ used to call me a 'long drink of water.'"

It hits Lewis that the picture that Dr. Amos Adler is now pointing to is a boyish Dr. Adler and the famous Bill Russell from their college days. They are beaming with pride holding the NCAA Championship Trophy. "Oh, my Goodness, Doc. You must have been on that USF basketball team back in the Fifties!"

"1955 to be exact, Lewis. I was the back up to Bill Russell—and believe me, he was the star and I was the bench warmer. He and KC Jones were amazing. I only got on the court to give Russ a breather. In those days, the NCAA would only allow two black players on the court at any time." Dr. Adler glances back at the photo. "But those were great times, great memories. But I don't want to take all your time." Dr. Adler leans back into his chair, places his reading glasses back on top of his head, and asks, "I've read Dr. Grossman's notes, but tell me a little about yourself. You are a teacher—English, right?"

Lewis is taken off guard. He thinks they should get right down to business. Instead, Lewis feels more like he is in an interview. "Um, yes. Well, mostly journalism. I advise the school's newspaper and teach Freshman English."

"Ah, English was my favorite subject. And I see you are a father."

"Yes. My daughter Hope is seven years old." Lewis leans forward.

"I remember those days well, Lewis." He glances over to his desk, which is adorned with pictures. "My grandchildren keep me and my wife very busy…and very happy. I am sure Hope does the same for you."

"Yes. *She's* the love of my life." Lewis instantly realizes his omission.

"Ah, yes. I see. You and your wife are estranged?"

"Yes. That's partially why I'm here."

Dr. Adler decides it is time to get down to the business at hand. "What brings you to see me, Lewis? What is bothering you?"

"You mean all the anxiety and sleeplessness?"

"Well, those are the symptoms." Dr. Amos Adler looks down at the notes from Lewis' referring doctor. *Panic attacks. Generalized anxiety disorder.* He rubs his goatee before speaking. "But, Lewis, for someone with your diagnosis, I must say, if you *weren't* panicking a little bit when meeting with a psychiatrist, *then* I'd be worried."

He lets the punchline bring a smile to Lewis' face as expected. Lewis beings to understand how this doctor can quickly radiate both confidence and calmness.

Dr. Adler continues, "We will deal with that soon. But what I'd like you to ask yourself is *what triggered it all?* Tell me your story. We have plenty of time. How and when did this anxiety start to dominate your mind?"

Lewis finally leans back, "Well, I am not sure of an exact time…I guess it was gradual. Well, that's not totally accurate. There was one particular night…"

Dr. Adler has tossed him a rope, and Lewis has begun to reach for it.

Chapter Three: 1994

5:30 p.m. The office of Amos Adler, M.D.

Noelani Kekoa drops her bag at her feet and lets her shoulders sag a bit. She takes a breath as Dr. Adler quickly peers down at his notes in her file. At the same time, he gently asks, "Noelani, how are you feeling now? It's been two months since you started on meds?"

"Well, Dr. Adler, I think I feel less anxious. I mean, I am sleeping better. My ex-husband John—he's still on my mind. I mean, you know—John's cheating and his trying to intimidate me with all the divorce issues. But sometimes I just feel the sadness. I guess, I've accepted that I was such a fool. Maybe I am just too naive, or just…whatever." Noelani looks at her hands. Her palms are sweaty. She is still far from feeling comfortable speaking with this particular psychiatrist, despite Dr. Amos Adler's reassurances. It has been a long time since she has been an ongoing patient in the psychiatric world. She decides to do something with her hands, so she pulls her ponytail forward and begins twirling her hair.

"I don't know. When I met John, he seemed perfect for me, you know. Independent. Willing to let me work at the yoga studio—he wasn't pushing me to make more money or have children. He seemed so laid back. But he knew I wanted to get married and, well, we did. I loved him…at least I thought

I loved him, or maybe I just loved the life I had with him and, well, we lived together and…. I don't know anymore, Doctor. I trusted him. I never saw the signs. I mean, John was just so good at lying to me, and I just didn't want to believe he would lead some secret life…or that I was not enough…enough to make him feel happy, satisfied….” She brakes, and frustration forces her to say, “I don't know the words. I just want to stop feeling the way I do.”

Dr. Amos Adler lets her unwind from a tightly knit ball of anger and betrayal. He knows the script all too well. She feels she was sleeping with the enemy. He knows the damage done. His remedy will take time. Noelani's third visit has become her chance to find some equilibrium.

Noelani's fears are palpable. She stops herself to try to not let the tears begin to percolate, but it is futile; her tears quickly overflow their boundaries, and the first drops spill. Her throat begins to tighten, so much so that she can only utter one sentence. “Doctor, I feel like I keep losing my mind.” She reaches for the tissue box she has stuffed into the enormous yellow bag.

Dr. Adler raises one eyebrow, and he glances at the folder next to Noelani's. He opens it and adjusts his glasses, nods, and returns to her.

“Noelani, this is not a matter of ‘losing your mind.’ It is a matter of you feeling abandoned, losing trust. Your mind and your heart work in different directions. You blame yourself. Everyone does. If I had a dollar for every woman—or man— who felt this betrayal, I could have retired years ago with my wife on your Hawaiian Islands.” He smiles.

Noelani's tissues pad her eyes as she nods and allows herself to melt and slightly smile behind the white, dampened tissues. She knows he is right on both counts. Her heart keeps racing no matter what her mind does to counter it. She knows the meds help.

"Noelani, it may seem strange to you, but your feelings of 'I keep losing my mind' come from a lack of confidence and that will go away as you feel more in control. Funny, but at my age, losing *my mind* is par for the course." He grins.

The humor is lost on Noelani. She is far too self-absorbed. "Why does it keep happening to me?"

"Some people cross a line, and the trust is gone. You were frightened, as anyone would be. But you're a fighter. Remember that. It takes time. By then, the meds will have stabilized you more, and the feeling of panic will be eased. It's a process." He pauses. "I was wondering about your father. You've never mentioned him in our visits."

"Oh, well, that's because I never knew him."

"Never?"

"No. All I know is that he was a sailor who got my mother pregnant. He abandoned her. She never talks about him. She only says that he left and that she never told him about me."

Dr. Amos Adler leans forward with his forehead wrinkled. "I'm sorry to hear that, Noelani. Very sorry."

"Yes, it's always been just my mother and me." Noelani fidgets and glances at the clock. "And that's fine with me."

"I see. Well, tell me how the transition to life here in San Diego is going. Is everything starting to settle down?"

Noelani updates him on how she is putting her world back in some semblance of order. She begins to sit more upright, and she leans into the conversation. She has stopped twirling her hair. Energy replaces distress for now. Nevertheless, Noelani knows she has not told her doctor the truth…and doubts she ever can.

Dr. Amos Adler slowly stands and smiles warmly. His deep-set, dark brown eyes may seem tired, but he radiates encouragement. He escorts her into the hallway that leads to the waiting room. "I'll see you next in two weeks, Noelani. You can always reach me if you need to, okay?"

"Okay, Doctor. Thank you so much. I feel much better," she concedes.

Dr. Adler returns to his desk, jots notes in Noelani's file, and places it on top of the one with the name, "Lewis Bennett." He then calls home to tell his wife, May, that he will be a little late for dinner—again.

Chapter Four: 1978

9:00 a.m. The Kekoa home. Maui.

"You're fifteen years old, Noelani! Fifteen. You're a child and behave like *Hupo!*" Noelani's mother, Kalani, can't contain herself. "You went to dance hula, and you tell me you stayed over at Kaleen's. But I call and find out you girls were *not* there last night!"

"Momma, I'm not a fool; we were invited to stay with other friends at their house." Noelani paces behind the kitchen counter.

"You lied, Noelani! Lied. You're lying too much lately. This is the last time. Were boys staying there? And what *friends* are you talking about? Kaleen's mother never saw you. She's as angry as me!"

"Nothing happened, Momma. We stayed at the dance assistant's house," Noelani pleads, knowing that this argument is not going to placate her mother.

Her mother puts her hands on her hips and makes her stand: "I will find out this dance person. You will not do any more hula shows. I won't let you stay at Kaleen's house again—unless her mother calls me. You make me look like a fool. You take your dance lessons, but then you come home right then. And that's it!" She turns and hears her daughter begin to cry, but she does not capitulate. Instead, she reminds her, "You're acting *lolo*, and you're my only child. And if I think we leave this island, then we will stay with your auntie and uncle—then that's what we do."

Noelani's rage overcomes her tears. "What are you saying, Momma? Leave Maui for the mainland because I did *one* thing wrong? I'm sorry I lied, but I swear—I swear, nothing happened."

Kalani turns. "Nothing, hum. Nothing *yet*, you mean. But I think this has been going on for a long time. These older girls—these stupid boys. You want to get pregnant? Is that what you want? Boys see how pretty you are *and how old you look*—they don't care."

Noelani's response rattles out so fast, like bullets spraying the room: "Did *my father* care, Momma? Did he care about you when you were 'a hula girl' and he was a 'sailor boy' with his *fancy* Navy uniform? Momma, you were eighteen when he got you pregnant. Who are you to tell me anything—"

For the first time in her life, Noelani's mother slaps her daughter's face. Slaps her with a force that wounds them both. The emotional gash will be a reminder of the damage done.

This isn't the only time that Noelani has felt the sting of her impertinence. This isn't the only time that her mother has felt misgivings about her own decisions. She knows their financial future is in jeopardy on Maui. A seamstress of her talent is in demand in Los Angeles. Her brother has already made inquiries, and it is just up to Kalani Kekoa to finally decide in which world she and her daughter will dwell.

* * *

9:00 a.m. *The Bennett home. Daly City, California.*

"Lewis, can you explain *why* you are choosing *San Diego State* over *all* the other choices? I thought you wanted to go to Cal

Berkeley?" Lewis' father is baffled. He takes off his Giants hat and rubs his bald head.

"Okay, dad, I haven't told you yet. Yesterday I did get my letter from Berkeley, and they put me on the waitlist. I don't know if I even want to go there. And I just don't know that I want to stay here—in San Francisco. When I visited San Diego with you and mom, I *really* liked it."

"We all did," Linda chimes in as she steps from the kitchen into the den. "But we didn't think you wanted to go so far away."

Lewis sits up on the edge of the ottoman, leaning forward. His red flannel shirt overlaps his jeans. "But I do, Mom. It's not *that* far. And San Diego is just so...*different* from here."

"But what about the other UCs you applied to—UCLA and Santa Cruz?"

"He didn't get into UCLA, Matt," Linda reminds her husband, annoyed because she knows the rejection embarrasses her son.

"Okay, UCLA was probably my first choice, but I didn't really like Santa Cruz. I mean, it was good and all, but—"

"But the beach, the party school," his father interrupts disdainfully. He stands up, slaps his baseball cap on, and paces from the bookcase to his chair. He quickly realizes it is a knee-jerk reaction and not what he intends. He has always respected his oldest son's maturity. "Sorry, I didn't *really* mean that."

"Dad, any school is a party school if that is what you're going there for. That's not me. I like the journalism program, and the PBS studio is on campus. It's a good English and drama school, too."

His son concedes, "Okay, yeah, I want to go to a school where there are beaches, where the water is not ice cold—and maybe I could, I don't know, learn to surf—whatever. I just feel comfortable in So Cal." Like any high school senior, Lewis pleads his case. He pushes his long auburn hair behind his ears. "Look, Santa Clara and the other private colleges are just too expensive. You guys don't want to admit it, but it's true. And Jenn is going to be a junior next year. Then you'll have us both to pay for."

Lewis' parents look at each other. They know San Diego State will be far less costly, unless their son lives at home, which they realize is not practical with the commute time. That is a non-starter for all three; after all, they agree "the college experience" is about leaving home and becoming independent. Nevertheless, talk of money ruffles his father's pride. "Money is not the main issue here, son."

"Your father and I want to talk about this. We know that *you* are the person who has to be happy, and, well, maybe we should all just give it a day or so to settle it. We want you to be sure, *really* sure, that you don't want to wait on Berkeley—or go to Santa Cruz."

"Or leave Northern California," his father chimes in. "Let's give it some time. That's all we ask."

"Okay, but I've mostly made up my mind, guys," Lewis murmurs.

His parents both roll their eyes. His father heads directly to the fridge. He needs a beer. His mother heads to the bathroom. She needs aspirin.

Chapter Five: 1982

3:00 p.m. On the front steps of Lewis' apartment near San Diego State University.

Lewis has been waiting for forty-five minutes. He knows her comings and goings, but once she has disappeared into her cramped, first-floor studio apartment, he has no chance. She's been there for five months, and not once has Lewis seen one guy clinging to her, which he thinks is hard to fathom—unless she's so ridiculously shy that she just never talks to anyone.

At least he knows her name: Lotte. He ponders the strange name *Lotte; is it short for Charlotte—like the web? Who names their daughter that? No wonder she goes by Lotte.* He also knows she is a business major in her junior year. That's all he could get out of her last week. He's tried the "Hi, how are you?" routine and the "Wanna grab some coffee?" line to no avail.

So he waits on the front stoop of their apartment building.

* * *

Most San Diego State girls seem to fit the stereotype: long blonde hair that is rarely natural, tanned from hours at the beach, and extremely social at "Happy Hour," as well as weekly sorority and fraternity parties. In sharp contrast, Lotte's hermitic life matches her modestly well-worn apparel. Not that

Lewis really cares much about girls' wardrobes. Like most twenty-one-year-old seniors, Lewis stirs for what lies underneath the baggy SDSU sweatshirt and the torn-at-the-knees jeans. Lotte's hair is chocolate brown and curly. Her runner's tan reveals toned legs and arms, and to Lewis Bennett, this is merely one reason to be intrigued.

Lotte runs and runs. Every day. Her Sony Walkman is her only companion. Lewis thought about trying to run with her, or at least asking her if that would be okay. But judging from the time he sees her leave to the time he sees her return—all from his third-floor window next to the kitchen—he knows his ego could not withstand the obvious: she would leave him panting on the pavement. Being on the "sports beat" this year for the university's newspaper does not an athlete make.

Finally, she becomes a tiny figure in the distance. Lewis' palms begin to moisten. He has an ace up his sleeve, but he knows that means little if Lotte won't even ante up to the game. She approaches, and it is apparent that she is slowing down, then walking, finally she notices Lewis.

She stops fairly close to him and pulls her curly hair back again so the ponytail is tighter. She is catching her breath. The Walkman has been disconnected.

"Whew."

Lewis thinks, *She speaks!*

"Good run?"

"Great. Started out hot but better now." Her breath is still choppy and her face is flushed, but like many young women, she is not perspiring noticeably. "You locked out?"

"No." Lewis decides it's now or never. "No, I am just sitting here waiting for you."

"What? What did—did I do something wrong? I *did* pay this month's rent, right?"

"Lotte, um, no, no. I'm not a rent collector. I was waiting to ask you something."

"Oh, okay—um, what?" Lewis senses this is *not* going to be easy. There has been no small talk. None of the usual conversation that two college students living two floors apart may have. Lotte is all business.

"Well, you know, I thought about asking you if you wanted a running buddy."

"Yeah…" Lotte shifts her weight to one side and looks askance as young girls are apt to do when they are impatient for a point to be made.

"Okay, well, like, there is no way I could possibly keep up with you."

Lotte laughs. "No, duh."

Lewis understands its implication: *Of course, you can't possibly keep up with me.* But he persists. "So I was wondering if you wanted to see a movie about running? *Chariots of Fire* is playing just down the street, and I heard it's great. You know, a true story about the—"

"Wait, Lewis. Yeah, I know what it's about. But what is *this* about?" She's challenging him.

"Lotte, I'm just asking if you want to go to the movies." Lewis repeats the obvious.

"So, like, on a date?" She is taken off guard by what would be apparent to most young women.

"Um, we could call it that. We could also just call it: 'Lewis asks Lotte if she wants to stop studying and have a nice time eating popcorn and watching other people run—with triumphant music in the background.'"

"Oh, um—I think—well…okay, I guess. Um, I have to tell you something a little embarrassing." Lotte begins to act as if she should stretch her hamstrings out. One leg then the next. Lewis can't help but notice how lovely her legs are.

"Wait," Lewis can't contain himself, "so that's a *yes* on the movie—date thing?"

Lotte takes a big breath and hesitates.

Lewis is befuddled by this adorable, obviously smart girl. Then his mind comes to a dead stop. *Embarrassing? Why?*

"Yes, yes, on the movie date thing, but—" Lotte looks over his head so as not to make eye contact. "I have no money, and I can't pay you back. Well, eventually I can, but—"

"Lotte, we're all poor. It's not a big deal. We'll go to the early show. It's four bucks. We'll sneak in food. Seriously, is that what you are so weird—" he winces as the word comes out and quickly corrects his ill-advised vocabulary, "I mean, nervous about?" He hopes he didn't blow it.

"I know, *weird* is probably the right word. Listen, Lewis, you are nice. I mean, I know you have been giving me hints that you want to get to know me. But you *don't* know me, and if you did, then you would understand why I am the way I am. Okay?"

Lotte then sits beside him. She stares at her shoes. They are old. She wants to hide them.

Lewis breaks the silence. "Okay, look, Lotte. Let's just figure out a time to go and not worry about anything. Money is not even an issue. Let's just go and, and—whatever. I tell you about my boring life, and you can tell me anything or nothing about yours. And thank you—because, because you are—shoot, I'm running off at the mouth. I'm just glad you want to go with me, okay?"

Lotte smiles. Her eyes turn to his. "Thanks for—well, it's just I like to pay my own way and all, but—oh, damn!" She jumps up, breaking the mood. "I just realized I'm supposed to meet somebody in like forty minutes!"

"You need a ride?"

"No, we're meeting at the library. I know, you probably think I'm a nerd."

She heads to her door. But then she turns and says to Lewis, "I'm meeting my boyfriend." She holds the door half open to see his face.

A beat.

"I'm just kidding, Lewis." She shuts the door, smiling coquettishly.

He can hear her laughing in the hallway.

* * *

Lotte licks her Cherry Garcia ice cream cone as she walks toward their apartment building, their shoulders bumping occasionally. She has not laughed this much in a long time. She hasn't let down her guard in so long that she can't remember the last time she did.

"So, you liked the movie?" Lewis asks.

"Yep. And I *love* this ice cream. I have never had Jerry's ice cream."

"Ben and Jerry's."

"Oh, I forgot ol' Ben. I'm going to run an extra mile to work this off." Lotte looks up at Lewis, who, at six feet, has a solid eight inches on her. She likes tall guys—not that her social life allows her to even make choices about men.

"You're not going to have to run, Lotte. You're already very…petite."

"I won't be if you try to fatten me up." She gives him a stern look, then smiles.

"Thank you for the movie and this," she says, holding her cone up reminiscent of the Statue of Liberty. The gesture seems appropriate since she feels the freedom the ice cream cone represents. They reach the steps of their apartment building, where their journey began. "Wanna talk?" Lotte asks as she bites into the crunchy cone. Lewis devoured his blocks ago.

"Sure. Here?" Lewis has already begun to sit on the steps.

Suddenly, Lotte feels bold. She wonders if her self-denial has fueled her actions. "No. Come on, we can talk better in my place…but no judging, okay? It's really occupied by hobbits." A nervous giggle.

Lewis tries to disguise his surprise. Lotte was reserved walking to the movie theater. Throughout the movie, Lotte was quiet. He has never made any overtures that anything more than friendship and company is desired.

Lotte drops down on her raggedy, faded orange couch. Throw blankets conceal the wear and tear. Everything is very neat and organized—but bare. She has scoured Goodwill. Normally, she does not let anyone see her world behind the front door, but something has triggered her to move aside the barricades she has built. Shedding protection is inevitable when one is coming from far down under and aiming for higher ground.

"This is nice. You have privacy—no roommates to deal with," Lewis says, sensing that Lotte is frugal, even by his standards.

"And no space, either—not to mention no TV, a fridge the size of a laundry basket, and carpeting that has…never mind." Lotte realizes she is incriminating herself. She plops the last bit of her cone into her mouth and licks her lips slowly.

Lewis notices. He quickly sits down on the couch but almost has the wind knocked out of him. The source of the rib-jarring push is the rock-hard cushions. "Wow. These could be used," his voice deepens, "as floatation devices in the event of a water landing." He smiles.

Lotte winces. "I know. Kinda hard. It's a sofa bed. I think they always come that way. That's another advantage to my private 'studio'—it's all here, in 420 square feet." She looks away. It's the running shoes. The bare bones. The minimum "assets" she will never let her parents see—not that that would matter. They think she is crazy for getting into debt by going to what they think is an "expensive" university. Why not just stay home, they say, and watch *Happy Days* reruns? Maybe get a job at the grocery store as a checkout girl?

Then Lotte decides that teetering on the precipice is no fun. She never has any fun. She never stops running. Running away from all that can control her, all that can expose her, all that depicts where she hails from and why she pushes her family away. Instead, she wants to jump.

Her mind races, feeling impulsive in that moment. *I don't wanna talk anymore. Talking about what makes me live like this is futile. I want to lean in and kiss him, longer and harder than any boy I've ever kissed. I want the sweet, ice creamy taste that still lingers on my lips to melt into his mouth—my tongue to dart out quickly, its tip to brush against his—*

With little warning, she starts to move toward him, but then, as if a wind has blown a door shut with an ear-bursting slam, Lotte's eyes widen, and she must turn away from Lewis.

"What's the matter, Lotte? I was just joking about the couch. I'm sorry," Lewis says plaintively.

"Lewis, no, no—I'm being stupid. You didn't do anything. It's me. I'm just—a private person. I don't know—I'm weird—whatever." She knows her eyes are tearing up; she tries to look away from him.

"Hey, no worries. I just want to hang out with you. We don't need to talk about anything, you know, personal," Lewis insists. He quickly changes the subject and hops off the couch to lighten the mood and give her space to compose herself. "Hey, is that a baseball glove?"

She looks up. "What? Oh, yeah. Some guy gave it to me because he wants me on his team at school—the 'business softball team' or something. They need a girl. I suck—I told him, but he stuck me with it."

"He was probably flirting is my guess." Lewis tilts his head but does not turn and make eye contact.

"No. I am just a token girl for their league's 'girl rule' crap. It won't work, though."

"Why not? I love baseball." He finally turns to her, relieved she is not crying, though her rosy cheeks stand out.

"I hate baseball. So boring."

"No way! Not if you know the game. Come on, have you ever played?"

"Nope."

"Why? You can't say you've never been asked."

"I can't play because I am left handed."

"Oh, well, that's good. Being a southpaw is great!"

Lotte looks at him quizzically. "A what?"

"Southpaw. It's a baseball term for a lefty. Boy, you need me to take you to a game someday." Lewis smiles and sits back down.

"Um, I don't know about *that*."

"We'll see. Have you ever played catch?"

"No. I *never* had a glove."

"Never?" Suddenly, it hits Lewis—the way she said *never*.

With that, Lotte abruptly stands. Lewis follows, as he feels it necessary. "Thanks for everything today, Lewis. It was fun."

"Yeah, it was. I'm really glad you liked the movie and the ice cream."

"It's the best. Those Ben and Jerry guys…well…bye." She steps toward the door. Opens it. He steps through, turns, and before he can say anything, the door begins to close. Then Lotte pushes it back open and says, "He wasn't flirting with me, Lewis. I know flirting."

"You sure about that?" Lewis leans into the door casing a bit.

"Yeah." And with catlike quickness, she steps forward, brushes her lips against his cheek, and retreats behind the door while making sure he hears, "And I know you are."

The door closes as she leans her shoulder into it, as if girding herself against forces she can barely control. She holds her breath, waits a bit, and hears him walk up the stairs.

Then she walks to her miniature bathroom and lets her eyes release the tears.

* * *

The following morning, a left-handed baseball glove appears on her well-worn doormat.

Chapter Six: 1982

4:30 p.m. Dr. Eva Chan's office. Los Angeles.

Young children often adapt to change quicker than adults, but Noelani's touchdown on the mainland is far bumpier than her mother's. It takes much longer for Kalani's daughter to see any trace of blue sky. This upsets Kalani so much that she, too, can't sleep at night. It is as if the wind is simply not blowing the clouds away for Noelani, even though her name means *heavenly mist*. Many times, her mother cannot tell if that mist is from heaven or the result of demons haunting her daughter.

Noelani's depression began when her mother decided to move them from Maui to LA. Kalani had her reasons—and they were not limited to her daughter's recent behavior. Her finances were a major concern; they were getting poorer by the month. Kalani's career was also limited in Maui; her skills as a seamstress were not in high demand. When her brother contacted her with both a job offer in LA's garment district and a place to stay until she and Noelani could get on their feet, Kalani quickly made up her mind.

However, she badly underestimated how difficult the move would be for Noelani, who faced a new school, new friends, and the feeling of being an intruder in her uncle's home. Downtown LA is a far cry from the salty, laid-back Kapalua beaches. Back home, Kalani knew her daughter was free to walk anywhere, talk to boys—flirt with them, mostly—and breeze into her dance studio knowing she was at the top of her class. In LA, Noelani's world turned upside down.

* * *

Kalani sees that Noelani is so dramatically different; this isn't simple homesickness. "She won't get out of bed. She's not eating. She says, 'I hate school!'" Kalani tells her brother and sister-in-law. "She's this way for too long, too long. I'm scared for her."

They all agree Noelani needs more help than they can provide. So Kalani seeks out counselors and eventually psychologists, trying to stem the tide of her daughter's tears and despair. Little works. Besides the emotional turbulence, Noelani bounces from one dance school to another. She feels the "dagger eyes," as she calls it, from the girls jealous of this new, mysterious dancer. The *new girl* feels alone on her inner-city island. The dance teachers see her talent, but little enjoyment flows in her movement, and they have little time for encouragement.

During her senior year of high school, Noelani comes close to bottoming out when she tells her mother she wants to quit dance. Her grades fall, as well. All she wants to do is sleep. That is when Kalani follows her brother's advice and takes her to see a doctor, who recommends that Noelani be treated by a psychiatrist who can treat her symptoms and determine their causes.

* * *

Dr. Eva Chan's office is as bright and modern as one might expect from a 41-year-old doctor who specializes in teenagers dealing with depression. It helps that she is a mother herself.

Up until now, Noelani has been distant with all other practitioners. Her reluctance has been one barrier; another has been her fear that something is wrong with her and that there is little that she—or anyone—can do to help.

Dr. Chan's waiting room isn't anything like the utilitarian ones Noelani has become accustomed to. It has the ambiance of a salon. The music is light and soothing. Dr. Chan does not have her degrees hanging on the wall, but rather portraits of her family.

Dr. Chan has asked Noelani to come in by herself; Kalani stays in the waiting room. Dr. Chan's first greeting to Noelani is a warm handshake, with a top hand over their clasp. Her smile radiates confidence in herself, but for Noelani, it pulsates an aura of protection and safety, like a warm blanket that one could wrap around oneself to shake off the cold jitters that often accompany anxiety.

Noelani sits on a white leather chair opposite Dr. Chan, who rolls her matching white chair toward Noelani. It becomes apparent that the space between them will be minimal. Dr. Chan gives Noelani a minute to survey the room. There is a single glass bookcase with knickknacks, a picture or two of her daughters at various locales. The books are very different from what Noelani expects to see: *The Joy Luck Club, The Hiding Place, The Princess Bride,* and *Ordinary People.* Dr. Chan's wardrobe even has a flowing lightness to it: a white and pastel sundress that implies openness and gentle serenity. Noelani thinks to herself that Dr. Chan's taste is anything but intimidating. This thought is immediately supported by the way Dr. Chan speaks to Noelani.

"Noelani, it is so nice to meet you. I'm Dr. Chan, but please call me Eva if you wish. If you feel more comfortable calling me *doctor,* so be it. But I am here to help you understand how you are feeling and why you feel this way. So relax. Take a breath. You can even smile." Dr. Chan models each move.

Noelani follows her instructions and closes her eyes, taking a breath, something that dance instructors emphasize. She doesn't smile, though.

Dr. Chan continues, "I have an idea of how nervous you must feel being here, seeing me. You must think something is wrong with you. Well, let me assure you of two things: first, hundreds of young women just like you feel anxious—some depressed. In my fifteen years of working with them, each story is different, but most have similar causes. Okay?"

At this point, Noelani's indifference becomes an asset. She nods. She does not argue.

"You don't sleep well, right, Noelani?"

"I can't get to sleep."

"And then you stay awake for hours, I bet, huh?"

Noelani nods.

"You're sweating. You're worried, right? You don't think this feeling will go away."

"It won't…it doesn't go away."

The tissues are too much to hold in one hand, so the other hand begins to wipe the soft Kleenex into the mascara that begins to slide down Noelani's cheeks. "Dr. Chan, I worry about…worrying. My brain won't stop."

"I know, honey. I know. You are not alone. So many teenagers feel the same way, and they keep it bottled up. You're lucky your mom and your family care so much that they brought you to me."

Dr. Chan's warm voice softens everything she communicates to Noelani. "You're blaming yourself. You think something's wrong with you."

For the first time, Noelani looks directly into Dr. Chan's eyes—not to judge her, but because Dr. Chan has arrived at the crux of the problem. "Isn't there, Doctor? I mean, I try to stop worrying, but the more I think about stopping, the more I don't. Even when I am supposed to be happy—or when I dance, even—the worry is still there. Sometimes it goes away, but only for a day or two—and then it's back. So, I think I must be—I mean, *isn't* there something wrong with me?" Noelani falls back into the white leather chair, exhausted from finally pouring it all out.

Dr. Chan is quick to respond before Noelani's confession begins to harden. "Not really, Noelani. You are experiencing anxiety, but all of this is treatable. Medication will help you get through the harder times and make you ease up on yourself, too. We all have these feelings, but some are more acute and longer lasting, especially for teenagers. Everyone's brain chemistry works differently. But for teenagers, those changes can be dramatic." Dr. Chan makes sure Noelani looks up into her eyes before she implores her, "Trust me. Will you do that?"

Noelani frowns and whispers, "Will I have to take these drugs, like, forever?"

"I can't predict that, Noelani. But we will start with the lowest dosage possible and see if that brings your anxiousness down several notches. It takes a week or so to take effect. But I promise we will monitor it carefully."

"Do other girls my age take…medication?"

"Yes, they do. We will see each other every week for a while until we know you are feeling better. Okay?"

Noelani nods.

"One more thing." Dr. Chan touches her forearm. "My guess is that right now, you feel a little relief."

It is as if the sun suddenly bursts through the morning mist. Noelani asks herself, *How does she know that?*

She accepts the medication Dr. Chan advises without further reservations, partially because she thinks she has nothing to lose, but mostly because Dr. Chan, who at that point insists that Noelani call her Eva, seems to genuinely understand her. It's almost as if she can read her mind.

Noelani smiles. Then she does something uncharacteristic

of most of the teenagers Dr. Chan sees on their first visit. She scoots to the edge of her chair, reaches out with her left arm, and begins to close her eyes. Dr. Chan pivots in her chair, leans forward, and begins to rise out of her seat, pulling Noelani up from out of her doldrums and into her space. It is then that Noelani embraces Dr. Eva Chan and sobs.

Dr. Chan whispers into her ear, "The clouds will begin to break, Noelani. It will take time—weeks, maybe a month or so—but you will see blue sky, sweetheart. You will." She feels Noelani's head nod.

Pulling away so she can make eye contact, Noelani says, "Thank you so much Doctor…Eva."

Dr. Eva Chan closes with this advice: "For now, the best thing you can do is dance. Dance. Noelani, dance your heart out. Because that is where you feel most at home. Trust me."

And that is when Noelani's dance begins anew.

Chapter Seven: 1982

1:00 p.m. A week after their first date. Del Mar Beach.

Lewis and Lotte grab the essentials from his beat-up '76 VW and head to Seagrove Park, above the Del Mar beach. There are people beginning to set up chairs on the far end for the classic beach wedding at sunset. But for now, Lewis and Lotte have a fair amount of turf to call their own. They spread out the blanket and unload the picnic basket, which Lotte rummaged from a thrift shop when Lewis suggested a picnic.

"Hey, do you like Chinese?" Lewis asks as he drops down close to her hip, still wary of her need for "space."

"Nope."

"Really? How come?"

"Do I need a reason, Mr. Journalism?" She wraps her arms around her knees. She is wearing cut-off Levi shorts with white strings hanging down; her shorts cut high up her thigh, revealing enough to make Lewis keep glancing down. It is a perfect spring day in San Diego. Lotte's baby blue V-neck Chargers top, which she also found at a thrift shop, is a compromise between a need for a tan and a need to not look like she is advertising herself.

Lewis has taken all this in, trying to be a witty conversationalist but not gawk at her perfectly toned, petite form. He wears a Padres shirt with three-quarter-length brown sleeves and board shorts that double as a bathing suit.

"Well, I don't know anyone who doesn't like Chinese food."

"Well, I'm the first." She tilts her head at him, knowing that he's going to pursue this and then start in on every other ethnic restaurant. "Okay, look. I worked nights at a Chinese place every weekend for like two years. I smell Chinese and I wanna barf, okay?" *That's that!* she seems to say.

"Okay, then. No on Chinese. Yes on Mexican?"

"Yes, duh. I lived in El Centro, Lewis. We have the best Mexican food."

"Oh, yeah. Where exactly is El Centro?"

"Try the desert. In the summer, we called it 'Hell Centro.'" Lotte takes out the sandwiches and places them on the paper wrappers. "It sucked."

"Oh, okay. I'm getting the picture. Aren't these sandwiches good?"

Lotte nods and tries to say something in mid-chew. Knowing she looks silly, she swallows. "Yeah. Check out the surfers. They are pretty good, too."

"The waves are breaking in nice sets."

"You surf?"

"No. San Francisco is not that great for surfing, and the water is like ice. Some guys are into it, though. I'm a baseball guy." Lewis glances back at Lotte to gauge her reaction.

"But baseball is boring," Lotte complains as she straightens out her legs on the blanket. She knows this will get Lewis' attention.

Staring at her legs, he manages to stay on topic. "How can you say that, Lotte? You've probably never been to a Padres game in your life."

Lotte opens the iced tea. "Um, doesn't it last for like hours and hours? And aren't the Padres terrible?"

"Ah ha! You do know something about baseball! Yes, it is a couple of hours—and yes, the Padres are kinda not good, but—"

"But what? Watching boring losers for hours—um, not exactly an exciting date, Lewis." She removes a pickle from her sandwich. She hates pickles, too.

"You are forgetting the hot dogs, peanuts—beer!"

"Lewis, I'm twenty, and they card people. That much I know."

"Okay, but there is popcorn and really good BBQ. C'mon, if you get bored, we can leave early." Lewis can't admit that he has been addicted to baseball since his dad took him to see the Giants play in Candlestick Park.

"So is this the price I pay to date you?" Lotte is teasing—barely.

"Yeah, I guess so, but it is a small price to pay to be with a charmer like me—don't ya think?" He offers her the pick of the first potato chip from the bag.

Lotte reaches in, snags the biggest one, fakes taking a bite, and instead tosses it at his face. It bounces off his nose and falls to the green grass. Lotte laughs and points at the fallen chip. "Ha, you were supposed to catch that in your mouth, Mr. Baseball! Isn't that what they call an *error*?"

Lewis tosses the chip up in the air and does catch it, or at least most of it, then spits out through the crumbling chip, "When the pitcher throws the ball, one has to catch it." He winks and then parlays his move by taking her shoulders and pretending to tackle her to the grass. But he is met with some slight resistance. "I'm also a football fan, and with that Chargers shirt on, I do want to tackle you."

Lotte coquettishly protests, "What makes you think I would *let* you tackle me?"

"Ah, always playing hard to get."

"Well, if you wanna 'play ball' with me, you gotta play by *my* rules."

Lewis smiles at her. He wants to kiss her, but to his surprise, she leans forward and swiftly kisses him. He lingers with his eyes closed for just a second longer. She notices.

Again the wind blows, but the breeze is softer, calmer. The sky is blue, the grass is green, and the ocean waves are breaking, leaving a long trail of white water coasting to the sand.

Lotte knows that Lewis has stepped up to the plate.

And Lewis knows he has definitely not struck out.

Chapter Eight: 1995

4:00 p.m. Two weeks since their last appointments. The office of Amos Adler, M.D.

Still self-conscious being in a psychiatrist's office, Lewis approaches the window. He tries not to look around the office at the other "patients." The young woman with the colorful fingernails is still there behind the window. She is typing and oblivious to Lewis' pitiful look that pleads, *Will you please look at me so I can get this over with and sit down and hide behind a magazine?* She merely holds up a finger, now painted fire engine red. She again has him paralyzed. He waits…and waits. Another woman comes in with some folders. Fire Engine Red pulls her microphone away and tells her something about getting a ride home. He waits. Despite his need to be under the radar, Lewis looks behind him.

She is there. The woman with the leggings—still black—with the bag that could easily be construed as a bean bag. Lewis tries to recall her name: *Begins with an N…hmm. Hawaiian.* He cannot boot it up.

She does not look up, but he notices that her jet black hair is not pulled back like it was two weeks ago, when he bumped into her before his first appointment with Dr. Amos Adler. Instead, it is in some type of wrap—a bandanna, perhaps. Lewis remembers one thing about her as he turns away, but just as that thought is forming in his mind, a fire engine red fingernail has slid the window back and is tapping against the glass as if to say, *Ahem! You are not paying attention to me, Mister!*

"Yes?"

"Oh, sorry. Lewis Bennett. I have a 4:30 appointment with Dr. Adler…I'm a little early."

"Yes, I see that, Mr. Lewis. Dr. Adler is running a little late."

"Bennett."

"What?"

"It's kinda funny, but you made the same mistake last time I was here. My last name is Bennett, not Lewis." Lewis smiles but is unaware of two things: Fire Engine Red has turned to her computer screen and isn't smiling one bit, but the woman in the black leggings has looked up and is smirking.

"Right. Bennett. Got it. Long day. Anyway, your copay is due. Ten dollars."

"Can I use my VISA?"

A long sigh of despair escapes from Fire Engine Red, as this will necessitate effort from the part of her hand that is not pointing at him. "Ooo-kay. Whatever."

With those pleasantries completed, Lewis must make a decision: where to sit? He could sit by the morose teenager. *No.* Near the woman with the two kids who are complaining about how long it takes for their sibling to get "outta there." *Definitely not.* There is an empty chair next to the strikingly beautiful woman with the black leggings whose name begins with an N. *No. Besides, the bean bag takes up too much space.* He compromises and sits one chair away from her, but then immediately rises up again to get a magazine. *Us Weekly* features "the newest hit movies of the summer" and "the hottest, steamiest sex scenes" to come. He sits back down with *Us Weekly.* He glances at her. He wants to say something like "Hello" or "Funny bumping into you—what's the chance of that?" *No.* He clears his throat.

She turns toward him, saying, "Sorry, my bag is in the way. Let me move it."

"No. No. It's not. I'm fine. It is a big bag, though," he says. "As bags go. I think I remember it—and you—from last week." He smiles.

She smiles back. "Um, yeah. Kind of silly I suppose…but it's all my stuff. And I remember you, too. You were very nice. Did you have a nice Christmas, um,… holiday?"

"Oh, yes. Thanks for asking. You?"

"Yep, had to work a bit more than I wanted to but it was nice." She looks back at her magazine. "Lewis, right? Not Bennett?" She winks, indicating that they are now co-conspirators dealing with Fire Engine Red.

Lewis replies, "Yes, Lewis. But I shouldn't be too judgmental because I can only remember that your first name begins with an N." Again, he winces. *God, I hope she doesn't think I am an idiot.*

Noelani shakes her head. "My name is very unusual. It's Noelani."

"Noelani." Lewis whispers it louder than he intended, like it was something on the tip of his tongue for a long time and it finally jumped out like a frog on a lily pad. "I've been trying to remember it when I saw you here. Anyway, hi—again."

"Hello."

Lewis wants to say something else, but just then, the door opens, and a black teenage boy, head tucked into his dark gray hoodie, exits. Lewis notices that he rubs his nose with his far too long sleeve. The boy's father is waiting outside the office, near the large window. Dr. Amos Adler looks at Lewis and Noelani and whispers, "Very sorry—I just need a minute." He follows the boy, steps outside, and speaks to the father. Lewis and Noelani—and the entire roomful of people, even Fire Engine Red—look out the office's window. The father, dressed in a three-piece tan suit, nods and firmly shakes hands with the doctor. His son seems to shrink in their presence, but the father puts an arm around him and nods at him as well. The boy's head pokes out from the hoodie, and his eyes meet his father's. The boy nods at his doctor, and they turn away to head down the stairs. Dr. Amos Adler watches for a second or two, straightens up, pushes his reading glasses to the top of his head, and pivots toward the door.

He steps in and says to Noelani, "Please come on back, Noelani." Then to Lewis, he adds, "Very sorry, Lewis. Couldn't be helped. Can you wait, or do you wish to reschedule?" He strokes his goatee.

Noelani looks back from the door she has opened and gazes directly at Lewis. With a flick of her hand, she waves to him.

Lewis immediately says, "No problem, Doc. I'm fine."

"Good. I want to talk with you." Dr. Adler follows Noelani into his office.

Lewis thinks, *Noelani. Now that is a name I have to remember.* He thumbs through the magazine, not really looking at it. Then he realizes it is upside down.

Fire Engine Red sees this and rolls her eyes.

Lewis' eyes linger on the door as he wonders what Noelani's troubles could be. After seeing the miserable teenage boy and his concerned father, Lewis cannot help but feel lucky as his mind's eye pictures Hope.

Chapter Nine: 1982

10:00 a.m. The Kekoas' first day in their own home. Downtown Los Angeles.

"This is a big thing for us, Noelani," Kalani tells her daughter, who is unpacking her boxes of clothes. "Finally, our own home."

"Yeah, but I have to audition in an hour. Oh, shoot—where are my jazz shoes?" Noelani frantically glances around her bedroom, the first room on the mainland that she does not have to share.

"There—in the box at the bottom of this pile." Kalani moves around the boxes to reach the one her daughter needs. She knows today is more than just moving day; it is Noelani's chance to be accepted into a new dance company with a well-known director who has just come out of retirement. Noelani has heard that the company will have a contemporary emphasis. Kalani senses that Noelani is both excited and nervous, for today's audition at the Fourth Street Dance Studio has the potential to make Noelani's dreams come to fruition.

As mother and daughter continue to unpack Noelani's boxes, they listen to IZ sing "I Am Hawaii" and are reminded of Maui. For both of them, becoming acclimated to life in Southern California has been a culture shock. The Hawaiian way of life—its music, food, traditions—disappeared into the urban rhythm of Los Angeles. The sweet fragrance of island flowers and the slow, patient flow of life on Maui dissipate into LA's hazy smog and faster pace of life.

Nevertheless, the City of Angels provides Kalani with a number of welcome opportunities. As a master seamstress, Kalani sees that LA has a carefree, sunny fashion vibe that makes it the ideal setting to launch her own line of Hawaiian clothing. As Kalani works to build up her clientele, the theater district's need for skilled seamstresses keeps her afloat financially. All together, Kalani's hard work and impressive list of boutiques that routinely demand her latest floral designs has materialized financially into a condo that she and Noelani can call their own.

Good fortune has also blown its way to Noelani. Two months ago, her anxiety began to scatter, just as Dr. Eva Chan predicted. The medication lifts Noelani's mood, and the sky above her begins to lighten like a new day over Maui, bright and rosy in hue. Then, unexpectedly, a fellow dancer tells her that a new dance company on Fourth Street is going to hold open auditions. Noelani asks around and learns that the company's director had a reputation for being warm and encouraging. To Noelani, this is a far cry from the stern, conservative dance teachers Noelani often faces. Noelani hopes that today, her body, as well as her spirit, will soar over the hardwood floors of the Fourth Street Dance Studio.

* * *

11:00 a.m. The Fourth Street Dance Studio. Downtown Los Angeles.

It takes Dee fewer than five minutes to understand the talent that glides before her.

"Noel, girl, you got it, sweets!" Dee's voice rings out loud and clear at Noelani's audition. "You do. You just got to let that Hawaiian mojo rattle your bones!" As Noelani sweeps across the floor, Dee gushes, "You're taking my breath away, girl!"

Dee Gates is a self-described "vintage" dancer. At sixty-three years young, Dee is a petite African American woman with expressive eyes that transfix her students. She is barefoot, as she typically is when at the studio. Dee wears an African-style top that runs from neck to knees, forest green with black embroidery. Her cream-colored leggings accentuate her dark brown ankles and feet. Dee's afro is held back by a gold kerchief, and she wears wooden hoop earrings. Her appearance belies her age, and as she watches Noelani dance, Dee is reminded of her youth.

* * *

Dee Turner and Henry Gates were high school sweethearts who met at University High School in West LA in the early 1940s. Dee wore Henry's letterman sweater, and Henry attended all of Dee's dance recitals. They wed right after high school graduation, and Henry was shipped off to the Army in 1942. The Army figured out that Henry had a knack for fixing anything mechanical, so he was assigned to the "fix whatever shit was broken" division, as he and his fellow soldiers called it. He never shot a gun, never saw action, and never failed to write Dee each week. When he came home, his skills served him well. He opened his own business in West Los Angeles as a general handyman but soon became a master plumber.

Meanwhile, Dee furthered her dance studies and made ends meet waitressing at night. Her dream to become a professional dancer was limited by the color of her skin. Even the great Jackie Robinson's breakthrough in Brooklyn with the Dodgers wasn't opening doors three thousand miles away in Los Angeles.

Dee and Henry were frugal and financially astute, buying

a home two years after Henry returned from the war. In the 1950s, they welcomed twin girls, who grew fast and studied hard under the tutelage of Dee, who by that time had transitioned into the career of teaching dance.

She and two business partners opened a dance studio in the 1960s, and business flourished as America embraced the new African-American sounds flowing from Detroit. The music of Motown became the soundtrack of Henry's and Dee's marriage. Dee could always cajole Henry onto the dance floor with her as soon as she heard the Temptations sing "My Girl."

Dee and Henry saw their fair share of struggle, poverty, and all the ills that went along with racial discrimination. The LA riots that followed Martin Luther King's assassination made a lasting impact on them both. But they loved Los Angeles. Henry's handiwork and Dee's good taste transformed their home that was built in the Fifties from a fixer-upper into the pride of the neighborhood. As their businesses grew, so did their relationships with community members. The Gates family helped to secure their neighborhood and its children at a time when Southern California needed stability the most: in the early 1980s, when gangs and the drug epidemic were on the rise.

In 1980, Dee and her business partners finally closed the studio they founded decades ago. Her partners longed for the "golden" years of retirement; however, at sixty-one, that "gold" was not the honey that Dee found desirable. One year of retirement soon brought a degree of loneliness for her. Her two grown daughters were both living on the East Coast, and neither had provided grandchildren yet. Their New York and Washington, DC, homes made visits few and far between, and Dee and Henry found the cross-country trip more than they could handle. Nevertheless, Dee remained a dynamo, as Henry thoroughly understood.

* * *

Henry Gates, one year older than Dee, is stocky and sturdy. Even at his age, his forearms are thick. No one would dare challenge him to an arm wrestling contest, lest they have their wrist twisted into a pretzel. Henry has a trade that transcends retirement. A master plumber is always working. He is by nature a "tinkerer," always fixing all sorts of mechanical things. At this stage of life, he never charges his friends, except for the occasional beer, which he shares with them at Dodgers games. Henry figures work keeps him busy, and it feels like he's doing God's work now, paying others back for the good fortune that he and his wife have had all these years.

Henry can be best described as a man who rarely stands still. He jokes that if he did, rigor mortis would set in after an hour, so Dee would have to bury him pronto. He is proud of his daughters and hopeful that things will stay just the way they are, except he prays for grandchildren before he "kicks the bucket." Otherwise, the man abhors too much change.

Little bothers him—except, of course, one nagging issue: Dee.

Henry doesn't like her attitude when she "retired." He knows his wife is a teacher to her core. She loves kids and misses them frolicking around on the dance floors. Henry can see the writing on the chalkboard. Like a bee, Dee is ready to sting. She has so much "pepper," he says, that she just has to "sneeze it out." He has a hunch what Dee has in mind.

Thus, within a year of closing up shop and parting ways with her business partners, Dee began to search for a new studio, a small one that Henry could "fix up." She finally finds her new nest on Fourth Street, and Henry receives a list of to-do's. As Dee reestablishes herself as a business owner, she welcomes a sea of fresh faces into her world. One such face belongs to a lissome Hawaiian young dancer named Noelani.

* * *

5:00 p.m. The Kekoas' home. Downtown Los Angeles.

For Noelani Kekoa, the horizon glows a glorious yellow, even amidst the smoky gray sky hovering over the City of Angels. When the name *Noel Kekoa* appears on the top line of Dee's chalkboard, Noelani runs to her new home and gushes to her mother, "Dee put me at the top of her list of dancers at the auditions! She knows people, Momma! And let's hope—"

"Dance is your gift, Noelani. Dee sees it. She understands you. You stick with her. I have no worries about cost. We got enough money for once," Kalani insists.

For a young woman barely in her twenties, hope is adrenaline.

So *Noelani* becomes *Noel* for the time being.

Chapter Ten: 1982

*9:00 a.m. Three weeks after their first in a series of dates.
Lewis' apartment.*

A note is taped to Lewis' door. It reads:

> *Lewis ~*
>   *Gonna make chili and cornbread tomorrow. Wanna come
> down for dinner?*
>   *~ Lotte*

* * *

"Wow, this is really good, Lotte." Lewis finishes his second
helping of chili and his third piece of cornbread, which has
butter melting over the crunchy top. "I mean, seriously."

Lotte watches him wolf down the last of the cornbread.
She smiles. She has been cooking for her family for as long as
she can remember. At first, her mother, Carol, would give her
instructions for simple meals like spaghetti, but as Lotte got
older, she just told her what to cook. Her mother didn't get
home until 7:00 on most days, and her father, Ed, was useless
in the kitchen—or he made sure it appeared that way. Being
the oldest girl, Lotte had to bear the burden of cooking, and
until recently, didn't think it was unfair. After all, her mother

was part of a cleaning service, and she came home exhausted, and her father, being a mailman, was on his feet all day. Was it too much to ask for her to do her "motherly" duty?

Unfortunately, Lotte's sister, Katie, five years her junior, always made excuses for why she couldn't help in the kitchen. She seemed to inherit her daddy's ability to not be around or else stumble through the most mundane chores, such that Lotte would often just grab the potato and peel the "damn thing" herself. Their brother, Tommy, was always out playing sports that never seemed to go out of season.

But all this is not to be shared at a dinner table with Lewis—or with anyone: girlfriends, relatives, and most certainly not other guys she dated. It remains her secret world.

Lewis, however, as an aspiring journalist, cannot hide his curiosity. "So, um, did your mom teach you how to cook? I mean, did you cook with her in the kitchen?"

"Some."

"I bet it's a big deal at Thanksgiving, huh?"

"Not really."

"Really? I mean, in my family, it's a big deal, you know… the turkey, the gravy, the stuffing. And my dad makes, believe it or not, *pies*—like, from scratch." Lewis' reminiscing seems to make little impression on Lotte.

"That's nice. Ours is…um, low key." Lotte wants cooking to disappear from the interrogation. "I'm glad you liked the chili."

"Come on, Lotte. We can't just talk about the weather or cooking or other trivial stuff." Lewis picks up their plates and walks to the sink; he begins washing the dishes.

"Um, what are you doing?" Lotte stands next to him, trying to scoot him away from the sink.

"What does it look like? I always wash the dishes at my house, and as your guest, it's the least I can do. Besides, you're being so quiet, I need to do *something*—otherwise, I feel like I am just blabbing along."

"I told you, Lewis, I am not—well, I'm private about things," Lotte stammers.

"What are you *not* 'private' about? I mean, seriously, I told you about my mom and dad and living in the Bay Area. I told you what I think I want to do when I graduate and stuff." He starts drying the dishes. "Where does this plate go?"

"In my hands. I'll put it away later," Lotte insists.

"Okay, so…what's the story behind the cute girl I am definitely flirting with three floors down?"

"Boy, I guess you're gonna be a good reporter. Why does it matter about my parents or my family?" Lotte puts up a shield, figuring the best defense is a good offense. "I mean, it's nice you have great parents and a really nice home and all. But, that's not—" She stops.

Lewis picks up the thread, "That's not your story."

A beat.

Lewis treads carefully. "Lotte, I just want to get to know you better. I'm not, like, judging you or anything. So what if things were different for you? As a matter of fact, I like the Lotte who just cooked me that awesome dinner. I don't give a crap if your parents aren't perfect. I mean, mine can be a pain in the ass sometimes."

"Oh, I'm sure that's not true."

"Yes, it is. They didn't want me to go to San Diego State. 'It's a *party* school.' That's what they insisted."

"Yeah, well, they're right."

Lewis tries not to show his frustration, but he cannot help himself. "You know what? You're just changing the subject."

Lotte's last line of defense: feign ignorance. "What is the subject?"

Lewis rolls his eyes and tosses the dishtowel down. "Never mind, I give up. I'm just gonna say that I think you are a very special person, and I think you don't want me—or maybe anyone—to know how special you are."

Lotte lowers her shield to at least peek over it at him. "That's not true. It's just—I'm not that special. I'm not anything remotely special. I am as ordinary as…white bread. And that was about all we had in our house…" Her final words trail off, as if she's singing a song that is about to fade away on the record player.

Lewis hears a sound: a small crack in her shield. Lotte finds herself falling into her own truth.

* * *

By the time she finishes, it is well past midnight. The tissue box is empty. Lotte's eyes are red, and Lewis is holding onto her for dear life.

"So, your brother, Tom, is married to Cindy, and they have a kid?"

"Two kids, and she is probably pregnant again."

Lewis tries to wrap his head around her brother's situation. "He's twenty-two and working at Jack in the Box, right?" Lewis' eyebrows are raised, as if they are trying to suspend Tom's financial reality.

"Yeah. And Katie bailed on school and is boy crazy and dates guys who are jerks." She takes a breath to continue the list. "That doesn't seem to matter to her as long as she has a boyfriend. She's freaking terrified of being alone and having no money. She works at Walmart, and I guess that's all she wants. I mean, they are just so—so 'whatever happens, happens. I just wanna be happy.' And 'happy' to them is kids and TV and driving to the beach to camp on holidays."

Lotte has rambled past her tearful, angry diatribe on why she's paradoxically angry at but loyal to her lackadaisical family. She proceeds to the denouement of her discontent. "Since I want more than to live in a *fast food, daycare, desert* type of world—that's insulting to them. I'm, like, beyond their comprehension. I'm a freak. Why not just find a guy, get married, have kids, and just be okay with it all?"

"Your parents—they're not okay with what you want? I mean, really?" Lewis shifts so that his arm, which has been wrapped around her shoulders for the last hour, gets some feeling back and the tingling mitigates. He patiently hears Lotte's confession, as her layers of self-protection slip away like some baked-on crust in a frying pan that required soaking. Nevertheless, the stains on the surface can never be scrubbed away.

"My parents are sweet and naive, Lewis. I know they love me. So do my brother and sister. But they think I'm nuts. They are so simpleminded—or maybe so laid back—that sometimes I think they are asleep to the world. They make me want to scream sometimes. They are so afraid to get out of their comfort zone. Like I said, my parents were so confused when I said I applied to big time universities. They were like, 'Why not just go to community college?' And I just looked at them like, 'Shit, why'd I even bother getting a 3.9 GPA? Why did I take the hardest classes?'"

Lewis returns his arm to its original position; but this time, he pulls her tighter to him.

"Anyway, they told me that they would pay for books, but that was all they could afford. Even that—buying my freakin' books—was something they complained about so much that I finally just said, 'Fine, forget it. I don't need your money.' So I was on my own if I moved out and went to a real college. SDSU was the best I could afford." Lotte came to a dead stop. "And now you know the rest."

She leans into him, slowly at first. Then she shifts her weight and shimmies closer. Eventually, his chest presses against hers.

Lewis decides that he will follow her lead. He knows how vulnerable Lotte is at this moment.

Again, as is her way, she takes him off guard. Her passion is rising faster, and she knows she cannot stop herself—nor does she want to. Every movement between them accelerates at a pace that takes their breath away.

They are pressed together so much that one of them must give in and fall back into the hard, firm couch. Lewis reclines. Lotte climbs onto him, shedding her t-shirt, unbuttoning his, and all the while kissing him deeply. She unwraps her hair out of its tight ponytail; her curly hair cascades around his face like a waterfall. She is fierce.

Lewis pulls away for a moment and says, "Are you sure? Are we…safe?"

Lotte pushes off his chest so her back is arched, reaches behind her, and unsnaps her bra. She nods vigorously and whispers into his ear, "Yes, Lewis. Don't stop." She leads their dance to the music's crescendo, leaving them breathless.

Chapter Eleven: 1995

4:30 p.m. The Office of Dr. Amos Adler

Noelani has just looked back at a man Dr. Adler has called *Lewis,* asking him to wait, if possible. This handsome man, whom she has spoken to briefly, seems cordial and accepts the delay. Noelani catches his eye and mouths, *Sorry.* He looks at both her and Dr. Adler and says, "I'm fine."

Their smiles flicker, hers then his. Then she scurries down the hallway and into Dr. Adler's office.

She sits and drops her ever present, enormous yellow bag. Before she can say anything, Dr. Adler speaks: "Again, I apologize. I have known that boy's family for years, and, well, the situation was complicated and I needed to also speak with his father. Okay, now," he drops his glasses down to the tip of his nose, quickly scans Noelani's chart, then continues, "how have you been feeling since…hmm…a two weeks ago? The holidays are a tough time for some."

Noelani takes a breath and nervously begins her ritual of twisting her hair. "Well, better. I think. A little. I know we talked about this when I first came to you—about my ex husband, John, and his affairs, but what bothers me still is how he—anyone—can lead such a secret life and think they can get away with it."

Dr. Adler reassures her: "Noelani, don't beat yourself up.

John's actions don't reflect on you." Normally a listener, he decides to recap the pivot points that brought her to him. "Remember when I first saw you, and I had spoken earlier with Eva Chan—Dr. Chan—whom you had seen for years?"

"Yes. I think I was sixteen when I started seeing her. Yes."

"And remember how worried you were to see me—the new, old guy?" he smiles warmly as he smoothes out his salt and pepper goatee. "I will never forget the look on your face when I told you why Dr. Chan recommended me—that *I was Eva Chan's mentor* back when my wife and I lived in Los Angeles. You looked at me, and your eyes just popped, like you couldn't believe your good fortune—because for so many years, Dr. Chan was so supportive. Am I right?"

Noelani can't help but smile, remembering what she thought back then: *This old, extremely tall, black man is who Eva recommends now that I'm living in San Diego?* And now, years later, Dr. Chan is still looking after her. "Absolutely, Dr. Adler—and you are not 'an old guy.'"

He laughs a bit louder than she expects. "Oh, yes, I am. See my grandkids here?" He points to an arrangement of pictures on his desk. "Anyway, my point is that there are two things that I know about you, Noelani. First, like most people who occasionally have ups and downs with depression, it came over you in your early teens—and for a good reason, leaving your home—we know all that. But what I have not told you—and I'm sure Dr. Chan reminded you of this back then—you are gifted with something that many women wish they could have: beauty."

Noelani feels uncomfortable. It is not faux humility; it is the realization that Dr. Amos Adler's diagnosis has landed right on the target's bull's-eye.

He releases his arrow. "However, your natural beauty, matched with your innocence, has left you the victim of two men who have damaged you—badly. Their betrayals have led directly to your anger, and ultimately, you have blamed yourself. You must understand that some men will use you, marry you, and deceive you—because to them, you are a possession. Both your ex-husband John and that other boyfriend—"

"Michael."

"Yes, him. Those guys are users, Noelani, and I know you know that. You can't blame yourself."

"Yes, I know. Well, maybe I don't *know*, but I am starting to finally open my eyes to this—this *thing* I do. I want—I need—*stability*, and I know—I know other people can't hold me up."

Dr. Adler leans forward. "Yes. And when they abuse you and your trust, you become like a tree that has grown roots just deep enough to hold you up: you bend. But here is my point: you do not break. I know you want the wind to stop— your mind to stop worrying—and it will. Some days it may blow stronger and some days, it's as calm as can be. You need to trust your power to stand up to the wind. What term do they use in yoga? Warrior. You are a warrior."

Noelani feels the urge to speak the truth to her doctor, so she begins to feel out what that will taste like: "Okay. Thank you, Doctor. I always like when you remind me that I am stronger than I think. But let me just say that—sorry, but I have to get this out of my head—how could John think I would never know? And how could I have been so naive? I mean, thank God for my business partner, Lisa. Lisa's husband Phillip saw John at that conference and figured out what he was doing at all these sales shows. I mean, he found out that the sexual affairs had been going on for *years*. Lucky for me, it was always out of town, so I wasn't walking around town having women look at me like I'm some pathetic woman who doesn't know her marriage is a farce." She pauses to look away from him and get a hold of her emotions. All of this leads to a point of no return. *Can I tell him what really happened?*

"Anyway, Lisa told me that Phillip confronted one of the women John had been sleeping with and told her that John was a married man. Then she told Phillip that *she was married, too*. And then she told him that John and many other people 'on the sales circuit' have these secret sex lives. Apparently, they act like it's 'just part of the business.'"

Dr. Amos Adler lets her unload her baggage, but then she approaches the finale.

"And then John got caught, and lied, and… got really mad." She pauses, realizing what she is saying to him. An alarm goes off, warning her. Her heart starts pounding. She feels some beads of sweat escape around the crown of her head as the truth begins to fall from her lips. She exhales. "And he lied to my face and said it was the first time. And I told him what I knew about his bragging about 'a woman in lots of cities' crap. And then John stupidly told me, 'Well, everyone is married—like, the women, too.' And he thought that made it right!" Noelani knows her voice is getting louder as her anger rises. Suddenly, the alarm becomes so loud that it drowns out her voice. There is a ringing in her ears. Noelani knows the perspiration has spread to her entire body; she can feel her clothes sticking to her. She takes a full minute to compose herself. *I can't tell him. I just can't.* She inhales the words she is about to say and instead she whispers, "I'm sorry for going on, Doctor. I swear I'm never going to be so naive again."

Dr. Amos Adler has witnessed this scene hundreds of times. He nods patiently. He has noticed the abrupt about-face in her monologue and her anxiety is on full display. Calmly, he says, "This is the first crucial step, Noelani. Let the wounds heal. It will take time. But I want you to think about something very important: trust. I know you have put up walls now—to men, in particular—for protection. It's understandable, but don't let those walls trap you. A time will come when you will want someone to share your life with, and those walls can't be so high that no one can scale them. Just keep that in mind, okay?"

She nods reluctantly.

He glances at the clock. "We will take things slowly. Keep up with the meds. We can talk about reducing them when you feel more balanced. Let's stretch things out, though. How about three weeks until your next appointment?"

Noelani jumps up, worried that she has taken up too much of his time. She knows she is worked up, but she also feels that relief she has always experienced once she has seen Dr. Adler. She tries to quickly put her face back together. Tissues pad the damage. Her inner alarm bell is quieting; its cause recedes, much like the lump in her throat.

Dr. Adler patiently reminds her to call him if she has any problems. They walk down the hall, and she thanks him. He gently takes her hand, saying, "Three weeks, now. Talk to the girls in the office, okay?"

The door opens, and Noelani spots that Lewis fellow—who appears to be nodding off.

Dr. Amos Adler says sympathetically, "Lewis, sorry—come on back."

Lewis stands, shuffles past the doctor, and heads down the hallway. But before he can get far, he hears Noelani say, "Oh, no." She reappears in the hall, and the two brush past each other. Noelani looks at Lewis, her eyes pleading for forgiveness. "I'm so sorry—can you believe I left my bag?"

Lewis grins. "Not sure how you could have forgotten it."

"I know, right?" She tries to squeeze by again, but the bag creates a sticking point. "Oops. God, I have to get—"

Lewis cuts her off. "No worries. I'm sure everything in there is just what you need."

Fire Engine Red pops her head out of the window and says, "Miss, I'm off in five. If you want to make an appointment, it's now or you'll have to call."

Noelani looks back at Lewis. They both roll their eyes again.

Lewis asks Noelani, "Can you make my appointment after yours? This time works for me, and she'll be gone when I get out." Lewis nods toward Fire Engine Red.

Noelani smiles knowingly. "Of course. Lewis, right?"

"Lewis Bennett. Yep. Thanks."

"Okay. I'll have her leave a reminder card on the window." Noelani heads to the window, glances back at Lewis, then hefts her huge bag back on her shoulder.

* * *

Dr. Adler watches them patiently and smoothes his goatee. He muses: *How much baggage human beings carry.*

Chapter Twelve: 1986

Noon. Saint John the Evangelist Catholic Church. Encinitas, California.

Lewis' baptism and confirmation compel him to exchange wedding vows in a Catholic church. That and the fact that the wedding is paid for mostly by his parents, with a modest contribution from the bride and groom.

Lotte's parents pay for the flowers. They feel guilty, naturally; however, that is all they can afford. Even so, all the bouquets and arrangements are more than they expected.

Lotte fought the "embarrassment wars" for years, ever since the day she got on a bus and headed to college, worked night shifts during the school year, and then tossed her life into the cauldron of corporate America each summer and every semester break.

Stubborn is a quality she writes on employment applications. She makes it clear she is determined to do the job right, at all costs. This pleases potential employers, who say, "You're hired!" She is never fired. She just moves onward, and for the longest time, slightly upward.

Lotte does not feel any ill will toward Lewis' parents for ponying up the money for the wedding. On the contrary, that is part of the allure. Lewis' parents juxtaposed to hers could have fit the plotline of any 1980s sitcom: *Unambitious, uned-*

ucated homebodies, satisfied with the simple life—playing with their grandchildren while watching TV every night—meet well read, intellectual somebodies who invest time, money, and energy to serve others.

After all, how can a father who has been a mailman all his life and a mother who sporadically cleans houses measure up to a father who is an environmental attorney and a mother who works for the Board of Education? How can El Cajon ever compare to the Santa Rosa wine country? Lotte does not want to feel this cruel juxtaposition; she hates herself for bitching about her past and her family. She knows she has to be the bigger person and take the high road, but when one's ambitions are ridiculed and the road is so rutted, it's easy to become bitter. On this day, with Lewis at her side, she promises to let the past be the past and move on to her idea of greener pastures.

* * *

What Lotte does not see—but Lewis knows from the start—is that despite the stark differences between their parents, both sets have one critical thing in common: they love each other more than any job, any amount of money, and any material possessions.

Lewis' parents cannot be more understated about all the wedding to-do's. They figure this is their son's wedding to a lovely, devoted young woman who makes their son happy. What more can a parent ask for?

Lotte's parents cannot be more understanding of the fact that this is the most important day of their daughter's young life. They adore Lewis and know he doesn't have a trace of snootiness in him; he is as modest and as charming as any groom. What more can a parent ask for?

* * *

They both hear the priest speak of *love and honor.*

Lewis remembers that night on Moonlight Beach. He was the first to say, *I love you.* She waited for him to commit before uttering those words.

Marriage seemed to be inevitable. They dated. They lived together. They knew each other's history. They saw each other's faults. They had a plan for where they wanted to live and what they wanted to do professionally. As for having children, Lotte made it clear that they had a long way to go before they would be settled enough to prepare a nest. "It will take us both quite a while to get on firmer ground financially," she claimed.

Lewis and Lotte, in their early twenties. One hot, one cold. One with passion, one with ambition.

The priest reminds them, *From this day forward...* And then the timeless question:

"If there is anyone here who objects to the marriage of these two people, let them speak now or forever hold their peace."

Lewis' mother and father squeeze their hands tightly.

"Do you, Lotte...? Do you, Lewis...?"

They do.

They kiss.

The rice is tossed, the champagne is popped, and the band plays "their" song, a popular one by Foreigner.

It would take a keen ear to detect the ominous rhetorical question embedded in the song chosen for their first dance. So for three minutes, Lotte and Lewis sway back and forth, as they will for years, always searching for the answer:

"I want to know what love is."

Chapter Thirteen: 1986

Noon. The Third Street Dramatists' Playhouse. Hollywood.

"Wisely and slow. They stumble that run fast."

Friar Lawrence's words echo in the empty theater as he looks sternly at Romeo, who will not heed his sage wisdom; no Romeo ever did, and certainly not this latest incarnation playing him. Of course, he looks the part and has all the passionate hunger of the tragic hero. He has one flaw, though—but that cannot be easily spotted by Noelani. All she can see is what this actor wants her to see.

For three weeks, Noelani has sat in these rehearsals, mesmerized by both the play and its principle male player, Michael Krauss. It was on a lark that she auditioned for a small role. She has no real lines, but nonetheless, the role is important, as she takes part in the dance that introduces Romeo to Juliet. Her mother's clients told her about the opening, and after taking one look at her, the director decided she would be a lovely asset to the cast. She could double as a maid, a townsperson, or a church attendee. There was but one significant objection to her presence.

* * *

"Frankly, Don, I think the girl playing my maid, what's her

name? Well, it doesn't matter, she is far too young," protests the actress playing Juliet.

"Her name is Noel," the play's director Don Mason lets out a sigh of frustration.

"Well, she looks like a child…next to me," his leading lady responds.

"For God's sake, Danielle, you're playing Juliet who is thirteen! You have almost two decades on Juliet."

"That is not true, Don!" the actress flares. "I can play fifteen to twenty-three, and you know it—and that's not the point."

"What, pray tell, is your point?" the director scoffs.

"Well, this Noel is, frankly, she seems too young to be my maid. I mean she's …"

As directors do, he stifles her with one stroke of his clipboard. "Damn it, she is too *pretty*; that's what you are saying, right? Well, I like her. She's smart and not yet filled with 'attitude.'" He pauses before he says something he may regret since Danielle, the actress playing Juliet, is quite capable, however vain. She is a diva who must be handled with care.

"Please, Danielle, don't worry about a little bit player. Just get ready for your next scene. We are already behind. Of course, you, my dear, happen to be one of the few who know their lines, unlike Mr. Romeo."

Danielle decides this is not the sword to fall on; she has other issues with this production, which she sees as too amateurish. She lets out a sigh and turns away, making sure her sway is seductive and her bodice allows for enough cleavage to rise. "Whatever. It's *your* play."

* * *

And that is how Noelani Kekoa finds herself in the first row at rehearsal, gazing at a Romeo four years her senior. At twenty-two, she is a community college graduate and one of the best dancers in Dee's Fourth Street Dance Studio. She also charms the customers in her mother's tiny but trendy clothing boutique. She still makes the runs to the theater companies with costumes. However, now that she has gotten the urge to dance in the footlights with acting companies, Noelani forgoes dance shows when necessary.

As the production closes in on opening night, she races home to show her mother the first printing of the play's program. "Mom, look! Here I am! Do you like my picture?"

Her mother's reaction is muted.

"Don't you like it?"

"Yes, but…"

"But what?"

"Why aren't you using your *real* name?" Kalani fidgets with a seam that is being too stubborn.

"What are you talking about? Oh, I see. You don't like the fact that I used *Noel* instead of *Noelani*, right?"

"That's right." She refuses to break eye contact with the material that she is molding to fit her wishes.

Noelani tries to tug her mother's face away from her work. "Why is that such a big deal, Mom?"

"Why is it a big deal? Hmm. Are you not proud to be Hawaiian? Look in mirror. You are from our islands. Why hide that?" Kalani starts to shuffle away.

"Mom, you are making me *lolo*."

"Hmm. *Now* you talk like a Hawaiian? But you don't admit it to your new friends?"

Noelani pivots, exasperated, "Never mind, Mom. I just don't want to be limited to playing the 'Hawaiian girl,' okay? It's a stereotype."

For the first time, it is Kalani who turns and faces her daughter. "It's *part* of who you are!"

"Not in this play and not in the future, and don't play

dumb, Mom. You know I have been *Noel* in a few dance shows. What's the problem with this now?"

Kalani speaks to some clothing on hangers: "I looked past it then. Maybe I shouldn't have. This is different."

"Why?"

"Because you don't know who you really are!" Kalani stops short as if she finds herself wading into waters that she has avoided for so long that she can't predict the current's strength and where it could lead. Instead she brushes her words away like lint on a dress. "Enough talk. I have work to do. Call yourself whatever you want."

The distance between the two women grows larger than any tape draped around Kalani's neck can measure. And that gap travels back to the islands—and Kalani's secret she refuses to reveal.

* * *

Michael Krauss is Malibu made flesh. His parents were born and bred in show business. His father, Allen, is an 'Agent to the Stars,' as his business card proclaims. His mother, Kimberley, is the chief accountant at one of the bigger television studios; she produces the steady, prosperous paychecks. Their only child is expected to play his part, despite his penchant for cutting classes and surfing and chasing bikinis whenever time allows. And in winter, it's the skiing and partying.

Money and influence can get a young, handsome actor into the right school, and Pepperdine University fit into his schedule. Most of the time, acting classes did not make it onto his calendar, which explains why this small community theater is where he has settled. Diplomas and discipline are not his strong suits, but that does not stop Michael from writing *Pepperdine* in the cast credits and frequently dropping the names of prominent drama coaches—who were merely his parents' dinner guests. Michael has learned that conforming to his father's version of "integrity" gets you places.

The director of this production, Don Mason, knew that casting the son of Allen Krauss would stir up curiosity and attract some theater veterans to his show. Besides, Mason believes that Michael looks the part of Romeo. As a novice director, Mason thinks that if he can impress upon the spoiled upstart even the slightest trace of Romeo's passion and naiveté, then Mason will make the 'director's cut,' so to speak. This is his fool's errand. But alas, one cannot ask for the moon; one must put bottoms into seats.

The fear that haunts Don Mason's playhouse is that Michael will never learn his lines. This, of course, makes Michael the butt of many jokes, especially since he plays Romeo. At least Mason knows that he has a dependable Juliet and a fairly seasoned company of elders surrounding this façade of Verona.

* * *

As the opening of the play draws closer, so too do the star-crossed lovers—just not the ones for whom the tears will be shed.

During the Elizabethan dance number at the play's opening, Romeo is supposed to be smitten by the lovely, pure Juliet. Instead, this Romeo finds his eyes magnetized to the young maiden who dances in and around his leading lady. Worried she will make a silly misstep, Noelani concentrates on the dance so much that she ignores Romeo. The more she ignores him, the more he is entranced. The more Juliet is overlooked, the angrier she becomes. Finally, she stops and looks at the director.

"Um, Don, why are we doing this scene?"

Don Mason realizes that without his approval, all has come to a full stop. "What? What are you talking about, Danielle?"

"Have you been paying attention, Don, to the fact that Mr. Romeo here is not trying to woo me, but seems far more interested in little Miss Nobody over there?" Her finger thrusts out like a sword toward Noelani, who drops her hands from her dancing partner, an older gentleman who has enjoyed placing his own hands on her petite waist. Noelani looks to the floor, as it is the only place to escape Juliet's wrath.

Michael, in an apparent act of contrition, steps into the dancers' circle and proclaims, "It's true, Don. I am so sorry, Danielle—everyone. I just zoned out. I was, um, trying to remember my lines, and when the cue came, I totally forgot what I was supposed to be doing. Really, I apologize, Danielle."

Danielle, hands on hips, is unmoved. "First, that's bullshit. You were looking at *her*—and you have been every damn rehearsal, Michael. Second, you probably are half telling the truth because we are two weeks away from opening—less than that—and you still don't know your lines! If you don't get your shit together, Michael, we are all going to die here, you ass!"

Noelani has tried to make herself invisible. Even though she does not know the play very well, she knows Juliet is right about how Romeo has been struggling with his lines. She often hears the others whisper, *Bullshit!* when they know he has flubbed yet another line. Usually, she is quite aware of men looking at her, and she enjoys the attention. But being a novice among veterans in a terrifying setting like this has made her aloof to Michael's attention.

However, once she is in the audience watching, as she does for the better part of the play, she is fixated on Romeo. Whether he is off script or not, he is mesmerizing. He moves the way a young lover should. She toys with the thought of Michael being her 'guilty pleasure'. His blonde hair has been dyed sandy brown. His emerald eyes glow, and his legs, now in black tights, show off the muscular structure one associates with an athlete. His hair often slides down over his eyes, and when he pushes it back, Noelani cannot help but wonder how it would feel to run her fingers through his hair and caress his lips, exactly what Juliet is supposed to feel when she sees her Romeo. *What does it matter if he stumbles over his words?* Then she remembers the Friar's warning about stumbling and falling.

The director announces a break for lunch and immediately goes to his Juliet to apologize. Romeo stands behind him, seemingly nodding in agreement—until he glances over his shoulder, catches Noelani's eye, and winks.

Noelani blushes and hurries off set. Once she is out of view, she hides her smile behind her mask, the prop she uses during the dance. Its shape: that of a lioness.

Chapter Fourteen: 1986

11:00 p.m. New Year's Eve. Lewis and Lotte's bedroom. Encinitas, California.

Lotte's head rests on Lewis' shoulder. Fulfilled, she has collapsed on his chest. They are both breathing hard, and the voice of Dick Clark, standing on top of a New York skyscraper, is almost inaudible in the living room. They lie in shadows but are startled as a firecracker snaps and whistles near their window. Lewis smiles. Lotte resents the disturbance as she slides off Lewis' frame, only to nestle herself around him as she pulls her hair back so she can see him better.

Rather than stay at a friend's party, they decided to escape and celebrate their six-month anniversary in the manner they enjoy the most: breathless and buried under the tossed covers in their tiny apartment just across from the train tracks, less than a mile from Moonlight Beach. Their intimacy has been the priority that dominates the evenings: however, in daytime, it is conversations that tiptoe around their future that are unavoidable and stressful.

They shower together. As they are getting ready for bed, they poke their heads into the living room and hear the midnight countdown. "Happy New Year," Lewis whispers into Lotte's ear. Lotte responds with a kiss. They crawl into bed, hold hands, and say *goodnight*.

Though she closes her eyes, Lotte cannot sleep.

Since the time they dated, Lewis has been her life preserver. Just when she felt she could no longer paddle and keep herself from sinking into the dark waters of failure, Lewis' optimism, warmth, and sense of family—all the stability he brings each day—has given her more confidence in herself than she could have ever imagined.

But that is not what is keeping her awake.

* * *

It started a few months after the wedding, when they had a serious talk about their plans.

"I don't know, Lotte. I would love to work for the newspaper...or even be a freelance writer, but when I have been subbing for Mrs. Libby, well, I just love the kids. Especially the journalism classes—and getting the school newspaper out today was a blast."

"Yeah, but she is only gonna be out until the new year starts. What will you do then? I mean, part-time work with the local paper and subbing..." Lotte has just come home from a grueling day making lots of calls on various doctor's offices. Big Pharma has its benefits; the money is one of them, but the days are long, and her need to prove herself to her new, demanding boss takes its toll. Her feet are aching. She is rubbing them vigorously.

Lewis takes the hint, grabs some lotion, scoots over to her, and begins on her sore calves.

"Oh, my God, Lewis. Thank you...that feels great," she moans as she sinks lower into the couch.

"Well, I'm getting great reviews from the teachers and the kids. The VP at the school has asked me to help with Homecoming. I have an appointment with her later next week to see if there are any promising openings at the school next year, with all the pregnancies and all. The staff seems very fertile."

"Um, great…Watch out for my toes; one of them is smashed from my heels."

"Speaking of fertile…um…" Lewis seems to tread carefully, but Lotte is not fooled.

"I know. I know. Lewis, I know what you are getting at, but we are barely making ends meet now. We are not going to get in over our heads in debt—I have seen that movie, and it ends badly. Look, we both want a family, but right now, my income is what we count on. We are young. We have plenty of time." Lotte looks at him carefully. "We gotta know where we are going first."

"Where we are going?"

"Well, I mean, my boss is talking about accounts in LA or Phoenix, and I think he thinks that if I work out, I would cover a wider area." Lotte's boss espouses the typical middle management mantra: Work the newbies hard and see who can take it. Pick the best, make sure they are "easy on the eyes," and then get them on the lucrative accounts. Lotte has figured him out and knows his game.

Lewis thinks out loud, "I guess they may want you to travel, huh? Not for a while though, right?"

"Right. And believe me, I want to say here. Encinitas is perfect. But a lot depends on your job, too." Lotte relaxes back, her point made.

"Right. Well…gee, your thighs seem to be awfully sore, you know." Lewis begins to work his way up Lotte's tanned kneecaps.

"Lewis, what are you up to? *Lewis. Lewis.* Stop! Okay. I love what you are doing, but save it for later. I am starving, and I don't feel like cooking. And I don't feel like talking about the future, a baby, moving, or your job. I am just dead."

"I'll go out and get Mexican, okay? The usual?" He begins to tug on his sandals. Juanita's Carnitas is just across the railroad tracks.

"Yep." Lotte begins to close her eyes.

Lewis grabs his wallet and keys. Just as he reaches the door, he turns to tell her he'll be back in a few minutes. It is pointless. She is already snoring softly.

* * *

Now she lies awake in bed. The New Year's festivities faded into the murky darkness long ago.

Her naps are more frequent now, and sometimes Lewis must wake her up and reheat the food. He is always worried that she is pushing herself too hard. What Lewis does not know is that right before the Christmas break, Lotte had been offered a position in LA. She can stay in San Diego and commute, but that seems daunting. They could move, but that's not something she can cope with now.

That alone is not why she cannot sleep.

It was Thanksgiving. With all the excitement of a *real* holiday with Lewis' parents in San Francisco, she made a terrible mistake. She still remembers staring at her suitcase in disbelief. It was nowhere to be found.

Chapter Fifteen: 1986

11:00 p.m. Opening night of Romeo and Juliet.

Noelani is beaming with pride. She holds hands with the cast as they take their final bow. Michael is center stage with Danielle—Romeo and Juliet, in all their glory. Somehow Don Mason, using guilt, bribery, or threats of Michael's actual demise, has gotten his Romeo to come within a reasonable proximity to Shakespeare's actual dialogue.

Thank God, Noelani thinks, as she has seen the entire cast's fury beat down on Michael during rehearsals, with Danielle almost walking out on them more times than Noelani can count. Noelani now understands that Danielle is a *real actress* because of her work ethic, and she overheard her warning Michael, "This will be done right, or you will never see an LA stage playing anything but a jackass—and I am not talking about *Midsummer Night's Dream,* you dimwit." Noelani winces at the memory.

Noelani marvels at how Danielle could turn all that off and routinely transform into the lovely and smitten Juliet, as if she is merely turning a car's ignition and cruising forward to the next scene. *Simply amazing* is the only way Noelani rationalizes the transformation before her. Noelani sees in Danielle discipline and integrity. And despite the tension between them, she can't help but go to her as the cast leaves the stage and stop before her, stammering, "Danielle, oh, my God, you were so incredible!"

"Honey, what did you expect?" comes the chilly reply. Then Danielle offers a slice of dry, coarse advice: "Noel, you realize the poison he drinks is contagious, don't you? Of course you don't. You are just a mere child, my dear." Then, perhaps because she sees in Noelani the innocence she once embodied, Danielle tilts her head back halfway so Noelani can see her right eye. "He's no Romeo, nor you his *only* Juliet." She then disappears with a flock of well-wishers, vanishing into the blackness of the curtain's shadows.

No such pomp surrounds Noelani's Romeo. Michael stands with just a few older women, clearly decades past their prime, so much so that even the "work done" on them can't fool even the most naive acquaintance. Naturally, they *adore* Michael, not for his portrayal of the doomed lover, but one can only surmise for their own ulterior motives. Michael plays along, though his eyes peek slightly over the women's dramatically colored hair, seeking some refuge from the onslaught. One of the women places her hand on Michael's torn shirt and chest.

This sets off an alarm in him such that it compels him to yell out, ridiculously, "Don, where is the cast party? Oh, please excuse me, ladies. I see our director is gathering the cast. You know, the post-show critique and such. Please excuse me." Michael backs away and literally skips, un-Romeo-like, to a gaggle of cast and crew members in the darkened upstage area. The women are left behind, muttering something to the effect of, "Oh, of course, Michael. Yes, by all means. We'll keep tabs on you, dear."

Then he espies the lonely figure he is searching for.

Glancing back at the disappointed ladies, one of whom is fanning herself, he makes sure they do not notice his sharp detour. He grabs Noelani by the arm and murmurs directly into her ear, "Come, my lady. Follow me."

Noelani, taken aback, follows orders and is whisked to the farthest corner, under the green *Exit* sign. Whereupon Romeo has her twirl so she is face to face with him. Noelani's eyes are dilated from the pitch blackness; to Michael, she is a twenty-three-year-old, star struck beauty. In what appears to be a melodrama on the silent screen, he kisses her passionately. And although Noelani's good sense that this over the top "love scene" demands a good slap in the face and a *What do you think you are doing?* scoff, she gives into the silly soap opera "romance" and relents. She craves this guilty pleasure. Her lips move subtly from stiff to supple, then more fervently from eager to erotic.

Michael gently but purposely bites her lower lip. And the hot-blooded poison races through her veins, with no balcony to stop his advance.

Romeo has his Juliet.

Chapter Sixteen: 1987

2:00 a.m. New Year's Day. Lewis and Lotte's bedroom. Encinitas, California.

Lotte's face is hot. Her perspiration soaks her nightshirt. She slips out of bed carefully so as not to wake Lewis. She reaches the bathroom and looks in the mirror. *Calm down, damn it. I just missed a day. Wait, no—two days. Shit. It was the day after Thanksgiving, too. I am so stupid. This can't be happening. It's impossible. My period should have started last week at least. Still, calm down. Jesus, it's 2:00. I gotta get to sleep.*

Lotte changes nightshirts; this one is lighter, cooler. She wipes the sweat off her brow and fans herself. She is starting to cool off.

"What's the matter, Lotte?" Lewis appears in the mirror. Lotte nearly jumps out of her skin, dropping the fan.

"Oh, my God, Lewis! You scared the crap outta me!" Lotte tries to calm herself. "Why are you sneaking up on me like that?"

"I'm not. I just reached over for you, and you were not in bed…and the bed sheets are wet. Are you sick?" Lewis touches her shoulder.

Lotte shakes off his touch. "Don't touch me right now, okay? I'm fine. It's just, just—night sweats."

Lewis raises both eyebrows. He steps back and withdraws

his hands. "Okay. Okay. I'm sorry. I just thought that maybe you were sick because…I don't know, you didn't eat much, and you said you didn't want to drink. Are you sure you're alright?"

Lotte wants to give in and tell him the truth, but why? It's silly. She can't be pregnant. Besides, *that is what he wants*. She knows that holding all this in is what is causing this panic. He always makes her feel safe, feel loved. He is the calm one.

"Lotte, what's the matter? I know something is wrong. Is it the whole job thing? Is it…?"

She shakes her head, signaling no, but she can't seem to speak.

"So what *is* wrong? Talk to me, Lotte. Please. Whatever it is, we can deal with it." Lewis' voice is so measured, confident.

Lotte tries to say something. She must force the words out through her now chattering teeth.

"Lotte, you are shaking! Come on, sit down on the bed and tell me what happened." He takes her hand, and she does not refuse. She perches herself on her side of the bed, half sitting and half standing. He is next to her, with his arm around her shoulders. He sees the beads of perspiration on her forehead. "Honey, please tell me what is happening to you."

Lotte nods, gathers resolve. She can't stop now. Suddenly, her eyes well up, and the teardrops plummet to her rosy cheeks. "Lewis, I did a really stupid thing. I forgot…to take…my birth control pill. No. No. My birth control *pills*. Lewis, I—I'm so afraid I might be pregnant." Lotte's right hand immediately goes to her mouth as if to say that the word *pregnant* is indescribably dangerous.

"Lotte, relax. You're okay. You are probably just having a panic attack worrying about it. You said you missed a day?"

"Yes. I mean, no. I forgot at Thanksgiving. I forgot to bring them with me…on the plane. I looked everywhere in my suitcase, but I left them at home. I didn't tell you, and we didn't have sex at your parents' house those three days…"

"Yeah, and…?" Lewis is trying to put the puzzle together.

"Then I just…just thought, well, three days. That's a big, big deal," Lotte stammers. She is now crying with full force, so much so that what comes out of her mouth next is inaudible to Lewis.

Lotte takes a big breath just as Lewis has told her to. "But then, remember before Christmas? I said I had the flu—kinda—and I put you off? You know, about sex—for like two weeks? Okay, well, the doctor said to wait until I started a new cycle and—and when I started, I thought I started—I thought it was safe…but…"

"But what, Lotte? Tell me, please."

"But I hadn't started. I just had some spotting on one day, and I was so relieved because I knew you wanted to make love to me…and it was Christmas, so we did. Twice. And then I realized my cycle had not started. When I screwed up with the pills, it messed me up, and we didn't wait long enough…and I'm—I'm late."

"Your period?"

Lotte can only nod. She grabs the tissue box by the nightstand. She pulls out a handful and plasters them to her eyes and nose. From the mound of tissues, Lewis can hear a muffled, "I'm so stupid. Stupid!"

Lewis waits. Thinks. His mind races for something to say. "Lotte, Lotte, listen to me, okay? Have you done a pregnancy test?"

"No."

"Okay, then you don't know anything, really. You may have just gotten so stressed that it has made your body react. I mean, the chances of you being pregnant are…and even if you are pregnant—"

She cuts him off. "I know what you're gonna say. My period should have started last week, or it should have happened before Christmas. Oh, Lewis. I am so confused—I'm not thinking straight. This could mess up everything—our plans, my job. I'm so not ready for a baby, Lewis. I'm freaking out."

"Well, then, don't worry. When—I mean, *if*—it doesn't start soon, you can take the pregnancy test—" He stops abruptly. Lewis turns to face her and gets down on one knee. "Lotte, if you are, then you are. And we will embrace what has happened—if it even has."

"What do you mean?"

"I mean that I love you, and I'll love whatever happens. It's not your fault. And you know how I feel about a baby. Lotte, please don't worry. We will be fine." He gently brushes her hair and peels away the tissues that have become her mask.

Lotte can feel something strange happening. Her body feels cooler. Her teeth are not chattering. She leans into Lewis' body. They hold each other.

Lewis remembers, only much later, that never once did Lotte use the word *love*.

* * *

Lewis and Lotte's bathroom the following day.

"No!" Lotte stares at the stick. Again, she is sweating. This is the second try, this time with a more expensive kit. The box says it's ninety-nine percent accurate.

Lotte knew. She knew all along.

Pregnant.

Oh, my God. What do I do? What will Lewis say? I know what he will say. "Honey, we are having a baby!" He will be excited—until he sees my face. This is not what I wanted now. Maybe ten years from now, when we are settled. I'm twenty-five, and by autumn, I will be a mother. I don't—I can't... Lewis will be home in an hour.

She walks from the bathroom to the bed. Sits down. Turns her face to her pillow and sobs.

* * *

Lewis opens the door, softball bag in hand, and yells, "Lotte, I'm home! Lotte, you here?" He turns the corner and steps into the bedroom. Lotte has just pulled herself from the pillow, trying in vain to wipe away her tears. He knows.

"Lotte, honey, I know. I know. It's going to be alright." He quickly slides beside her and holds her. She is shaking. He knows she is choking through words of apology, but the only word that matters is *pregnant*.

Minutes go by. They just hold each other. Lewis is determined to not say anything until she is still. He will wait her out. Finally, she tucks her head lower into his chest, and her breathing slows. He lets this phase take its turn, as if she is going through stages of grieving. *Grieving.*

When she finally looks up, he takes her face in both hands. "Lotte, I love you. I will love the baby. I will never, ever stop loving you. We can't always plan everything. You are not your sister or your brother. You are never, ever going to be like them. We will take this one step at a time. We will be fine."

Lotte looks at him desperately. Her eyes tell him that she wants to believe him, but she can't seem to control herself now. She mumbles, "What's the plan now, Lewis? I screwed up all our plans."

"You didn't. I had an equal part in this, you know." This is Lewis' effort to bring some lightness to her despondency.

It doesn't work.

Lotte bites her lip and forces herself to say what she thought she would never say: "Lewis, I've been thinking. It's still possible... I mean, I know this isn't what we planned, but I've thought about maybe—at least *considering*—an abortion."

Lewis is stunned. This has never crossed his mind. Not even through some vague implication. He wonders if this has been Lotte's secret Plan B. For the first time, he is scared. He looks away from her and gazes into the adjacent mirror. Lotte's face is contorted. He sees not a glimmer of joy.

"Lotte, you can't be serious. Lotte. Lotte. You—you're not thinking clearly. This is our baby. Your baby. Let's just stop—right now. Let's just calm down and take some time. We need to think things through. Lotte, whatever we do, we can't do anything out of fear. And we shouldn't decide anything right now." He holds her hands tightly, waiting for affirmation.

Lotte nods. She hugs him with all the strength she has left. Her panic has eroded what confidence she had. "I am so... confused, Lewis."

"I know."

"I feel so guilty. So careless." She stands.

"You are not either."

"I gotta go."

"Where?"

"To the bathroom."

"Are you okay?"

"Yes... No... I just gotta pee."

"Oh. Good. I thought you might have to—"

"Throw up? No. I did that already."

Chapter Seventeen: 1995

5:15 p.m. Lewis steps into the office of Amos Adler, M.D.

Noelani's fragrance still faintly infuses the air of Dr. Adler's office. Lewis hasn't noticed it before; perhaps the waiting room disinfects most who enter. But her presence has not escaped; even the seat across from Dr. Amos Adler is still a bit warm.

* * *

When Lewis entered Dr. Adler's waiting room, he hoped he might have a minute or two to exchange more than a quick "Hello" with Noelani as she checked out at the window, but the young receptionist, today decked out in Florescent Blue, tried to nip that in the bud. She demanded Noelani's attention in order to make her next appointment; and when Lewis stepped up to the window next to Noelani, she rapped on the glass and said, "Privacy, please!" Noelani glanced at him, and they exchanged what has become "their look." Lewis retreated to a chair in the waiting room.

As soon as Noelani finished making her next appointment, which Lewis noticed she repeated at a louder volume than necessary, Noelani looked directly at him and said, "Funny meeting you again, Lewis."

"Well, you were the one who made my appointment, remember?" Lewis grinned.

Florescent Blue would have none of this fraternizing on her watch. All traces of joy must be eradicated from this tired, dated waiting room, and it's her duty to make that crystal clear to anyone who does not obey the rules. In a voice as dry as the Sahara Desert, she said, "Ahem—Mr. Bennett? Can I help you now?"

Noelani looked at her, then back at Lewis apologetically. "Gotta run. Bye."

"See you—Noelani, right?"

Just as she reached the waiting room's exit, the door to Dr. Adler's corridor opened, and Lewis believed he heard her say, "Good memory, Mr. Bennett."

Unfortunately, though, this response overlapped with Dr. Adler's gentle greeting: "Lewis, come on back."

So he did.

What neither Lewis nor Noelani knew was that Dr. Adler then stepped to the window to check the appointment book. He slid the glass window open. To Florescent Blue, whose demeanor instantly turned much more pleasant, he said, "When Mr. Bennett comes out to make his next appointment, schedule him right after Ms. Kekoa, if that is possible for him, okay?" He slid the window closed again. Florescent Blue waited until he turned and strolled down the corridor before she rolled her eyes.

Meanwhile, Lewis had entered Dr. Adler's small but comfortable office and had taken his usual seat. He noticed the *I love you, Grandpa!* drawings taped up on the wall near the doctor's family pictures. A couple of birthday cards stood side by side. He waited a bit for the good doctor to enter.

* * *

Lewis wonders, *How many people have sat in this seat just*

today. How many people has Dr. Amos Adler tried to mend? Lewis almost feels like he should apologize for all the turmoil the poor old man must face. He also wonders what could be troubling this woman who preceded him. His Walter Mitty expression is quickly replaced as Dr. Adler begins the session.

"So, Lewis, you are my last patient today, and we have plenty of time. How have you been since I saw you?" he looks down quickly at his notes.

"Gosh, Doctor. You have had a day, haven't you? Par for the course?"

"Yes, well, some days are more stressful than others, Lewis—or is it Lou?"

"Lewis. Yes, well. Hmm. I am starting to...what's a good word? *Process.* Process it all and such. I think." Lewis grins. He feels the need to be a "happier ending" to the day for the dutiful doctor.

"Lewis, do you know that you are not the typical person I see?" Lewis cannot read Dr. Adler's face; it seems to express a mixture of hope and something troubling. "You see, you are here because of an action, or a series of actions. You have had no history of depression or even anxiety. No, Lewis, you are merely a temporary visitor to my domain." He spreads his long arms out; they seem to encompass all his territory. "You're someone just trying to process something that has, as they say, pulled the rug out from under them."

"Ah. I see. Is that good?" Lewis is still on pins and needles.

"Generally, yes, as long as you keep pushing forward, trying to understand what happened and why. So let's review. You told me last time that you felt you were 'losing your mind,' but the truth is you are very upset because you are feeling distanced from your wife, Lotte—that's her name, correct?"

"Right. Yes. Lotte. Did I say I was losing my mind? Wow, I was a little freaked out, I guess. Um, *distanced* isn't the right word for it, Doc. *Divorce* is more what I am dealing with—at least part of it."

"I see."

"Maybe I should back up. After we got married—me and Lotte—things got tougher money-wise. I was still subbing and trying to decide between teaching and the newspaper business. And so, we were basically living on one income—hers. Then Lotte got pregnant. It was *not* planned. That's another story—but we managed. Then I got the job at the high school, but she was sort of forced to take a job at the Phoenix office selling pharmaceuticals—marketing drugs to hospitals and doctors." Lewis is trying to keep this short, but he knows he is not telling all that he should. He feels guilty about it, but there is a stubborn side to him that will not allow him to show himself completely. Dr. Amos Adler senses Lewis is not being forthright. "I'm confused, Lewis. You wanted to have a family, I assume, but just not at that time?"

"Correct. I mean, it was fine with me, but…"

"Your wife was not prepared, I take it."

"Yeah, that is one way of putting it."

Dr. Adler tries to follow the thread. "Why did she go to Phoenix? How did you work that out?"

"Oh, well, her boss—a typical mid-manager—figured she was great at sales, and he had too many people in San Diego and not nearly enough out there. He told her, 'Work for me in Phoenix or leave the company.' So our backs were against the wall with the baby and all. But—and this is the important part—Lotte was so valuable to him that she got him to agree to at least pay for her hotel and travel for the first year. Lotte knows how to get her way, Doctor."

Lewis pauses to take a breath.

"So, she would leave Monday morning and come home sometimes on Thursday night. And that worked."

"But that must have been really difficult for Lotte, being a new mother. It was hard for her to be away from her infant, right?"

"Yes and no. It's complicated, Doc. She was so focused on her job and worried about money. And at the same time, um, she just didn't have the same...hmm, the same *feeling*..."

Dr. Adler peers over his reading glasses and clarifies: "You're speaking of maternal instinct."

"Exactly. Weird, huh?"

"Actually, Lewis, no. It is far more common than you would think. I have worked with many, many women who feel that way. But go on."

"Oh. Interesting. Well, meanwhile, I was really consumed with school—running the newspaper, correcting papers, trying to keep my head above water. You know—first few years as a teacher. After a year, she was making so much money for them that they continued the arrangement the following year. At that point, we were much more solid financially, and she was getting all those sales perks they give—trips to places like New York and Europe."

"Ah. Did you go with her?" Dr. Adler looks up to the ceiling in thought.

"Um, yeah—New York. After the second year, I think. But then the Europe trip was with her girlfriends from the office. At least that's what she told me. Anyway, the argument began about who should move and who should quit. We even thought about moving to the Bay Area—near my folks—and both of us starting over. But that wasn't *really* what Lotte wanted."

Dr. Adler asks the leading question, "She wanted you to move to Phoenix with her, I assume?"

"Well, yes...and no. We love San Diego. She knew Phoenix's climate was awful for half the year. And things were manageable...for a long time. At least I thought so. You know the expression, 'Absence makes the heart grow fonder?' That was true for the first two years, like I said. But then—I don't know—she started not coming home on Thursday nights, saying Friday meetings were needed. And that bled into Saturdays sometimes. And—"

Dr. Adler leans forward. "But you never offered to go out there during school vacations, for example?"

"Well, I did. But it was complicated…"

"I'm missing something, Lewis." For the first time, Dr. Amos Adler takes an approach that he rarely uses. He pushes his patient to start laying all his cards on the table. "See, Lewis, I see a great many men and women who are distraught over a divorce, but you—I have a suspicion that your panic attacks are coming from a place that you are trying very hard to contain. Hmm. So, let me ask you bluntly… Lewis—what are you *not* telling me?"

Lewis has the look of a guilty man who must confess to his interrogator what he wishes that he could keep secret.

Chapter Eighteen: 1987

Midnight. New Year's Day. Pulling into Mammoth Lakes.

Noelani is leaning against the front window of Michael's parents' Volvo. She has slept on and off during the six-hour trip, and her dreams drift from reality to fantasy. The reality is that she has agreed to go with Michael to his parents' ski condo and try to ski for the first time. Naturally, this is exciting, but she is nervous. Michael assuages her fear by telling her, "Noel, you're gonna be a natural. I'll teach you. We'll start slow and work our way up." Noelani takes him at his word. After all, many of her friends do this. *It can't be that hard, can it?*

Her thoughts, however, are a murky blend of what has happened since the play opened, quickly closed, and how Michael's presence became part of her weekly schedule, much to her mother's chagrin. But lately, Kalani has had less and less sway over the twenty-three-year-old dancer. Kalani's appeals range from caution to outright indignation.

"He's too spoiled. I don't trust him."

"He's not fooling me. He brags and he thinks I say, 'Oh, yes.' But I know that he's selfish and I worry if he is a nice man or just using you, Noelani."

"He doesn't work hard, Noelani. He's living off his parents. He's older than you. A real man stands on own legs!"

Noelani does not completely ignore all these comments,

but she also thinks her mother doesn't see Michael's other side. He is generous. He buys her jewelry and clothes and attends her dance performances. He adores her Hawaiian heritage, though he refers to her as Noel, and he makes her feel sexy and desirable. When they sleep together, their sexual appetite is ravishing. In the bedroom, he contradicts the self-centered appearance he gives off to others. He wants her to experience how much her body can respond—what pleasures can be reached with his efforts. At times, she simply gives herself to him like the flowers bend to the spring breeze. And when her eyes open, she sees his gorgeous face and his smile of satisfaction at his conquest.

Then there are his connections. He moves with confidence, and due to his parents, he has experience in the entertainment world. He says he knows people who know people, and he has promised that Noelani's talents will not be limited to Dee's studio. He has taken her places: a night at the Laguna Beach Ritz-Carlton, the Greek Amphitheater to see the Go-Go's tour finale, and, of course, Rodeo Drive. Naturally, heads turn when Noelani walks into any hotel or store, and Michael notices—and makes sure others do, as well.

* * *

Michael announces that they have arrived, and Noelani rouses herself. For an island girl, the cold is bracing. She owns no clothes for these frigid temperatures, but Michael borrowed some winter jackets and such from friends—women who just happen to be the same size and shape as Noelani. These women clearly have expensive taste. "Tomorrow will be a day to hit the slopes," Michael says. But for now, he squeezes Noelani and winks, "The Jacuzzi will thaw you out tonight, Noel." She is far too tired for anything but a hot shower, but Michael's persistence means that Noelani does not fall asleep until well after 2:00 a.m.

* * *

The morning sunlight gleams off the white powder outside their window. Noelani has not seen a winter wonderland remotely comparable to Mammoth. She stares at the trail map and realizes just how massive the mountain is. Michael explains that near the main lodge, there is a perfect place for a beginning adult skier to learn, so there is no reason to be intimidated. Noelani tries to keep that in mind as she looks over the trail map, which seems to have death-defying drops. From the lodge, all she can see are lifts, a few trees, and skiers dotting the side of the mountain. The people higher up the mountain look like ants scurrying among the patches of moss green trees. The higher up she looks, the more the trees appear to be a blend of white and green, like that twisted spearmint gum. It is breathtaking.

It isn't until 10:00 a.m. that the two of them start outfitting her. Some of Michael's female "friends'" ski pants fit well enough, but they traverse the rental shack for boots, skis, and such. It is all exciting to Noelani, and despite her general weariness, the combination of the cold, the nerves, and the adrenaline keeps her on "high alert." Today, Michael says, will be spent on the "bunny slopes," with him explaining the basics. One thing becomes obvious: Noelani's fearlessness makes her a very quick study on skis.

Michael gives her some very basic tips and lets her get her bearings. The boots seem very confining to her, but at the same time, Noelani thinks that at least her dancer's ankles are not going to twist.

"It will feel really weird for a while, but you'll get used to it," Michael insists. "Besides, you look good. You are moving very fluidly, Noel. Great."

"Okay, well, this seems doable. So how do we get to the chair lift?"

"We ski there. Use your poles and push off with the inside of your skis. Perfect. We will get on chair 11—Sesame Street. It's really flat, and if you want, you can watch some people taking a group lesson."

Getting on the lift isn't too hard for Noelani, as Michael guides her to the blue line. She sits back into the chair. "Oh, my God, Michael—this is amazing."

"And this is for beginners. I have a feeling you will catch on very quickly."

"We'll have to see about that," Noelani warns him.

But he is quite right. Noelani glides down trails that she thinks have the funniest names: Woolly's Wood, Apple Pie, Disco Playground. Each time, she laughs at how exhilarating it is when she comes to the end of the trail. She can't wait to take the chair lift up again, but after the third time, she finds herself both hungry and a little fatigued. Despite all her years of dancing, some muscles are not used to the strain of skiing. "Michael, this is so much fun." She catches her breath; for the first time, she realizes the effects of the elevation. "Whew. Can we stop and have lunch? Gosh, between the cold and the thin air—"

"I know. Tough to get used to it. I'm hungry, too."

They grab lunch, and after repeating the simpler runs, Noelani gains strength and balance. Her confidence brims. She is quite satisfied with just staying at this level, but Michael claims she will easily master more challenging runs. He leaves her for a bit to scout out the other runs. He is a little bored with just following her shapely form. He is amazed that she has fallen only twice, and even then, her laughter at the powdery spill has told him that she is game for the next day's adventure.

But there is something else he plans to introduce to his island girl.

* * *

"What do you mean, 'You don't want to try it?'" Michael is incredulous.

"What I said. I'm not into cocaine, and I don't need it to have a fun time with you, Michael."

"But how do you know if you don't even try it?"

Noelani leans back against the white pillows of the over-stuffed couch. She refuses to look down at the glass table with the similarly white powder posing as the centerpiece. "I don't need it. I am fine just as I am. I love being with you—and besides, I am a dancer, and what I put into my body matters."

"Oh, come on. You've got to be kidding me, Noel. 'Your body's a temple'—seriously? Look, you're scared. You think it will make you an addict. It's not like that, believe me."

Noelani's mind is racing, as Michael seems unwilling to stop pressuring her. As he keeps trying to convince her, his voice is strangely muted. Noelani's mind races back to the day when her mother said, "*I no trust that one. He wants you, then poof, he's gone. No. I don't trust Mr. Fancy Pants.*" The anger Noelani felt toward her mother that day is now directed toward Michael. *Why won't he just let this go?* She crosses her arms and counterattacks. "Michael, are you saying that I— just as I am, not all coked up—that I am not enough? That I'm not sexually pleasing, not adventurous enough? Michael, I went down those slopes and wasn't afraid. Okay, I was a little, but what more do you want from me?"

He takes his time to assess how hard to push. This is the first time she has refused to play along with any of his 'games.' He leans back on the couch and looks up to the ceiling. He lets out a sigh. "Okay, okay, Noel. I guess this is what you want. I will just…understand, I guess. It seems like a waste. But I don't want you to be upset."

"Well, I am trying not to be."

"Right, well, forget the coke. Let's just open the champagne and relax, okay? Tomorrow we can ski all day and have a nice dinner at the Mammoth Mountain Inn." He stands and goes to the kitchen, opens the champagne, and pours her a glass. He fills his own, brings the bottle with him, and reaches for her hand. She rises from the couch and takes her flute of champagne.

"A toast," Michael kisses her hand, "to the rest of the evening's pleasures."

Their glasses ring, and they proceed to the bedroom. Noelani smiles, proud that she has stood her ground. She sits on the side of the bed and downs her champagne. Michael quickly refills her glass. She places it delicately on the nightstand, then unbuttons her top and slowly reclines back. Michael's body shadows and soon engulfs her.

* * *

Hours later, Michael slides out of the bed and lines up the cocaine while Noelani apparently sleeps soundly from the day's exertions.

Chapter Nineteen: 1995

5:35 p.m. Lewis remains in the office of Amos Adler, M.D.

Dr. Amos Adler repeats the question. "Lewis, I know this is tough, but again—what are you not telling me?"

Lewis inhales and exhales. He looks around the office and lets out a sigh. He stares at the photographs on the doctor's desk. "I couldn't just leave for Phoenix, Doc. I was the one raising Hope. And we needed to stay home, here in Encinitas."

Dr. Amos Adler faintly smiles, trying to encourage his reluctant patient to open up his tightly secured baggage. "Your daughter? How old is Hope now?"

"She is six, turning seven soon." Lewis looks up at the doctor, hoping to not see a frustrated look on his face. What he sees is anything but.

"Oh, that's a wonderful age—but naturally, time consuming."

"You got that right, Doc."

"Mmm-hmm. But there are three years that I—that you—are not explaining. Were you separated?"

Lewis is beaten. "No. I love Lotte. And up until three months ago, I thought she was coming back. For two years, we agreed that we would hang in there. I knew she loved me—she still does, in her way. The plan was to bank money and buy a house here. So we did. But then…"

Lewis looks at his hands. "Then she called me and said it's over. She wanted a *divorce*."

Silence follows such that each man can hear the other's breath. At Lewis' first meeting with him, Dr. Amos Adler first wanted to deal with the symptoms of panic and disorientation. He knew there was a marital issue, but this revelation—and Lewis' unwillingness to "come clean"—tells him much more than Lewis would understand. He suspects there is more to this stoic man's fear. After all, Lewis has dealt with this situation for years. Why would the end of a teetering relationship cause so much desperation?

The doctor begins, "*Divorce*. Well, Lewis, I assume you know what that means. And I assume you will have to speak to Hope about this. Understandably, that will be difficult for you and your wife." He adjusts his reading glasses, looks at his notes, and tries to calculate if his next question is worth the risk of alienating his patient. It is a delicate proposition. Normally, he allows the patient to "come to him with their issues," but in Lewis' case, the issues are stuck between his mind and his heart. Dr. Amos Adler smoothes his goatee and notices that Lewis glances at his watch.

"Lewis, you are my last patient today, and I am not concerned about time. I am concerned about you. My wife, God bless her, knows I'll call her when we are done. She keeps the dinner warm for me." He chuckles, hoping that a glimmer of relief will bubble to the surface of the man sitting across from him. But he suspects that that will not be the case.

It is not. "Lewis, from my experience, I suspect you are still not quite done telling me about what may be another issue you are trying to cope with. Am I right?"

Lewis knows he is perspiring. He feels the sweat running down from the tip of his hair near his ear and from his brow. He relents. His life's troubles have come down like a landslide.

"Doctor, I have been diagnosed with something I can

hardly pronounce. It's called *serpiginous choroiditis.*" Lewis'
eyes well up with tears. He wipes his forehead with his shirt
sleeve. Then he rasps, "I may be losing my sight."

Chapter Twenty: 1987

8:00 a.m. Hotel room in Mammoth Lakes.

Noelani sips coffee, wrapped in a plush terrycloth robe. She looks out the bay kitchen window. Silence. She has a few quiet moments to take in a world that until yesterday she had only seen on TV.

Noelani refills her coffee cup and makes a decision. She does not want to fall in love with Michael, but he has enabled her to break away from the cycle of dance and work, not to mention the hovering eyes of her mother. Besides, she believes last night's incident proves that she is in control of the relationship.

The ice is melting in the corners of the window, as the sun is already breaking through the dawn's silvery sky. Some puffy clouds are off to the north, she thinks—it seems to be the north. Her compass has been off since Michael proposed this weekend adventure. It has been even more askew since he offered her cocaine last night. She suspects that he returned to his pile of white snow later, after they made love. But she can't be certain. Regardless, she decides to drop the subject and just let him sleep it off, although this is their last day here, and she would love to ski this morning.

Yesterday, Noelani got a taste of the skiing social world. At Mammoth, there are "regulars" who have a network of friends who, not unlike surfers, have a way of talking and an understanding of the rules of the slopes. Michael knows many of them; they ask about his parents. Most of the people she meets have a timeshare at this resort, and Michael, it is implied through their whispered conversations and knowing looks, has entertained his fair share of girls. Nevertheless, they are very friendly to Noelani. They ask if she skis; she says no, but that does not raise an eyebrow. Apparently, Michael has introduced many other beauties to this mountain paradise.

The mountain itself is overwhelming to her. So many trails. The beautiful gondola rides appear spectacular to her—and a bit scary. As Noelani pours out another cup of coffee, she reflects on how Michael treated her the day before. To Michael's credit, he did not push her; however, she took to skiing as easily as those days in Hawaii when she was first on a surfboard. Balance. Strength. Her ability to shift her weight and gain speed contributed to her advancing to the easiest of the "moderate" slopes. Michael explained to her that Wednesdays were less crowded and that the better skiers would be out there. The slopes were going to be much busier today, when people want to get a jump on a long weekend. He also explained with a look of disgust that more *teenagers* would be out today.

"So?"

"More snowboarders."

"And that is bad? I saw them today."

"Yeah, but they knew what they were doing. The kids are just doing stupid stuff. But don't worry—we will stay away from them, and I'll keep my eyes on you." Michael's confident statement had sexual overtones, something he displayed by touching her often and occasionally inappropriately, especially when he was talking with his friends. She felt like he treated her like a Bond girl—and that was annoying. It made her wonder if that was what she was to him. But for this morning and the rest of the trip, his faults could be overlooked.

People are moving now. Loading skis onto cars; laughing with their coffee mugs in hand; discussing what they are going to do today. She can hear their muffled voices, which brim with excitement and adventure. The roads have been cleared, the snow pushed aside. She remembers seeing quaint, bustling stores when they drove through the center of the village. She would love to do some shopping—even if she cannot afford to—before they leave. Perhaps buy a memento for her mother.

* * *

Finally, Noelani pulls Michael from bed with the enticement of a shower. She tells him they have very little time left here, and if they want to ski, it's now or never. "So quick showers, Michael, you understand?" She teases. Within the hour, they are suited up and ready to go.

"Let's just do one easy run like yesterday, so I get my legs under me," Noelani tells him.

"Okay, but you'll be bored." Michael is eager to get higher up the mountain. In short order, she realizes he is right, and they ride Stump Alley Express, the high-speed quad, to the top and ski right down the expansive pathway. Noelani falls only once, when she sees a skier come too close and tries to cut away.

"You okay?"

"I'm fine. I just saw that guy, and it made me cut and slip. No worries."

Michael protectively explains, "People are supposed to keep fifteen feet away from each other, but that's not the way some people ski. They get out of control and get right on top of you."

"It's no big deal. Let's go!" Noelani wastes no time getting down the rest of the run. "Let's go again. I really liked that one."

"Alright, we'll take chair 3; it's called Facelift. But we'll cut across to some better trails. You will love it, and hopefully it'll be less crowded." Michael guides her to the chair lift. As they approach the top, he tells her, "Tips up—and this time, after you get off the slope, follow me because we are going to cut to the right." They ski across the mountain to a run called Coyote. It is much thinner and nestled with trees on both sides.

Michael stops before they turn onto the trail. He sees the look on Noelani's face. "Don't worry, Noel. We will take it slow. Try not to snowplow too much. Just keep sweeping left and right. Use your legs and pivot. You've got this."

Trepidation flutters in her chest, but she is determined. She notices that it is much less crowded. They turn left. She feels a mixture of euphoria and apprehension as she advances down the slope. When she reaches a stopping point, where Michael, who has been just in front of her, is waiting, she high fives him and hugs him.

"Oh, God. That was fun! Scary but fun! Whew!" The cold, crisp air billows around their faces.

"I knew you could handle it! Now we just go down here to Comeback Trail. It'll take us back to Stump Alley. It's beautiful. We'll be right beside trees. Gorgeous. Follow me."

"Okay, Michael. I'm going to take it slow and enjoy it all." She readjusts her goggles, drives her poles into the powder, and again veers left. There is a quick drop; she gains speed and fights to slow herself a bit. Then it levels out somewhat. Noelani likes to always keep Michael in her view, but on this trail, the trees tighten the path, and she loses him at times.

Noelani hears some hooting and hollering off to her left and tries to see what the commotion is. She takes her eyes off the trail momentarily and realizes that's not smart. She feels she has tunnel vision—she is only able to see what is immediately in front of her because the speed is a bit faster. She tries to dig her skis' edges into the powder so she can track more parallel to the trail to control her descent. Then she hears yelling again. This time, it seems lower, and she realizes it is from somewhere behind the trees, probably on a trail next to hers.

She manages to slow herself down as she veers away from what sounds like crazy guys, some of whom are now further down the hill. She gets to the side of the trail and prepares to make the turn. Out of the corner of her eye, she spots Michael waving at her. She hits a small rut that drops her down, only to lead to a small mogul that makes her lose her balance for a moment. But she braces herself, and her right ski holds firmly. She slides toward the end of the Comeback Trail, where she sees a break in the trees on her left. Again, she sees Michael waving at her. He has stopped. She cannot see anyone else, but she again hears voices in the trees. As she maintains her turn to the right, her back is to the trees.

Michael sees what is happening. Snowboarders are whizzing through the trees in the soft powder. Two of them seem to know what they are doing and pass Michael, laughing at their antics. But the ones lagging behind them keep falling.

Suddenly, one of the snowboarders bursts through the tree line, his back to the Comeback Trail, looking only in the direction he came from, unaware of what is behind him. He hits the trail and immediately doubles his speed. He is out of control. He has no idea who is around him as he cuts diagonally across the same trail that Noelani is descending. She is starting to turn back. She is only about forty yards away from Michael. She hears him but cannot understand him. She leans to the right and pivots just as the snowboarder hits the bump she just rolled over. He goes airborne. He never utters a sound. Noelani only sees him seconds before he is about to hit her at full speed.

Michael can hear the sickening sound of bodies impacting, Noelani's sharp scream, and his own voice bellowing, "No!"

Part Two

"Love looks not with the eyes, but with the mind,
and therefore is winged Cupid painted blind."

—Helena, *A Midsummer Night's Dream*

Chapter Twenty-One: 1995

Sunday evening. Lewis and Lotte's home. Encinitas, California.

"Yes, Lewis." Lotte's voice is flat. Lewis cannot see her face, but he senses what Lotte must be feeling. He feels it too. Seven years has taken its toll. He thinks of all those vocabulary words he teaches his students: *heartbroken, distraught, impotent, and forlorn*, and one has the adjectives to describe the last three years of the marriage of Lewis and Lotte.

Phoenix. In Greek mythology, it is the long-lived bird that is cyclically regenerated—reborn from the ashes. That has been his hope. Lotte's too. But Phoenix, Arizona has burned them out.

That is part of the reason their first and only daughter is named *Hope*. Despite Lotte's lack of maternal instinct—and her anxiety that the baby would derail their plans to establish the lifestyle she wanted—Lewis always knew that deep down, Lotte could not accept motherhood in its totality. Lotte never settles for just what is acceptable, manageable. Lotte wants remarkable, exceptional.

"Alright. I understand. Lotte, we can talk about the details later." Lewis sighs as the phone conversation dries up like the desert that surrounds the high-rise condo that Lotte owns. It made financial sense. The days of traveling back and forth on weekends and living out of hotels were hard on everyone. Kahil Gibran's words of advice are passé to Lewis: *"And the oak tree and the cypress grow not in each other's shadow."* Lewis knows that he must accept that they were never born of the same timber.

The *goodbye* stings Lewis, and he believes it resonates with Lotte, too. He still loves her the way he always has. He still wants her to be sitting on Moonlight Beach in Encinitas with Hope, watching the California sunset. But the phone connection goes dead. Lewis thinks about what Lotte will do—or has done—to fill the void. She has "come home" sporadically. The trips were more frequent when Hope was a toddler, but as Hope grew, Lotte withdrew. Maybe the guilt was just too much. Maybe in the last year, the smiles on all their faces were just painted on because that is just what you do when "the relatives" visit. Lotte tried to bond with Hope as a mother, but the older both grew, their reality turned the painted smiles upside down, like the bizarre faces of clowns. All three of them were putting on makeup that ran down their faces as tears do when goodbyes are spoken. Lotte evolved into a "fly-in mom," with sacks of gifts—clothes and such to compensate. Guilt gifts.

Lewis sits on the couch, wondering how this will play out when he has to bring the farce to an end with Hope. He finds himself in a never-ending memory loop, like those TV promos for the music of days bygone. You just can't seem to escape that channel. You are hypnotized by the "hits" of the past. You remember where you were and how you held each other and how you dreamed of the joy that would eventually become your world. But in the end, Springsteen was right "Everybody's got a hungry heart." And just like the song prophesized, she went out for a ride and she never came back.

The first year, Lotte practically begged to stay on in Encinitas with her company. She promised to leave for whatever city they sent her to if they would just give her time with her baby. The company made small concessions that became unnerving to her and upsetting to her daughter. *Where's Mommy?* became the question Lewis had to answer so often that he grew angry and frustrated. But putting blame on Lotte, when they could barely make ends meet, was the last thing he would say. He felt it, though. He took walks with the baby, cursing how corporate America used their employees. He wished Lotte would just quit and work for another company. But it would be the same mentality with the same quotas to make and the same coldhearted attitude: *If you can't do it, there are plenty of good-lookin' gals to take your place, honey.*

Lewis knew that Lotte's financial fears would always instigate memories of her life back in El Centro with parents who felt that ambition was as unnecessary as a brand new car or a four star dinner out. From their perspective, as long as Lotte and Lewis had a passel of children playing in the sweltering heat in the backyard, with hot dogs on the grill and NASCAR on TV, they were in paradise. As Lewis walked down Encinitas' main street with Hope in her stroller, he realized that Lotte would not allow *her* family to become so damn mediocre. Lewis felt that he deeply understood Lotte's fear, her drive, her desire to be more, to have more, to know more, and therefore ascend to what she desired: higher ground.

Now, sipping a coffee, he wonders where she sits. Twelve stories up in downtown Phoenix. Upscale. Contemporary. *Was she really alone?* He doubted that, but they had never once discussed it—until now. He did not ask for a name. She did not offer one. But they both knew. They acknowledged that it was better to leave things unsaid until the bandage of time could be peeled off, leaving behind a scar, visible only when naked staring at themselves in the mirror.

"God damn it!" Lewis howls at the wind outside on the deck. His daughter will soon be home from a sleepover—her first real overnight at her best friend's house. *Do I tell her now? Now, when she jumps into the house, fully liberated from midnight fears of monsters under the bed? Does she need to know now that divorce is the unimagined creature lurking in the closet? It has been waiting for this day—or some day very soon—to jump out and scream, "You don't really have a mom like your friends. You won't ever have a sister or a brother in the family picture on the sofa table. It will just be Dad there for the flute lessons and the softball games. Just Dad for Thanksgiving and Christmas and your birthday from now on."*

Lewis sees the pink glow of the Pacific sunset. He can't help but be reminded of the many mothers who have cried in his classroom about their efforts to raise their children without their husbands. They sob for their children and for their ruined lives. Lewis knows these women feel alone.

Lonely. It has been seven years. He has never once taken off his wedding ring. The ring that says, *I am taken by the woman I love.* How many times has he pretended that Lotte is in his life? How many times has he made excuses when he shows up alone—if he shows up at all—to parties or movies with friends? People suspect, naturally. But Lewis, like many accomplished teachers, is a good actor. He models himself after Dustin Hoffman's character in *Kramer vs. Kramer.* And now that the finality of their fictitious life has set in, it all seems crazy. How could they have ever thought that this could have or should have worked?

He will not tell Hope today. Not tomorrow, either. Maybe in a week.

And he certainly has no intention of telling Lotte or Hope about his eyesight.

His life has become a blind man's bluff.

Chapter Twenty-Two: 1987

Around midnight. Mammoth Lakes Hospital.

Kalani Kekoa sits in the back seat of Henry and Dee Gates' Ford Explorer. She has tissues balled up in her hand; the rest of the box is in her purse. Henry is driving. Dee is nervously looking for the hospital's sign. She spots the brightly lit sign and tells Henry to turn. He obeys.

Henry pulls up to the entrance of the hospital, an A-framed, chalet-like structure. He stops, and it is implied that the women will get out and Henry will find parking. He parks the car and then rests his head on the steering wheel. He has never driven so long, at night, with so much tension. He fights the exhaustion, locks the car, and ambles toward the glowing lights near the front doors of the hospital. His breath is like a white cloud enveloping his face, but the frigid temperature smacks him so hard that he has no recourse but to move—and move as fast as his cramped legs can carry him.

Henry enters and immediately realizes that what looks like an old Swiss lodge is actually a state of the art hospital. He does not see either his wife or Kalani. Befuddled, he shuffles to the front desk.

A receptionist immediately realizes he is the missing piece of the puzzle. "Hello. You must be Henry."

"Yes, I am."

"I know where your wife and Mrs. Kekoa are. Please follow me. You look cold, but I promise you'll warm up quickly. I will get you some coffee if you like," she says. Her badge reads *Diane*.

Henry is so tired that his senses are telling him to just do as this kind woman says. He replies, "Yes, Miss. Coffee would be very nice. But let me follow you and see what's what. Thank you kindly."

They walk down a long hallway. Henry hates hospitals. He and his buddies often joke that if they go into one, they'll never come out alive. He tries to swallow that fear like a bitter pill.

They turn down one corridor and then another. He then sees the sign: *SURGERY WAITING ROOM.* The letters are red. He enters and sees his fellow travelers, sitting next to each other.

"Henry—oh, thank goodness you found us," Dee says to him. Out of habit, she continues, "Did you find a place to park?"

"Of course I did, Dee. Why do you think I am standing here? This nice lady—Miss Diane here—brought me to you. What's the situation?"

Kalani is so emotional she can hardly speak. "Not sure, yet. The doctor is coming over to talk to us. He's with Michael, I think."

"Oh, okay." Henry tries to get his bearings. Diane quietly exits. Henry notices that the women already have coffee. "Well, has anyone said anything?" Henry asks as he remains standing.

"Why don't you sit, Henry?" Dee pats a seat next to hers.

"Dee, I've been sitting for God knows how many hours. I gotta stand for a while." Henry tries not to show his annoyance. "Geeze, I gotta find the men's room."

* * *

When Henry returns, Diane has coffee, cream, and sugar for him. "Thank you, Miss."

"My pleasure. Please, if there is anything I can do, let me or the front desk know." She vanishes.

Just as Henry sits down in the waiting room, a doctor in a white coat and blue scrubs briskly emerges with Michael behind him. Michael wears jeans and a green flannel shirt, and in his hand is a heavy coat that he places on a chair. His movements are anything but brisk.

The doctor removes his wire-framed glasses and begins: "Please sit down, everyone. I'm Dr. Knowleton, and my staff and I have been treating Noelani since Mr. Krauss—Michael—brought her here with the help of the EMTs from Mammoth Mountain. I know you are all very worried—and rightly so—but just know that this is one of the top orthopedic hospitals in California and that your daughter," he looks at Kalani, "is in the best of care, Mrs. Kekoa. So please, let me take you through what we have already done. We have a good idea of what needs to be done in the morning."

The threesome's faces are a mixture of hope and fear. Michael's face is the exception. His expression is that of a man defeated and guilt-ridden. He interrupts the doctor.

"Mrs. Kekoa, I am so, so sorry. I don't know what to say. I'm sick. I just—" He sits next to Kalani and puts his face in his hands. His eyes are red, and it is obvious that he is shaken. His knees are bouncing up and down like a cylinder in a car's engine.

Now it is the doctor's turn to interrupt. "Mrs. Kekoa, I assume these are your close…friends?" He realizes that they cannot be family. They nod.

"Yes, I'm Noelani's teacher. My name is Dee, and this is my husband, Henry. We came from LA as soon as we received Michael's call that Noelani had been in a serious skiing accident."

"Yes. Oh, that was quite a trip," the doctor agrees. "So let me get right to it. The first thing you should know is that the ski patrol and Michael explained what happened on the ski slopes to me, and everyone agrees that what happened was an accident that was not—I repeat—*not* in any way either Noelani's or Michael's fault. I want you to know that. Michael can go over what happened later, but let's talk about Noelani's medical condition. She has a broken femur in her left leg. Fortunately, it is a clean break, and we have already reset the bone. She is young, strong, and healthy, and that bone will mend itself quite nicely. That is the good news. The more serious—but treatable—injury is to her ACL, her left anterior cruciate ligament. The ACL, which is in the middle of the knee, stops your shinbone from sliding in front of your thigh bone. Most often we find that it is torn, but in Noelani's case, I am afraid, it is ruptured—and a ruptured ACL is a more complicated and painful skiing injury."

He pauses to let all that sink in. All five of them take a breath.

"Right now, she is sleeping pretty soundly. We have sedated her and are giving her pain meds. We would like to operate to reconnect the ruptured ACL very early this morning. We would like her to rest, and we are working on the swelling. I must tell you that I can perform the surgery—and I have done my fair share of these—but we do not have to perform the operation here in this hospital. She can be ambulanced to one of your local hospitals if you like. Another reason I wanted to wait for you to get here is because we need you to consent to the procedure. Michael cannot legally give consent, since he is not her husband, you understand."

Kalani feels the need to stop the doctor. "Wait. Doctor. Wait. I don't want to move her. I trust you, Doctor. But I have to think." She turns to Dee and Henry. "What should I do? He is excellent doctor. This hospital's excellent. But I'm worried, Dee." Before either Dee or Henry can respond, she asks, "Doctor, how do I pay?"

"Kalani," Dee touches her friend's hand, "remember, you and Noelani have the same health insurance. Doctor, do you take insurance—of course you must?"

"If it is a major carrier, I do. But my office will be in contact with you to make sure. I don't want you to worry about that. And Michael and I have talked." This is Michael's cue.

Michael clears his raspy throat. "Mrs. Kekoa, I spoke with my parents. They feel terrible. Sick. They told me to tell you that whatever the cost of the deductible —or whatever is not covered—they will take care of it."

"No." Kalani's pride erupts. "No! Mr. Michael, I will pay. I don't need help, but your parents very nice to offer that, but I don't think it will be necessary."

Dr. Knowleton calms all of them. "I am sure once my case manager gets involved, the costs will be worked out. The important thing now is for me to inform you of the risks associated with the surgery—since Noelani will be under general anesthesia—and the possible complications. We will have some paperwork for you to sign, and if we are proceeding here at this hospital, I will need to get my surgical team together. A rupture requires me to basically do some careful sewing and mending. It requires that I…"

As the doctor explains, poor Henry cannot keep his eyes open. His head leans back against the wall. He begins to lightly snore.

All look up. Dr. Knowleton smiles and says, "I'm afraid either I am really boring, or Henry has exhausted himself getting you all here tonight." He looks at his watch. It reads 1:44 a.m. "Perhaps we can all agree to just fill out the minimum paperwork—just to get things started—and then everyone can get some rest. Fortunately, it is not a weekend—yet—and the hospital has some cots in another room that you can rest on until we wake Noelani up at around 6 a.m.—would that be alright?"

Henry's loudest snore wakes him up, and all look at him.

"Sorry, what did I miss?" Henry says sheepishly.

Chapter Twenty-Three: 1995

7:00 p.m. The home of May and Amos Adler.

"Are you *still* on that computer, Amos?" May Adler's voice sounds overcooked, just as she fears her dinner will be. At her feet, a German shepherd named Otza keeps a close watch on May and her husband, ever alert to any discord between the two.

"Yes, I am. Gimme a minute, May." Dr. Adler is hunched over his desktop computer with his head tilted up so his glasses can magnify the text. He hasn't mastered the ability to increase the font size yet. The words keep repeating in his ear from his last appointment an hour ago with Lewis Bennett.

He mutters to himself, "Serpiginous choroiditis."

In the last thirty minutes, he has grasped this much: *"Serpiginous choroiditis is a rare disorder that affects men more often than women. Symptoms usually appear during the early to middle adult years."* Another medical journal concluded, *"A sudden, painless decrease in vision in one or both eyes may be the first sign of serpiginous choroiditis. Patients may also notice blind spots in the visual field or flashes of light. Both eyes are commonly affected, although the second eye may not develop lesions for weeks to years after the first eye. The exact cause of serpiginous choroiditis is unknown."*

Dr. Adler sighs, but then, like a lightning strike, May's

warning booms from the kitchen: "Amos, I'm making your plate, and it's either going on the table or going in the trash."

"I'm coming. I'm coming." Amos pivots from his swivel chair and hop-steps to the kitchen as fast as his sixty-nine-year-old legs can carry him. Otza follows and nestles himself under the table, hoping for some scraps to drop. Upon sitting, Amos innocently looks up at May, and then smiles as he inhales the aroma of the steak, baked potato, and butternut squash. "Honey, it's a meal fit for a king."

May's retort begins with an *ahem.* Then she seats herself and eyes her husband. "I've got some things to say to you, Amos. First, I'm telling you right now that the steak is overcooked—"

"No, May. It's fine." Amos begins to slice into the steak. He tries to disguise the difficulty of cutting into it, but to no avail.

"Yes, it is. Don't try to butter me up. How many times have we had this conversation, Amos? I don't make things like your sister Lena. I do hair. I don't do 'the kitchen.'"

"May. May. May. Everything is fine. Really." Amos keeps his head down for safety's sake. As soon as May looks away, Amos lets a small scrap of steak fall to the floor. Otza quickly devours it.

"Well, *this* time it *would have been* if you had gotten off that damn computer when I gave you the five-minute warning." May uses her knife to make her point.

"You're right, sweetheart. I'm sorry. It's just something that perplexed me about work."

"Yes, I'm sure. How many times have I heard that in the half-century that you have been listening to people's troubles?"

"I know. Too many." He butters his potato, which he realizes is as hard as a rock. It is undercooked, but he is not about to utter a syllable about that. Instead, he counters with compliments on the squash.

"Yeah, I know, Mister Smooth Talker." Then she deadpans, "It's Lena's recipe."

Being the gentleman, Amos reminds his wife that she had *two* points.

"Yes, that's right. Hmm. Now, what was it? I hate when I forget something that you do that bugs me, Amos. Oh, wait! I remember. She pauses because she is still chewing the over-cooked steak. She keeps chewing. "You know what? I think this steak is just tough. I should have gotten the filet mignon."

They work their way through the meal, both savoring Lena's butternut squash.

Not wanting to invite disaster, Amos asks May about her day and covertly slides another—bigger—scrap of steak in Otza's direction.

"You are changing the subject."

"And that was?"

"It's the thing I can't remember. Oh, yes. Now I remember. Last week, I asked you when you are retiring, and you said, 'Ask me next week.' Well, it's next week, so I'm asking again. I mean, Amos, you're going to be seventy next year!"

"I'll retire when you retire, May." Amos smirks because he can anticipate May's response.

"Now, that is ridiculous, Amos. I cut hair for my friends. They are family. I've been with them for thirty years. You don't just quit on your best friends. Goodness, it's not even work for me. Snip here, cut there, we talk about who's doin' what to whom and when and where." May breaks open her potato with a plunging thrust of her knife but makes no comment on its rock-hard surface. "Me quitting—or 'retiring'—is not the issue because I'm not the one coming home late and carrying the burden of a whole bunch of people, now am I?"

"May—" Amos pauses before he continues. He wants to calm down the love of his life. He starts again. "May, you know I am not taking on any more patients, and I have cut back my hours. I've been thinking, and I'm going to tell my secretary to cancel all Friday appointments."

"Really? Hmm. When?" May looks under the table and sees that Otza has placed his head on Amos' foot and his tail on hers.

"I already told her." He lies. "And I am shifting some of my patients—a few—over to the other doctors whom I think can relate to them a little better." He looks her straight in the eyes and puts his fork and knife down.

"May, I know it is not easy being married to me. You have had to endure this for forty-seven years. But I know the time is coming, okay?"

With that, all the tension in his petite wife seems to slowly fade, just as it has through all the challenges they have faced over the decades. Their two sons are grown, and their grand-children are their favorite pastime. May can be mercurial, her husband placid. Their waters run deep, and their squabbles are like the shifting currents that pass over the rocks on a river. Like Dee and Henry Gates, Amos and May Adler have lived through the LA riots, Civil Rights Acts, assassinations, Black Power, and integration. One of their boys served in Vietnam and runs his own business, and the other was a JAG, lawyer-ing for the military. They are proud, and they are resilient. But mostly, after all the turbulence and discrimination and dreams deferred, they are still each other's best friend and in love. So May's next question comes as no surprise.

"What was so important on the computer that you were looking at?"

"Well, before I tell you that, you remember the troubled boy I've been seeing?"

She nods, dropping a tough piece of steak down to Otza. He reverses his position, recognizing that good fortune comes from both his masters.

"I saw his father today. He came in on the spur of the moment. Apparently, his son is being harassed by other *black* boys."

"Why? What did he do to them?"

"That's not the question. It's what he *didn't* do to them. At the high school here, as you know, the black kids are a small minority. Well, his son, I'll call him Junior, anyway, he has been hanging out with the guys on his baseball team. Many of them are white. And the black kids are giving him grief because he won't eat lunch with *them*. They're calling him *Jackie*."

"What are you saying, Amos? You talking about Jackie Robinson? Don't those black boys know what in the Good Lord's name that man did for them!"

"May, calm down."

"I am calm. I can be calm and angry. I have a mind to call their mothers and let them know exactly what those knuckleheads are saying to that boy...the one you called, Junior!"

May knows that what is said in her husband's office stays there. No phone calls will be made. She settles down and then asks, "So *that* is what you were looking up?" May is still confused.

"No. That's not why I was late. I was looking up a rare eye disorder that my last patient has. There is a good chance that his condition will lead to partial or complete blindness. He's in his forties with a daughter, and today he told me his wife wants a divorce."

"Oh, that poor man." May has heard many tales of woe but she is not ready for this.

"Yes. And to make matters worse—if it can get worse—he needs to read papers for a living. He is a teacher—a journalism teacher. He is scared out of his wits."

"Does the daughter or the wife know about the eye disorder?"

"No. This man is one stubborn mule, May. Proud. Bright. Independent."

"Is there a treatment—or is it caused by anything he can stop doing?"

"The treatment can slow its progression, but the disorder is different for every person. And there is no known cause of it. It just happens, and no one knows why." Amos pushes himself away from the table. "Crazy thing is that the Hawaiian gal I have been seeing—you know, the one who Eva Chan recommended?"

"Oh, yes." May slowly rises and gathers up their plates. Otza follows, alert to the possibility of more treats.

"Yeah, well," Amos says as he follows her to the kitchen with the glasses and serving dishes, "she is another person who just got betrayed by a terrible husband. And there is something about her husband that she's not willing to tell me, something that I haven't figured out yet."

He takes the plates, tosses the last scraps of meat to Otza, and turns on the hot water while May puts butter and such back into the refrigerator. It is their after-dinner ritual. Amos continues, "She was a depressed teen when Eva worked with her, you remember Eva Chan, right?"

May nods, "Well, of course I do, Amos. I have not lost my memory yet, thank the Good Lord."

"Me, neither. Anyway, this woman had been stable for years, even after marrying this guy. I told you about the skiing accident that damaged her leg so badly, right?"

"Oh, yes. That poor girl. I cannot imagine what her mother must have felt." May now wipes down the counter and the table, putting the placemats back in the spot they have been for decades. Otza tramps to the fireplace for warmth, curls up, and watches his masters. He seems to understand that the tone of their voices conveys distress.

"Yes. That was seven years ago. There is something about her now that disturbs me greatly. I don't want to push too hard, though."

"I'm sure you have your reasons." May stands next to Amos and shakes out the dishtowels. "Wait, are you afraid she may hurt herself?"

Amos sits down in his favorite chair next to Otza. He reaches down and caresses the dog's head. "No. I doubt that. I'm just afraid for her. You know what I mean? And I am afraid that even admitting the truth about what her husband really did may be more than she can handle."

Chapter Twenty-Four: 1987

3:00 a.m. Mammoth Lakes Hospital.

Kalani sits in the brown leather chair next to her daughter's bed, holding hands with her only child. Her eyes are closed as she prays for the wisdom to know what to say to the doctor in the next few hours. It is all so overwhelming. Kalani has not been in a hospital since she gave birth to Noelani twenty-three years ago. She thanks God for their health and blessings every day, but now He seems to have turned a blind eye to them.

Kalani opens her eyes and sees her crippled dancer. She is frightened for her, knowing that Noelani's dreams of becoming a professional dancer scattered to the winds on that snowy mountain. Kalani knows that her daughter occasionally feels depressed, and she thinks about contacting Dr. Eva Chan when she gets home. Kalani thinks it would be beneficial for Noelani to talk with her and settle her mind. Hopefully, that will prevent her daughter from experiencing night haunts again.

The tubes from the bags hanging from the bars scare Kalani. They go into the back of Noelani's hand. The nurses check on her every hour. They squeeze the bag, check the tubes, and look at the monitor. Kalani is sure the equipment is monitoring Noelani's heartbeat, but just to be sure, she places her hand on Noelani's chest to feel the beating. It is slow but steady. Then she looks at her daughter's leg—elevated, the doctor told her, to keep blood from pooling and to reduce swelling. Noelani's leg is trapped in a prison of black and white wrappings, and it is held up by loops attached to a metal bar. Kalani looks outside through a small slit in the window curtain. She sees a world that belongs in movies, not in real life—and certainly not in hers. She sees great piles of dirty snow, plowed to make way for cars. The stars are brighter than she has ever seen them, as if they are searchlights far up in the sky, making the night seem the darkest blue imaginable.

Kalani frets over what to say to Noelani when she wakes up. How can she tell her daughter that everything will be okay when they both know that Noelani's life will never be the same?

The door opens softly, as Dee noiselessly slips into the room, putting her finger to her lips. She spots another chair and slides it to the other side of Noelani's hospital bed. The women nod. Dee places her hand ever so tenderly on Noelani's left leg, her undamaged one. She can feel the warmth of Noelani's body. She smiles at Kalani. Then she makes the sign of the cross, bows her head, and prays.

When Dee raises her head, she repeats the gesture of crossing her heart. Kalani whispers, "She's asleep. She can't hear us. Why are you awake, Dee? You should rest."

Dee smiles and purrs, "No way. Henry is snoring." Both women smile. "Besides, I want to see our girl." Dee takes the temperature of the room, so to speak. "Are you scared, Kalani?"

Kalani nods and dabs her eyes with tissues.

"Me, too," responds Dee. "But the doctors here see this every day, I bet. They are so good. I know she's in the best hands. I know it." Dee finds a tissue package in her purse and hands it across.

Kalani nods and mouths, *Thank you.*

"She looks beautiful even in this…this bed. Look at her

face. So peaceful. Kalani, she is strong and young. She is a warrior. She will fight through this and get strong. I know she will. Henry and I will help you and her all we can, okay? Kalani, we love her, and we love you."

With that, Kalani bows her head. Then, with the strength that she has displayed from the moment she left Maui, to the time she hid the letters, to the decision to force Noelani to see Dr. Eva Chan, to her transformation into a businesswoman, Kalani rises from her chair. She circles the bed and embraces Dee. The two comprise a portrait of sisterhood.

Then they sit silently in their chairs as the clock on the wall tracks a slow, tedious path toward morning.

* * *

Henry is the only one who does not enter the room at 7:37 a.m. when the final preparations are being made to move Noelani into surgery. He listened carefully to the doctor's explanation of what will happen and how he will reattach Noelani's ACL, but it all seems like something he heard on a TV program. *Ligament. Cadaver. Incision. Adhesions. Grafts. Screws. Bones. Staples.* All of this reinforces Henry's view that hospitals are haunted houses and that the sooner he gets some fresh air outside, the better.

When Noelani is wheeled out of her room on a gurney, Henry grabs her hand. "You gonna be alright, Miss Noelani. I'll take care of your mom, okay?" A faint, disoriented smile appears on her lips as she rolls past. Henry's shoulders sag.

Michael comes out of Noelani's hospital room, with Kalani and Dee behind him. All four slowly turn down another corridor. "Let's get some coffee, everyone," Michael says. "You folks must be hungry. Let me get you some breakfast." No one really speaks, but everyone acquiesces to his invitation. They head to the cafeteria, where nurses and doctors are buzzing around like blue and white birds getting morning snacks for their little ones back at the nest. The foursome plops down and looks at a laminated menu.

Michael takes orders, although toast and coffee are all that everyone requests. Nerves do a job on appetites. When he returns, each person nibbles on their toast and sips their too hot coffee.

Michael smiles at his three breakfast companions, but only Dee and Henry return the expression. He feels the need to break the awkward silence and hopefully exonerate himself from all that has happened.

He tells them that Noel quickly learned how to traverse on skis. How much she loved being on the mountain. How much care he took to make sure she was safe and enjoying herself. How he saw the teenagers, wild and careless, in the trees and off the trails. He explains that that is not allowed and how sure he felt that Noel couldn't have seen them. How stupid and out of control they were. How he warned her and yelled at them. How she was blindsided. How he heard her scream.

Michael looks down, but Kalani stares at the top of his head. Henry and Dee sip coffee. Michael resumes his confession.

How he skied up the hill back to her. How he held her. How he crossed his own skis in the snow to signal other skiers and the ski patrol. How someone grabbed the guy who hit her. How quickly the patrol came down with the sled for Noel. How calm and careful the medics were with Noel. How he skied behind them and never left her side. How he hasn't slept since. And finally, with a flourish, how terrible he feels.

No one speaks for a full minute.

Then Dee says, "I am sure you did what you could."

Henry says, "Well, you can't blame yourself."

Michael nods. He waits.

Kalani says nothing until she asks Dee where the bathroom is. Dee leaps up to accompany her. Once they are out of earshot, Kalani turns to Dee, "He sounds sad, but that is the actor talking. He doesn't even know her name. It is *Noelani.*"

Chapter Twenty-Five: 1995

4:00 p.m. The office of Dr. Amos Adler, M.D.

In the minutes he has before seeing Noelani Kekoa, Dr. Adler peruses his file on her case. He is still perplexed by Noelani's unwillingness to share what brought on her panic attacks. He has his suspicions. He reads his notes: *She had a promising career as a dancer, but she was in a terrible skiing accident back in '87. Despite all her efforts at rehab, her dance career never materialized.* He sips his lukewarm coffee. *The husband, John McAdams—she never took his name, probably for professional reasons—had affairs on his business travels—she claims he says "everyone does it...it's not personal." She says that "he thought she knew." No children.* He jots down, *Ask about that. Never mentions her father.* He flips the page: *Yoga instructor. Plans to be a co-owner of a yoga studio.* His secretary Lemon Yellow fingernail pokes her head into his office. "She's here, Doctor," she nonchalantly informs him before sauntering back to her desk.

Dr. Adler enters the waiting room and notices that Noelani is chatting with his next patient, Lewis Bennett. He pauses and observes the easy banter between the two—the smiles. Usually, clients are nervous and hiding behind magazines. These two are clearly the exception. That's when he also realizes that Lewis is quite early for his appointment.

He clears his throat and smiles at them both. "Noelani, come on back."

They navigate through the office passageway, and once in Adler's office he waves to the usual seat, "Please, Noelani, have a seat. How have you been feeling?" he asks, as he replaces his reading glasses on top of his head.

She gathers her long, black hair and wraps it behind her. "I'm fine. A little bit nervous. But fine."

"Why are you nervous, Noelani? Has anything caused it?" Dr. Adler's eyes zero in on her non-verbal cues. Her face is his focus for this session.

"Well, I guess, what I am nervous about, um, *nervous* isn't the right word. *Anxious*…a little." Adler notices she is already twirling her hair around her hand. His concern is piqued.

"Okay, I'm anxious just *thinking* about my ex…," she stumbles to get her thoughts together. "John is upsetting me." Noelani begins, "First, I don't ever want to be in that house again. That's first. I don't ever want to see him again. My divorce attorney has told me to get my stuff out, and I have friends who can help me. I'm staying, for now, with my partner and her husband temporarily here in San Diego until I find my own place. Things are really busy with finding a new studio. Actually, my plan is Lisa and I will open our own studio here in Encinitas."

Dr. Adler has not seen her this jumpy, this talkative, but also so discombobulated. "Yes, I recall you telling me that and I understand your misgivings," his voice is deep and solemn.

"Anyway, my partner's name is Lisa Holtzman. We first thought of opening a studio in LA, but her husband Phillip has transferred to San Diego, and we have both heard that yoga is catching on here. Right now, Lisa and Phillip's condo is in Del Mar, not far from your office, Dr. Adler. And with my marriage falling apart…well, Encinitas is our goal. So whatever settlement my lawyer reaches, I want to set aside a significant portion so we can get our business started."

Dr. Adler knows that some clients 'fall into their own truth' by just talking it out, so he does not interrupt.

"My mother is worried about me being 'so far away.' She drives, but usually not on the freeway or at night. She treats San Diego like it is as distant as Maui. I tell her there's a train that goes right to Encinitas, where we are planning on opening our business and where I will be renting an apartment—soon, that is. I think I just said that, right? Sorry, I'm just… whatever."

Dr. Adler notices that Noelani's posture is different. Rather than sitting back in the chair, she is perched on the edge of her seat and leans closer to him. Dr. Adler makes an effort to be upbeat. "No. No, don't concern yourself with repeating things, Noelani. I'm an old guy. Sometimes I need to hear things twice. So says my wife." He chuckles. "Anyway, I can understand your mother's concern, Noelani, but she must be happy you are making a fresh, new start."

"You would think so, since she did the same thing with her business. I mean with us leaving Hawaii to go to LA, right?" Noelani's right hand moves through her hair and twists the ends tighter and tighter.

"I see what you are saying. And you feel confident that you and your business partner, Lisa, are on the same page with all this? And that your mother feels confident in you two as partners?"

"Definitely. Lisa is the one person I can trust. She and Phillip were the ones who basically saved me from John that awful night." Noelani abruptly stops.

Her eyes give her away. Dr. Adler senses that even one more word would push her off a cliff into a deep, dark chasm. Dr. Adler ponders her choice of words: *Saved me from John that awful night.* He knows for certain that she must be very scared.

Noelani takes a deep breath, attempting to calm herself and mask the emotions with which she is wrestling to stifle.

Dr. Adler fills the void. Noelani's mercurial relationship with her ill-tempered husband, John is the minefield he knows he must navigate. He has worked with many frightened clients so the key is to see how to defuse the fear and move to safer ground. He asks, "I assume John is living in your LA home, but, more importantly, he is staying away from *you*, right?"

Noelani is quick to reply, "No. I mean yes. He plans to move to Las Vegas, thank God. He said something like that's where his money will go a long way."

"Well, that should ease your mind; however, that does not seem to be the case. Why is that?" Now he is pushing deeper. She either comes out with it or not.

"Yeah, well. It would be better, but he is being a jerk. Fighting with my attorney and calling me, and saying lies… and other things, like 'We had an open marriage,' and that 'he thought I knew that'—which is ridiculous. Totally."

"I assume your attorney has advised you not to speak with him." Dr. Adler is making sure that that is the case.

"Yes. Yes. Of course. But one time, last week, he calls me, and before I could hang up on him, he shouts something like 'You're probably getting laid by some dudes at yoga as soon as I leave for work!'…and he called me some filthy name…and I hung up as fast as I could."

Dr. Adler watches as Noelani reaches into her bag for a tissue. Adler has heard this vengeful, threatening outburst towards wives or girlfriends more times than he can possibly count. He presumes that John is one of those men who simply hate to lose anything, especially to a woman. He wants his world to be just the way *he wants it*. And when he gets caught, he blames the victim and vocalizes his anger in an attempt to cut as deeply as possible. His concern for Noelani and her safety reaches a tipping point. He decides to say what many others in his profession would not.

"Noelani, two things I want you to hear, and they are equally important. Both of which you may have already done, but I would be remiss if I don't emphasize these actions. First, has your attorney advised you to have a restraining order placed on John?"

Noelani's mouth and nose are hidden behind her tissues. She nods.

"Good. Second, John may be vindictive, but he needs the money to sell your house and move on and he needs your signature to sell, I assume, so you have leverage." He pauses to let that sink in. "So you are *not* powerless. He will need to get this divorce settled so he can get on with whatever damnable life he wants to live."

Noelani again nods. Behind the tissues, Dr. Adler sees a glimmer of optimism, shaded by fear.

Dr. Adler knows that John's phone call was likely preceded by a physical assault. He also knows that Noelani may not be able to say anything more about this for now, but he makes one gentle attempt.

"Noelani, is there anything else you feel comfortable sharing with me about how John has treated you?" He pauses and opens his enormous hands in a gesture of safety. "Anything John has done, besides the overt infidelity? Has he *physically* harmed you, perhaps?" He lets that last question drape over her, hoping it will be of some comfort to tell him what happened.

For the first time, Noelani turns stone-faced. She purses her lips. "No."

Dr. Adler fights the impulse to narrow his eyes. He is deeply troubled by her reluctance to admit what is obvious to him. He knows her emotions are raw. He stops. He sees how her face is flushed.

She stares at her hands, and without looking up, says, "I don't want to talk about it. I know you mean well, Dr, Adler…. I'm not ready…. I just never want to see him ever again. Ever."

Dr. Amos Adler realizes that this may be all that Noelani will articulate. He somberly replies, "I understand, Noelani, I really do."

He knows she's fighting to hide her face from him. She is eager to leave before she cracks.

For now, he can only imagine the fractures that lie just beneath her surface.

Chapter Twenty-Six: 1995

The first-class cabin on a flight to Los Angeles. Just after takeoff.

Lotte is sorting through the mini photo album that she carries with her whenever she heads west. Sitting beside her is her "life mate," as she calls him: Anderson Rodriguez. He is in the aisle seat. His hand is on hers. Neither has a ring encumbering their finger. His hand is a russet brown and is well manicured. He is a native of Arizona.

Lotte looks up from her photo album as a flight attendant offers them champagne and an assortment of cheeses and crackers. Lotte cannot help but notice that the woman's smile and attention are fixed on her strikingly handsome partner. His voice is rich, confident, and courteous as he accepts the woman's offerings. Lotte is used to his magnetism, to which many women are drawn. It is what pulled her into his vortex two years ago, when Anderson Rodriguez, COO of Phoenix Solar Industries, asked her to join his company as VP of Marketing. This was after a passionate love affair that shook Lotte to her core and found her sleeping in the King's suite in Munich, Germany.

* * *

The secret world of Lotte Bennett is about to be exposed to Lewis in the most abrupt manner. It will not, however, be the theme of her journey to sun-drenched Encinitas, the place she has pretended to call *home*. Her residence is no longer a stylish condo in downtown Phoenix. She now lives on a sprawling ranch-styled estate near Scottsdale and, when necessary for work, in a penthouse in the heart of Phoenix.

Sitting beside her, sipping his champagne and reviewing some business documents, is the soon-to-be forty-year-old Anderson Rodriguez. He has an MBA from Columbia University and a family with investments in noteworthy real estate both in Arizona and Mexico, along with several energy companies. By Arizona standards, he and his family exude "old money."

He is four years Lotte's senior and has been driven to succeed, much like his parents and brothers. He is recognized as Phoenix's most eligible bachelor. He has taken many lovers as companions, but never has any woman had any lasting appeal or intrigued him like Lotte Bennett. Her back-story, with an intentional gap, fascinates Anderson, as it is both astounding and alluring to him. He values Lotte's grit, something he feels too many women sorely lack. He believes Lotte is loyal and loving.

His money and fame are secondary to her compared to what she feels she can and will achieve with him as her partner and lover. She is with an accomplished, distinguished gentleman who sees the world as she does, but comes from the other side of the tracks. She knows that her determination to independently succeed distinguishes her to Anderson. Besides her corporate dossier, her petite figure and sensual hunger for him—and his for her—have made their two-year romance sizzle.

When Lotte eventually came clean to Anderson about the heartbreaking reality of her secret life, including her many lies, her child, and even her husband, Lewis, Anderson's compassion for her was palpable. He confessed his own indiscretions and his own guilt. Anderson admitted that he had deceived several women and had left many more heartbroken.

He, too, was pushed by his family to "settle down" and "start a family"—even, if necessary, to cut back on work. After all, his father warned, *When is enough enough?* He resisted. His family did not understand his priorities. But in Lotte, he found what he needed—his Muse.

He met Lotte at a dinner party, where both ignored their plus ones and slipped off to discover the pleasure of each other's company. After six months of pretending she was a free woman, she burst into tears and admitted her sins. She promised to be honest with him, and he made that vow in return. Now, two years later, after building the lifestyle they mutually craved, it was time for Lotte to face Lewis and tear down the façade of their marriage.

A few things had to be clear: she was not abandoning Lewis, disowning Hope, or abdicating her responsibility to either of them. She knew she deserved the shame. But she would not be ashamed of her choice to live with Anderson Rodriguez without the desire or need for children or a wedding ring. But first, the truth must come out—face to face.

* * *

The photographs sit on her lap. Lotte tries to not be emotional when she sees how she has hopscotched each frame of Hope's life. She's not sure she can pinpoint the moment when she started to drift away from Hope—and when her family finally snapped in two. When did the outstretched hands lose their grip? Or was it just her hand that refused to hold on? And why? Mothers are indoctrinated in a simple lesson: love your children above all else. Sacrifice your life goals, your quest for learning, and your journey to a place of your dreams. Abandon these things in lieu of what your children need. Even your husband must be secondary to the needs of your children. When your children can stand apart and alone, the lucky ones—the mothers who have somehow managed to keep their figures, their youth, and their husband's attention and affection—those charmed women may then proceed down their own path. That is, if they have any idea, after decades, where in God's name that path leads.

She knows that Anderson pretends to read a magazine, but he's aware of how nervous and emotional Lotte is as she stops at each picture. He motions for two more glasses of champagne. He places the glasses on his tray. Lotte will sip hers soon enough.

Lotte stares at each picture of Hope. She has unconsciously curated the collection to exclude Lewis; she has cropped him out of most of the birthday, holiday, and beach scenes. It is only when she detects half of his face that she realizes what she has done. She is ashamed. She can't bear to look at his face. He had held her; he had loved her; and worst of all, he had trusted her. Lotte's stomach aches. She quickly turns the page.

With wild, blue-black hair that mirrors Lotte's, Hope bounces with the surf's crest on her boogie board. She races like a deer after a soccer ball, wearing a number 2 on her teal-colored jersey. She sits in her white snowman pajamas under the Christmas tree, hugging an American Girl doll in a colonial costume. She poses for the camera, about to blow out the candles on her birthday cake; Lotte crouches down beside her, her smile frozen in time. Lotte realizes that standing next to her in almost every scene is Lewis, whom she has made invisible. But he was responsible for most of these occasions. The smile painted on Lotte's face in each picture reminds her of how she pretended to perform her motherly duties for her daughter. To a trained eye, Lotte's guilt is as obvious as the suitcase that appears in the background of several photographs.

The last picture is the one that hurts the most. Hope is at Disneyland the summer after third grade. She and her best friend, Carly, are posing with Cinderella. Carly's mother took the photo and gave a copy to Lewis. He mailed it to Lotte, who knows all too well that she never took her daughter to the "Happiest Place on Earth." The remorse bubbles up into Lotte's eyes, and she quickly closes the album and reaches for the champagne. She twists her lips into a fleeting smile, doing her best to convey to Anderson that everything is fine. And then she buries the photo album deep in her purse so that she will not make contact with it again—at least not on this trip.

Anderson squeezes her hand. She looks up at him, then abruptly glances out the window at the City of Angels' skyscrapers, which have emerged from the clouds.

The captain makes the announcement: "Ladies and gentlemen, we are making our final descent into Los Angeles." A flight attendant chirps, "Please return your seat backs and tray tables to their full upright position. Fasten your seatbelt securely and stow all carry-on bags underneath the seat in front of you."

Lotte downs the rest of her champagne in one gulp and hands the glass to Anderson.

Chapter Twenty-Seven: 1995

Outside the home Noelani has shared with her soon-to-be-ex-husband John in Santa Monica.

Noelani's divorce attorney has advised her to take her possessions and move to Encinitas, if that is her intention, as soon as possible. Noelani realizes that most of the "stuff" in the house is John's; she never wants to see or touch any of it. She just wants her clothes, her books, her music, some of her kitchenware, and a few personal effects. She, Dee, and Lisa have been gathering and boxing while they know John is at work, presumably traveling. Noelani has not talked to him in two months. That is her attorney's department.

Noelani's mother is too upset to deal with all this. John is despicable, and it makes her too emotional. All Kalani has asked is for Noelani and Lisa to pick her up when they are done. Then they will caravan to San Diego, followed by Henry and Dee in his pickup truck. Dee has called him, and he is heading over to load up what they have.

As the last of the boxes and such are loaded into the vehicles, Noelani reminds Dee that she and Lisa will pick up her mother. Dee nods and says, "Henry and I will fight the battle of LA traffic. The sooner the better." Noelani and Lisa head south on Interstate 5.

Up until now, Henry has been quietly doing his duty. He

is dressed in his usual dark green work shirt and baggy khaki pants, which are splattered with paint stains. Dee frequently pleads with him, "Henry, please don't go out in public looking like that!" Henry's wardrobe is one of the few bastions she cannot conquer. He does so much for her that his reply always trumps hers: "Dee, I'll do any chore you ask of me, just let me wear what I wanna wear, woman." And that is that.

Dee walks over to Henry and says, "Hurry with the—" But before she finishes her sentence, she sees a black BMW tearing down the street toward them. They know the owner. Dee digs in her purse, grabs her cell phone, and walks away from Henry, who is tying down the last box.

John abruptly pulls into the driveway, opens the car door, and slams it shut with such force that it makes the BMW rock back and forth. "What the hell are you doing?" he shouts at Henry. Henry does not look up at him as he finishes the knot he is working on.

Being ignored is not what John expects. He strides right up to Henry and repeats himself with his volume kicked up a notch.

Henry pulls the rope, steps away to examine his work, and then calmly turns to John. "It's John, right? I'm Henry Gates, Dee's husband—you know, Noelani's dance studio employer?" Henry puts his hands in his pockets. He is not smiling, but he is neither intimidated by, nor irritated with, John's in-your-face attitude. Henry has seen his fair share of white man rage, and this particular white man knows little about how Henry operates.

John shakes his head in mock disbelief and points his finger at Henry. "I don't give a shit who you are. Why are you here, and what do you think you are doing at *my* house?"

"Well, I suppose your attorney may not have informed you that Noelani is moving out and taking her things. I'm here to help her." Henry's hands are still in his pockets.

"So you've been in my house? Who told you that you had any right to enter my house?"

"Well, son, Noelani entered what is, I believe, still her home—and yours, that is. I just loaded the boxes." At that, Henry brought out his truck keys and jangled them.

"Hold it. I have no idea what she took. I should have been here."

"Hmm. Well, I guess she didn't want you here, son."

"Don't call me *son!* I want to see what is in those boxes."

"Well, I started calling you *John*, but then you said you didn't care who *I* was, so I figured I should call you something else. As for the boxes, I've got two things to tell you. One, all she took was her clothes, her kitchenware, and her odds and ends. Lady stuff. She left all the rest for you." Henry pauses and nods toward the front door. "Go ahead, check it out. You'll see that all your furniture and TV and things are all in there."

"I—I will. But I still wanna see what she took."

"Well, that's my second point—fella. That's just not gonna happen."

"Yes, it is, old man. You aren't leaving until I see what is in those boxes." John's face has naturally reddened, but it is his movement toward Henry's truck that makes Henry intercept him.

"You are not going to touch a single thing on my truck." Henry's persona has become more imposing.

John takes a small step back. Two of his female neighbors, both of whom are friendly with Noelani, slowly move toward the scene. John glances at them and sees their scowling faces. He points at Henry and says, "I don't trust you. If I go into the house, you'll take off. So that's why I'm going to look in these boxes."

At this point, Henry has run out of patience. He moves toward John without touching him, though his right fist is closed tightly around his keys; the tips point out between Henry's thick, coarse fingers. "I'm very sorry you don't trust me. But unless you are blind, you can see that this truck does not hold one single piece of your precious furniture. Now, I am a patient man, but if you push this issue, you are not gonna like how it turns out for you—*son*."

The neighbors venture closer, moving toward Henry in solidarity.

John grabs his cell phone. "I'm calling my lawyer and the cops."

Just then, Dee appears from around the truck. "I have Noelani's attorney on the line right now, John," she says, holding her cell phone up to him. "He's heard every word you've said and has recorded it. He very much wants to talk to you."

John scoffs. "I don't give a shit what he wants."

Dee speaks into her cell phone: "You heard that? Right. I'll tell him." Dee turns to John. "Noelani's lawyer says he has the police on hold on another line. If you don't speak with him or allow us to leave without any more disturbances, they will be here within minutes to inform you that there is a restraining order issued against you. He seems to think this is not a good idea for you in terms of the settlement with Noelani. Here, talk to him," she implores, stepping close to John and putting her phone near his face.

"This is all bullshit!" John booms into the phone. "Bullshit! That bitch—" He turns his back to Henry and Dee, then pivots and concedes, "Listen, if I find one thing of mine missing, I will sue that bitch and—and... never mind. This is all bullshit!" John reaches the zenith of his exasperation. He starts to slide downward toward aversion. He slowly starts to walk backward. With a smirk on his face, he says, "You know what? I don't even give a shit. This is all just so goddamn ridiculous. Look, I don't even care. I just want you two and your stupid truck outta here." He yells one last time in disgust: "Just get the hell out of here! All of you. I never want to see you or *her* again. What a waste of my time!"

Henry finally grins.

John turns his back on him and storms toward his front door, mumbling obscenities and jamming his finger into his cell phone.

"C'mon, Dee," Henry says before turning to the two neighbors. "Sorry you had to witness that, ladies."

The women brush it off. One turns to Dee and says, "We've always known he is an ass. We've always felt sorry for Noelani. We're just glad you stood up to him—and stood up for her."

Dee returns their gratitude. "My husband and I appreciate your support." The two women head back in the direction of their homes.

Henry repeats, "C'mon, Dee. We gotta get on the road." They hop into the truck, but Henry cannot resist. He rolls down the window and calls out, "We never wanna see *you* again either, sonny boy." He puts the truck in drive and accelerates slowly, chuckling enough that Dee must hush him up.

"Henry, I swear, I thought you were about to punch him. You are so lucky I am the brains of this operation." She shakes her head, relieved that this confrontation between a white man and a black man ended without blows.

"He's the lucky one, Dee. Trust me." Henry pauses. "But that was smart calling her lawyer. I guess Noelani found one of those lawyers who actually answers the phone when you call 'em."

"Who said I talked to him?" Dee applies lipstick in the sun visor's mirror.

"What?" Henry's eyes bug out.

"His secretary just put me on hold. Never talked to the man." Dee turns to her devoted husband with a wry look. "Besides, I knew you wanted to coldcock that man, and although the Good Lord knows he deserves it, the last thing we needed was for you to go to jail."

Henry swivels his head from the road to his wife. "Dee, you *are* the brains, baby—and that's not all." He pats her thigh.

"Keep those hands on the wheel, Mister. We got some driving to do."

They burst out laughing. It takes about four freeway exits for their laughter to die out. Then they drive on in silence, and the LA traffic materializes before their eyes.

Chapter Twenty-Eight: 1995

Noon. Lotte and Lewis in Encinitas.

Lewis, who knows Lotte is driving down from LA, plans for Hope to be at her friend Carly's house so they can talk before Hope returns home. Hope knows her mom is coming to visit in the late afternoon and assumes she will be there for the weekend.

As Lotte enters, she awkwardly embraces Lewis. The two separate, and after mundane chitchat about LA traffic, how each other looks, and what's new with the house, they get to the heart of what really matters.

"Lewis, before we talk about Hope, I want you to know some details about our divorce and about my feelings for both of you. None of this is easy, and I know what I am going to say is probably going to surprise you and be hurtful to you. It hurts me." Lotte stops to ascertain how her opening address has impacted Lewis.

Lewis is stoic. "I understand, Lotte. Go on."

"Okay. First, you should know—and you probably assumed—that I have been in a long-term relationship with a very nice man. His name is Anderson Rodriguez."

"How would I know this? And why are you telling me this?"

"I am telling you this—wait. What do you mean? You think I have been alone all these years?"

"Well, I was. We were married, Lotte. Married." Lewis hits reset. "Okay, forget it. You had an affair. I don't need to know your personal business." Lewis regains his composure.

"That's right. You don't, and I'm not going to go there. All I am trying to tell you is that we are, frankly, well off. And I'm not saying that as any kind of put down." Lotte knows she is saying more than she should, but she can't help herself. "Look, I did not tell you this, but I have been working in upper management for his solar company for the last two years." She stops, remembering that Lewis rattles her sometimes. Most men do not have this effect on her. *Why does he? Why does he always make me feel guilty?*

"Well, that's nice to know," Lewis says sarcastically. "I guess there's a whole lot you've kept from me." She knows that he stops because he hates when he loses his temper. She admires that about him, but she also knows that concealing the truth is unjustifiable.

"You have a right to be angry."

"Thank you for informing me of my rights. Yes, I am angry. You could have—should have—been honest with me. Instead, we have played this game—for what? For Hope, I assume."

She sees Lewis tamping down his anger. "Yes, for Hope. But no—I don't know, Lewis. I meant to be honest, I just never—it just wasn't the right time. And now—"

"And now *is* the right time? That's bullshit, Lotte. Why is *now* the right time? Because you want to marry this guy?"

"No." She gathers herself. "No, we have decided that marriage is not for us, but we are seriously committed to each other. I don't want to get into all that." Lotte recomposes herself.

"Good. I don't really want to know about all his money and your new lifestyle. Keep the rest of your secret life to yourself." Lewis leans back against a couch cushion.

Lotte knows this is not going well. How could it? "I am telling you this because I want you to hear what I am going to say."

Lewis frowns. "Fine. Just say it, and let's get this 'business' over with."

"Right. Sorry. I'm very nervous. And—" Lotte catches herself. Swallows. "Okay, here is what I want the settlement to be—away from lawyers—just talking to the person I still care so much about. Okay?"

Lewis nods.

Lotte explains, "First, my lawyers are going to present this proposal—and I don't want to go into detail—but the remaining balance on the house will be paid off, and the title will be put in your name only. Again, money is not an issue for me and probably never will be. I want you to know that the burdens you have carried with money and all the sacrifices you have made for the last eight years will not be—"

Lewis interrupts. "Don't make me into some kind of hero. You've never made my life or Hope's life a burden financially, Lotte. You've been more than generous with money, but—"

It is Lotte's turn to cut in. "Lewis, please let me finish. Okay, look. What I am saying to my lawyers in the proposal is to continue substantial support for Hope. Frankly, *whatever* you two need. I trust you." Lotte stops and inserts, "Not that I want her to be spoiled." Her attempt to lighten the pressure of this moment makes no impact on Lewis. "So, I know the schools are great here, but if you want to send her to a private school, that's fine. It's on me."

"No, it's not. Hope's life is on me, not you. You haven't made it a priority to be a part of her life. You made that clear a long time ago. We don't want to go there—not now." Lewis speaks firmly but without bitterness.

Lotte realizes she has overstepped a boundary. She has intentionally avoided the planning and organizing of Hope's life; it has always been Lewis' responsibility. She has merely helped finance it. She's not sure what role she will have in Hope's life—it hovers between abdication and guilt. Nevertheless, she cautiously persists, "But we are nine years away from college decisions, and we can revisit this issue at that time. But again, I want what she wants." Lotte lets out a breath. She settles herself a bit.

Now it's Lewis who takes a deep breath. "Lotte, I get it. And I'm grateful. But you are not a player in this. Hope and I can make these decisions, and I intend to pull my financial weight." Lewis then shifts gears from business to family—or what is left of it. "But Hope needs to know that her mother cares about her and her future. That's what you need to discuss with her." He pauses for emphasis. "Honestly, discuss it with *her*."

Lotte nods. Her first bit of business is done—the easier part. She knows he might have exploded with resentment and anger, but that has never been his nature.

She proceeds. "Right. Before we talk about Hope, how are you feeling about everything? Oh, and how are your folks? I remember your father had heart surgery—"

"Triple bypass. Seven months ago. We visited him, and he is getting his strength back. Mom is a rock." Lewis now leans in. Starts to speak. Stops. Starts again. "As for our divorce, Lotte, my folks have always known that this arrangement was never going to work. They hoped it would because they wanted us to be a family. But they understand how things are."

"What do they understand?" Lotte's curiosity gets the best of her.

"They know what I know—at least, what I hope I know." Lewis now catches himself. Swallows. "That I loved you. That you loved me. But things changed for us once Hope came into our lives. You care about Hope. But that's not love. That's responsibility. That can't sustain any marriage. Look, we were—perhaps equally—stubborn about the direction we wanted our lives to go in. I get that you have always desired to achieve certain goals. All that stuff is—or has been—*your* choice. You have excluded both of us—Hope and me. I have my goals and my passions, and they are so far from what matters to you that—that the Grand Canyon literally separates us. I don't want your world, and you don't want mine. Equal guilt. I don't know. But I *do* know, deep down, that your independence is what you value most. I knew that being away from us was hard on you at first, but it was also a relief for you. It allowed you to focus on what you needed." Lewis abruptly stops and softens. "And I know you never stopped caring about us. That's what I know and what my parents know—but it is not what Hope knows."

A beat.

Lotte tries to find equilibrium. She knows everything Lewis has just said to her is true. She knows he is trying hard to be diplomatic. But his last blunt words are tougher to hear than she imagined. She purses her lips. "Lewis, do you know something?"

"What?" He leans back to recover from the emotional battle.

"Do you know I admire you?" Lotte looks down at the carpet when she can't say the word *love*.

"Well, look, we are so far past our feelings—I just feel regret, Lotte. My mistake was that I thought I could change you." Lewis feels spent.

"And I thought I could change you."

Lewis breaks the silence. "This is where we are and where we have been for a long, long time. All the deceit has made this day so hard."

Lotte winces at his final judgment. *My deceit.*

Lewis immediately tries to repair the damage his words have done. "We both have to bear responsibility for the damage we have done to each other—and to Hope."

Lewis waits for enough time to pass before he asks the question that identifies him as a person who, despite all the lies, still finds it in his heart to care about the mother of his child. "Do you love this other man—Anderson? Do you *really* love him, and does he love you?" Lewis looks directly into Lotte's eyes. They never break eye contact, although their vision has suddenly turned blurry.

"Yes. Yes." Lotte looks up toward the ceiling, hoping that the tears will roll back into her eye sockets. Her throat tightens, and she does not want to argue or explain or justify anything anymore.

* * *

Emotionally fatigued, they break for lunch, but neither has much of an appetite. They play with their food for an acceptable amount of time. Trivial subjects come and go, and then they glance at the clock before tackling the next round.

"Lewis, can I ask you something about your personal life? You don't have to tell me, since, as you say, 'it's none of my business.' But...have you met someone?" Lotte delicately places the question on the table.

Lewis takes his time to respond. "Hmm. Long story, but I will cut to the chase," he says as he takes a sip of iced tea. He sets down his glass and pushes back from the table so that he can cross his right leg over his left. "Lotte, for years, I just didn't have any interest or energy. Every week was consumed by teaching, taking care of Hope, driving her places—you know, soccer, dance, birthday parties—and then waiting for you to come home. I was satisfied—or at least I didn't spend too much time thinking about—things."

Lewis pauses. Lotte knows that it is not easy for him to speak about himself. "The last two years have been the toughest. Hope has never really understood our marriage, and I needed to make sure I didn't crush her innocence. Of course, she now has a pretty good idea that we are not the 'normal' family that her friends have—or think they have. I'm not trying to be a saint here, but, you know, you *are* her mom, and we *are* married, and Daddy shouldn't be sleeping with another woman. At least, that's the way I see—saw—things."

"I understand." Lotte's head tilts and her eyes narrow. She is unsure if she should pry any further. Instead, she takes the high road. "Lewis, I am so sorry that you had to deal with that burden and that loneliness. That is part of my guilt. And it is also why you—okay, I'm gonna say something corny now, so don't you *dare* laugh—but that's why you are her hero." She looks away, not wanting to see how that remark is taken. "And I appreciate you, too."

"Now there you go, trying to get me all emotional again. By the way, you said *gonna*."

"So?"

"That's the way you talked back when we first met. *Gonna*." He smiles. "Anyway, to answer your question, I was just a dad trying to also be a mom. I was lonely, yes—and when you talk about feeling guilty, well, that's my burden, too."

"How so?" Lotte knows how close she has pushed Lewis to the edge.

"Because." He shuts the door.

Lotte softly knocks. "Are you still together?"

"No." Lewis' eyes drop, and he concedes, "She'd like to be. But it's not the same. She's not—"

"Me."

"Yeah, that's about right."

"Well, Anderson isn't you either. But our relationship is solid, and our lives are on parallel tracks. I mean, he never wanted kids—and never will. This is hard to admit, but I just never had that maternal instinct. Jesus, I wish I did back then. I read about women who just didn't have it in them. It was so strange because all the women I knew *did* have it." She pauses. "Anyway, forget me, Lewis. I know there are so many women who would *kill* to be with you. I just hope you find the right person. My God, you deserve the best."

Lewis is silent during her monologue. Lotte realizes that when they are together, they are like statues, unwilling and unable to move.

"Well, I think Hope should be home in fifteen minutes. I'm going to clean up the kitchen."

Lotte stands. "I'm gonna freshen up." Then she laughs. Lewis joins her.

Gonna.

Chapter Twenty-Nine: 1995

On Highway 101 in Encinitas near Pannikin Coffee and Tea.

Noelani and Lisa have been with their realtor inside a small-ish, empty building down the street from an Encinitas institution since 1968: Pannikin Coffee and Tea. They have had breakfast there every morning while checking out apartments and possible studio locations. Lisa reads from the sign next to the front door: "Built in 1888, the Pannikin is located in this historic Santa Fe Railroad Station on Coast Highway 101." Lisa smiles as she compares their studio location to others: "Noelani, this place is perfect. We can have classes early; folks can walk to the Pannikin; and we will get lots of foot traffic right past our front door."

Noelani's hands are on her hips. "Agreed. The lease price is within our budget, but we'll have to do some work cleaning this place up. Thank God the hardwood floors are still in fairly good shape. We need to ask Henry if he thinks we need to refinish them. When he and Dee get here, we can bounce our ideas off them, and Henry can tell us what he thinks about the lighting and furnace too."

"Poor Henry. Between us and Dee, that man is always working," Lisa halfheartedly worries.

* * *

Noelani's apartment is literally on the other side of the railroad tracks, within walking distance of the studio they wish to lease and the Pannikin. In the 1960s, the railway station that is now Pannikin Coffee and Tea was a popular stop. However, when the trains started to skip this location and head straight to the newer station in Solana Beach, the abandoned brick red railroad station fell into disrepair. The current owners restored the quaint old building, adding bright 'Pannikin Yellow' paint, white trim and a flock of yellow umbrellas for the front porch seating. With the ground floor functioning as the coffee grinding station, the coffee shop is the go-to place for locals. Lisa and Noelani know that the aroma of the fresh baked cinnamon rolls is a killer.

As Noelani and Lisa sip coffee and consider the studio's possibilities, Dee and Henry, rather than driving as they did several months ago with Noelani's possessions, decide it would be less stressful to take Amtrak down to San Diego. The couple will stop in Solana Beach, a few miles south of Encinitas, for a brief visit—a day trip for them to see Dee's protégés.

* * *

After exchanging warm hugs and kisses, all four of them squeeze into Noelani's 1992 Honda Accord. As they motor their way north up the 101, they notice that the beach is at times a stone's throw away. Henry looks over at his wife and remarks, "See, Dee. *This* is where we should retire."

"Am I sitting next to my 'I-ain't-movin'-from-this-house-that-I-own' husband? You, who have told me umpteen times how you 'built this old house with your blood and guts?' are you the same Henry? I don't even recognize you, Mister!"

Henry, feeling Dee's wave of sarcasm crash over him, merely looks out the window at the beach and jokes, "Well, I could get a nice tan."

"What are you talkin' about? You're already brown, Henry. I know what you're really thinkin'. You're thinkin' about all those skinny girls in their bikinis parading around on the sand. So, that's another reason we ain't moving." Dee's obstinacy makes Lisa and Noelani laugh just like in the old days, when they were a part of her dance company.

With the window rolled down and the cool ocean breeze wafting through the car, Noelani's hair blows loosely. She feels free for the first time since she first started dating John. Those were the "honeymoon days" before things turned ugly. She glances to the backseat and shouts above the sound of the wind, "You two are a comedy act, really. You should have your own TV show."

"I don't know about that," Henry says as he leans forward, laughing. "Hey, Dee—look at that ocean! It almost comes right up to the road!"

Dee only exhales. "Hmm. Changing the subject. Hmm. We'll talk about this later. So, are we close to the studio, ladies?"

Lisa points to a building with a worn down, beachy look. It is part of a series of storefronts built in the early '60s. Hair studio on the left, surf shop on the right, and a record store called Lou's at the end of the line. "Here we are," Lisa proclaims with pride.

Everyone piles out, and Dee and Henry absorb the lay of the land. They quickly realize that this surfer town has a certain vibe that LA lacks. Things seem less claustrophobic and slower paced here, certainly not what they are accustomed to in their downtown streets.

Once they enter the storefront, both of them see the possibilities. Henry almost immediately looks for the power sources for electricity, and Dee examines the hardwood floors and the lighting. There are a lot of *um's* and *ah's* as the younger women rattle off plans for the yoga studio.

"The front desk will be here, lockers there. We're not sure if we will have any showers. We know the heat can be turned up for hot yoga. We want to run some paint colors by you, Dee. Oh, and Henry, we want to ask you if…" Questions ricochet around the room. *Is this up to code? What can Henry help them with? Who should be hired to do what?* And on and on.

* * *

After an hour or so, all agree to break for lunch in downtown Encinitas at the Beachside Bar and Grill. Dee and Henry offer advice and give their positive assessment of all the plans for the studio. Then the subject of Noelani's mother comes up.

"You know, your mom *does* support you on this, Noelani," Dee makes clear as she puts down her menu.

"Okay, but why didn't she come down with you guys?" Noelani asks.

Henry silently gazes at the menu's selection of burgers. Dee speaks to the mother/daughter issue: "Well, she just needs time is all. She'll be down here soon, girls. She will. She's also sad, though. You have always lived near her, you know—just around the corner."

"Dee, she has hired other girls to do the theater costume running—and she has hired girls to work at the store." It is hard for Noelani to disguise her frustration.

Dee patiently counsels, "Yes, Noelani, I know, but they're not *you*. And to tell you the truth, she's a little lonely. But she isn't quite ready to retire yet, like Henry and I." Dee looks at her husband for support. "Henry, isn't that right?"

Henry simply nods and says, "The bacon cheeseburger would be tasty—*mighty* tasty."

"Yes, but the cholesterol will knock two years off your life," Dee says as an aside. Then she continues her explanation of Kalani's situation: "Your mom wants to have a nest egg for herself—and help you buy a home when the time comes." Dee puts her menu down. With that, her point has been made.

Henry finally speaks to the issue: "She is worried about you, too."

There is much unspoken but understood by all four of them. The name *John* is not part of the dialogue, but it is on all of their minds. Dee and Henry have not told Noelani or Lisa about the altercation at the house. But they have told Kalani about the fight when they drove her back after getting Noelani settled at Lisa and Phillip's.

It was on that return trip to LA that Kalani confided in Dee about Noelani's history of depression and anxiety. They both realize how fragile she is—and always has been. Dee remembers those days when, as a young teenager, Noelani came to dance straight from Dr. Eva Chan's office. Kalani told Dee that Dr. Chan advised Noelani to see a therapist in San Diego whom she highly recommends if and when Noelani's delicate psyche requires help.

To keep things from getting too tense, Dee decides to change the subject to something she has little understanding of: yoga.

"So, ladies, why yoga? Why not a dance studio?" Dee asks. "I don't get it." Henry nods in affirmation. He has decided on a regular cheeseburger and fries.

Lisa takes the lead while Noelani broods about her mother. "Dee, as much as we love dance, that is not where our spirit and our passion lie. Yoga is not just a workout, like some think. For us, yoga is the means for the body to open up."

"But why not just dance or exercise?" Dee asks.

Noelani reawakens. Honestly, Dee, I started yoga right after I could get back on my feet after the surgery. If not for yoga, I can't imagine how I could have survived physically and emotionally."

Dee's eyes widen. "Yoga did all that for you, Noelani? That's impressive."

Lisa adds, "I met Noelani—what, six years ago? I was twenty-three; she was twenty-six. She was starting to teach at the yoga studio, and she trained me. We are lucky to have worked with some of the best yogis in LA."

"But I hear it's so *hot* in yoga. My, I could never do that. I am long past those damn hot flashes, ladies. I don't need to be in a sauna." As it is, Dee is using her napkin to create a breeze.

"We understand that, totally," Noelani explains. "That's why only some classes will be heated, while others will be room temperature. Here's the thing, Dee. We sit all day at work. Hips are a real problem for women in particular. Loosening the muscular structure allows the hips to open up, and if you have a good flow of poses, then all the major muscle groups are gently given permission to settle and be calm. Yoga is so much about moving your brain out of its constant loop and finally allowing time for yourself."

As he takes a break from dipping his fries into his ketchup, Henry mutters, "That's what I need—some time for myself."

Dee tilts her head just so and rolls her eyes.

Noelani keeps pitching their ideas. "Dee, the mind, the body, and the spirit are all one. The point of yoga is to calm the mind—to put away what we call the 'monkey chatter' of our daily lives. We believe that people are rarely at peace. Life is so fast paced. There is always something—"

Lisa breaks in, "—on the phone or the computer or the endless 'to-do list' that keeps popping up. Yoga is a time to center—"

As if on a relay team, Noelani continues, "—time for yourself. To let the mind rest. For Lisa and me, it is how we unplug. Yoga teaches us how to take care of our bodies. And in the end, yoga is part of the meditative process."

Lisa grabs the baton: "All the poses are designed to release tension and pressure from joints and muscles. That is why most studios nowadays use some heat."

Dee is very focused on what they are telling her. Henry, not so much. He is dialed into his cheeseburger and squirting more ketchup on his burger.

Lisa provides the metaphor: "We help people disconnect from the world for an hour or so, and at the same time strengthen their core, their posture, and their overall well-being."

Henry swallows his first delicious bite. "Sounds good to me. Hey, how long have you two been at this yoga business?"

Noelani answers, "I started soon after I rehabbed my knee, Henry."

Henry reaches for a drink, "Oh. Well, that's been a while now, right, Dee?"

Dee wonders, "Yes, it has. Would you pay attention, Henry? Noelani just told us that!" After chiding her husband, Dee returns to the subject at hand. "But remember, you ladies were in LA then. They do all sorts of newfangled things there. I'm not saying this is 'out there,' because I see the whole thing starting to grow around the country, too. But are you girls sure it will catch on here? This is a pretty—how do you say, *laid back*—place?"

"Well, that's the thing, Dee. It already has. There are a few studios doing business—good business—here. Encinitas is just the kind of place where people are paying attention to their physical well-being." Noelani smiles. "And we have a secret weapon."

"Oh, what's that?" Dee and Henry ask in unison.

"Our studio's name is Karuna Yoga. It means *yoga of compassion*. And we will have a Hawaiian theme. Tropical. A place where 'cool sand meets hot yoga'." Noelani's excitement is evident. "Lisa and I are not just yogis; we want our students to bond as a community. It's a crazy world, and it is going to get crazier with all this technology. We want to add the human touch."

Lisa smiles as she sips her unsweetened green herbal iced tea. "The music, the ambiance, the whole environment is going to be geared toward helping people understand their bodies and their minds. It can be a place where the soul is refreshed."

Noelani asks, "So what do you think?"

"Ladies," Dee proclaims, "if I were not pushing deeper into my seventies, I would be there. And you know, maybe I will try it. Unheated, naturally. So I think it sounds great! You are the dynamic duo! Oh, and the whole Hawaii thing is terrific. You know, your mom will be interested in that. Perhaps a little boutique on the side?" Dee winks.

"Yeah, well, it sounds like a girl thing," Henry says. "But I can do some of the plumbing and electrical work for you. Maybe Dee and I can come down for a week or two—stay in one of these hotels here—and like I said, 'get a tan' while we are at it!" They all burst into laughter. Even Dee.

Chapter Thirty: 1998

4:15 p.m. The office of Amos Adler, M.D.

Today she is Miss Goldfinger, Lewis thinks. The fingernails, he presumes, are false, although they look real. Here he is for his regular med check. Same time. Same day. Same window with the young woman with an attitude. She holds her fingernail up like a stop sign, and then waves him through.

For the last couple of years, Lewis has noted that the lovely woman named Noelani, with the monstrously large but colorful bag, has appeared either before or after his appointment almost every few months. There have been rare exceptions, naturally, and Lewis is always disappointed not to see her and make small talk. They are on a first name basis. He has discovered that they have more in common than just their mutual resentment for the receptionist—whatever color her nails may be.

Lewis observes that lately they seem to be a team, always back to back—usually Noelani is first in, and because of that, Lewis always comes early, brings a book to read while she is in with Dr. Adler; however, they manage to get in a chat that can last ten minutes or more, depending on the doctor's schedule. Their 'med checks,' as Dr. Adler calls them, are usually thirty minutes or so, but Lewis always hopes he is running late. Lewis surmises that Noelani is on to him, but she's always more than happy to talk, and on the rare occasion that he is first to see the good doctor, Noelani has come early, claiming she "mixed up appointment times." Lewis remembers the small kernels of their lives that each has been willing to share, and he almost had the courage to ask her to coffee. *But how strange would that be?* He thinks.

Besides, all he really knows is that she's from LA, has a yoga studio in Encinitas, loves the beach, and is originally from Hawaii. On his side of the ledger, he has revealed that he teaches at a high school nearby, also lives in Encinitas, and that he agrees that Dr. Amos Adler has helped him enormously with some "issues" he's been dealing with. Dr. Adler has been the common denominator in most discussions; his calm demeanor, his encouragement, and his warmth. In a nutshell, he's their 'go to' topic.

Lewis wishes he knew more about her, but he senses her need for privacy. *She probably has guys trying to pick up on her all the time—unless, of course, she is married.* Lewis has noted long ago that she wears many rings, on toes and fingers, but none appear to be a wedding ring on her left hand. *Perhaps she feels safe talking to me because I am wearing mine, even though I have never mentioned my wife.* So in the end, Lewis has accepted that this 'waiting room encounter' is just a friendly 'how-are-you' sit down chat. *Fair enough, I guess.*

However, on this day, Noelani is not in the waiting room. Strangely, Lewis has noted that fewer and fewer people are. And equally perplexing is Dr. Adler's request for him to stay after his appointment. *Does it have anything to do with Dr. Adler's health?*

The thought has crossed his mind that perhaps Noelani is no longer in need of his services. He thinks, *Good for her.* Nevertheless, he chides himself for selfishly wanting her to appear any minute from Dr. Adler's office.

Lewis begins to wonder if *he* really needs to see Dr. Amos Adler. He has seen so many doctors—eye doctors—in the last year. But the only one who makes him feel more empowered and less anxious is Dr. Amos Adler. Today is the first time Lewis meets Dr. Adler using his cane. It's not necessary—yet, but he has been told it will be sooner rather than later, and it's best to get used to it. It makes him feel pitiful, like a person in need of a life preserver. He refuses to carry it to school. His students already know about his condition, and he is far too proud to admit that anything significant is wrong. Besides, knowing a few of his smart-ass kids, they would probably hide the damn cane from him as a joke. *Kids.*

Just as Dr. Adler opens the door to call him back to his office, Noelani steps into the waiting room. She waves at Lewis and motions to her watch, as if to say "Sorry, I'm running late." Lewis tries his best to mouth that he'll chat with her later, and it seems to him that the message is received, since she broadly smiles back.

As Lewis walks down the corridor to the doctor's small office, he anticipates the first question he will be asked.

"So, tell me the latest on your eyesight, Lewis." Dr. Adler leans back in his well-worn, overstuffed chair. His wife May now demands he use a pillow for lumbar support.

"Well, Doc, I can still see you." Lewis smiles.

"Ah, still got that stoic, tough guy sense of humor," Adler volleys.

"Yep, that's me." Lewis smiles. "Brought this stick with me to hit you over the head if you ask too many personal questions, Doc."

Both men laugh heartily.

"Actually, they tell me I have to get used to it. Anyway, the important thing is that Hope has stopped worrying so much about me."

Adler gets serious. "Lewis, you did not answer my question. And this time, please be really straight with me. I need to know exactly how you are feeling. Oh, and I appreciate your willingness to stay after with my next appointment."

"Of course, Doc." Lewis gives him a look that teeters between mildly curious and slightly concerned.

Both men nod and there is a pause that Lewis finds awkward for some reason, almost as if it is Dr. Adler who seems anxious.

"So, here's the scoop. You know it started with fuzzy spots in one eye, and then the other. The last time we talked, I told you that some of the medications they gave me didn't really seem to have too much of an effect on the 'white snow,' as I call it. Occasionally, I'll have a week or two where what I look at right in front of me is dark. Like a black spot. It's annoying as hell, but the eye doctors tell me that the meds are slowing things down. So right now, my peripheral vision is not too bad. And I have learned to move my head and compensate." Lewis thinks that is enough. He does not want to admit that the black "spot" is sometimes much larger or that it has appeared more often and can last longer than a month. And he definitely does not want to talk about the injections that will soon be inevitable.

"So, are you driving?"

"Um, yes. I am hoping to get to the point where I can teach my daughter to drive."

"Well, isn't she a ways away from a permit?"

"Hope's eleven. She'll be twelve in the summer. So a couple more years, I guess."

"Hmm." Dr. Adler's voice sounds like the plan is dubious at best. He continues, "Lewis, let's get to what I need to know. How have you been feeling?"

In previous sessions, Lewis has confessed that the anxiety of losing a significant amount of his vision has been the reason he has stayed with Dr. Adler. He knows the anxiety can overcome him on the days when his vision is at its worst. "Well, Doc, I give myself 8 out of 10 on your happiness scale." He sniggers. "You always ask me to rate my emotional state, so that's where I am. The days that are nerve-wracking are when I have to contort so damn much to see Hope when she is talking to me, or when I have to read articles. Fortunately, I have trained the newspaper staff to have 'hawk eyes' in the copyediting department. They are so proud when the paper is clean of mistakes. My seniors are going to be missed, but they have trained the juniors well."

"That's fine, Lewis. Fine. But tell me how you feel when things are off the rails. I know you are at the lowest levels of meds. This is partly due to my concern that the meds can sometimes lead to weaknesses in concentration and memory in people with retina issues like yours." Dr. Adler smoothes his now completely silver goatee.

"Well, you remind me of that every time, Doc, so my memory is fine. Weakness—not an issue, except for ice cream." Lewis smiles, and Dr. Adler nods, implying he has the same weakness, but he does *not* smile. "As for the lowest levels of meds, that is what I have always wanted because I am so pig-headed. I've always told you I've never been a drug guy. But overall, I'm good—really." Lewis knows that he has to sound confident because the man sitting across from him is not easy to fool. He also knows that he may be fooling himself. So the next question knocks him for a loop.

"I think half of that answer is very encouraging, and half of it is bullshit, Lewis." Dr. Adler has never cursed in a session with a patient before. But this appears to be a very different session. He is not smiling, but he is not scowling either. "Lotte has never left your mind's eye, has she? You still have not opened yourself up to another relationship, right?"

Lewis' head tips downward before he responds, "Not really, Doc. I'm just—just—well, you remember the affair I told you about with the teacher at my school? Divorced—"

"Like you."

"Yep. She is nice, and we had some good times, but it's

just not happening—at least for me. The 'it' factor is missing. I enjoyed her company, but I stopped the affair in its tracks because the longer it lasted, the more I knew it would really hurt her. I was *her* lifeboat—and I get that. But she was not mine. For a while, I felt like a jerk."

Lewis sighs, then continues: "I have met a few other women on some dating sites. Funny—when I say *sites,* it's strange because the moment they realize that my *sight* is a big issue, then I feel like I'm damaged goods. Mostly, it's in my head. The women have been very understanding, but often they are in a different place than I am. A few have their sights set on some guy who is forty-something and can take care of them or help with their children or whatever. They look at me and see a guy who can't see and is certainly not going to be rich anytime soon. Oh, others like that I am a teacher, but Doc, I swear, they look at me like I am a missionary—like being a teacher is on the same plane as taking a vow of poverty. I feel like they take one look at me and think, *Oh, here's some poor teacher who makes half of what I make.* You know the line, Doc. *He's just a teacher.* So anyway—geeze, I am rambling on here. I guess that's what I do when I see you, huh?"

"That's what I do for a living, Lewis—I listen. It's very important for you to get all this out of your system."

"Yeah, well, I have friends I can talk to. They are always trying to set me up with people. I don't know. I'm thirty-eight, going to be forty soon. I have an eleven-year-old daughter who needs my full attention. I have an ex-wife who is—who has—made our lives much easier when it comes to money. But I'm just—I'm just *on hold,* I guess. On hold."

Here, Dr. Adler stops him. "Lewis, I am not cutting your session short. And I am not ignoring your situation. And, yes, you are 'on hold,' as you say. Waiting for the right moment and the right person is wise. It is. Trust me. But now I need to see someone, and then I want to call you back in."

Lewis is puzzled. "Why all the mystery, Doc?"

Dr. Adler does not respond; he merely rocks forward for momentum and smiles, waving Lewis to follow him to the door and down the hall to the waiting room. His only response is, "Trust me."

* * *

Miss Goldfinger holds up her fingernail, looks at the computer screen, and then flicks the window open for Ms. Noelani Kekoa. Noelani is tired of her power trip. Despite the window being closed, she says, "I'm here. Bill me for the copay." She then turns, whips her bundle of clothes and accessories around her, and plops down. Miss Goldfinger looks at her incredulously and switches fingers, indicating her contempt for people who do not follow her instructions. Noelani does not notice the affront.

The door opens, and Dr. Adler steps out. Behind him is Lewis Her smile is inverted when she sees he has a cane. Lewis does not see the look of concern on Noelani's face as she notices his cane for the first time. Realizing her rudeness, she quickly puts on a happier expression. She rises before the doctor's invitation to come into his office.

"Hello, Doctor." Noelani says, as if standing up and meeting him generates the "Hello, Doctor" every time.

"Hello, Noelani." Dr. Adler turns to Miss Goldfinger and says, "Heather, please give Mr. Bennett some coffee or water—whatever he needs."

Miss Goldfinger's hands rise from the keyboard as if to say, *Oh sure. Whatever you say, boss.*

The doctor turns to Lewis. "Lewis, I am sure you and Noelani have seen each other here many times. Noelani, this is Lewis Bennett."

An awkward moment quickly morphs into polite pleasantries as both say, as if as a duet, "Of course! Yes, we have talked many times before." They softly shake hands. Noelani notices that she is the one who stretches her hand out towards his.

Dr. Amos Adler takes control. "After my session with Ms. Kekoa, I wish to briefly speak with you *both*, if you don't mind."

This is unprecedented for Dr. Amos Adler. Noelani is mildly surprised, but she tries her best to disguise it. Dr. Adler adds, "Don't worry. You two, I'm not dying." He smiles broadly. Lewis and Noelani look at each other with a trace of relief.

Lewis takes a seat. Miss Goldfinger asks what he would like. He says water. And Noelani follows her doctor down the corridor.

* * *

Noelani sits across from Dr. Amos Adler and immediately realizes she does not have her bag. That alarms her. But she knows it is right next to Lewis, and she knows he will see it. *No worries,* she thinks. *I don't need it. Just a routine med check.* This will be a short appointment, she figures, because there isn't much to say. Everything is fine. So she is thrown for a loop with the first thing the good doctor says.

"Noelani, I have heard good things about you from my wife."

"I'm sorry, Dr. Adler—your wife?"

"Yes. My wife, May. She is a busybody. Don't tell her I said that. But she knows what is going on around town, and she tells me your business is flourishing. Even some of her friends have attended your classes—the not hot ones—and May says they love the whole experience. She tells me she is going to try it next week." Dr. Adler looks like the Cheshire Cat, smiling as if he is holding all the aces. He lets the moment breathe.

"Oh, well, um, that's so nice of her—and you—to say." Noelani tries to figure out what is going on. The usual opening question is, "How are you feeling, Noelani?" This is a significant departure from the script. "Um, yes, Lisa and I are so happy with our studio. Our yogis are just—well, they are just so encouraged." She knows *encouraged* is not what she wanted to say, but it was the first thing that popped into her head. "And my mother is retiring and plans to live with—or near—me. Temporarily. She is going to open a little boutique as a part of our studio." Noelani seems almost bubbly.

"That is wonderful." Dr. Amos Adler nods. "You've had the studio for several years now, right? Has it been two or three years?"

"Three."

"Ah, yes. I bet you feel much better emotionally now. Every session we have had recently has been very positive, I believe."

"Yes, as a matter of fact, it has. I cannot remember the last time I felt, you know, those dark clouds or the anxious moments. So I think the meds are working perfectly. Things are really—nice—right now."

"Well, that's what we have been striving for, Noelani. I'd like to ask you about something that we have not talked about in quite a while. I bring it up because you are in such a good place both professionally and emotionally. I know that your ex-husband is an afterthought for you. He has never contacted you since the divorce settlement, right?"

"Um, right." Noelani's radar is picking up strange signals.

"And you have naturally buried yourself in the work of starting a business, I'm sure. So permit me to ask how you have been doing socially in terms of relationships."

Noelani leans forward with a look that screams, *What are you getting at?*

"Look, Noelani, let's not kid ourselves. Your ex husband John scared you so badly that it took us a year just to touch on the subject. I backed off it when I realized just how anxious it made you. But I am out of time, and you are ready to grow. You're past ready. So I'll just do something I rarely do—I'll be blunt. Are you dating? Are you more comfortable with men now? This concerns me greatly because your ability to trust men is at the heart of some of your emotional issues."

She sighs and looks down. She reaches for the tips of her hair. He waits her out.

She begins, "I have my issues. Yes, I was—I still am—very afraid of making the same mistake. I don't know why I married John. I was young. I know we've talked about this before, but John was just there at what I thought *then* was the right time. But I was also—I don't know—hearing a clock ticking in my head, reminding me to settle down. Maybe have children—which he didn't want. I know why now, but that's water way under the bridge. Funny—I made the same mistake twice, Doctor: falling for imposters. My first serious boyfriend, Michael was an actor, too. Not a very good one, but in my eyes, he was just what I thought I wanted. And then the ski accident and within months I was alone. John comes along and his successful businessman act was so smooth, so believable. John was very good at selling—I bought into his whole act. I was pretty naive...I just didn't see what was obvious to others." Noelani has to make up her mind. She decides that a half-truth is all she can concede right now. "I have dated a few guys. I have a rule. They cannot be clients. The guys who come to yoga try to hit on me. I make it very clear that I am not interested. I have dated some of Lisa's friends. But I just don't want to be involved at all. I just don't," Noelani says with a shrug. "Is that weird?"

"I don't know. You are the only one who knows the answer to that."

Typical psychiatrist response, Noelani thinks. She continues, "I guess I still have things I need to work out in terms of trusting men. It's been that way my whole life, Doctor. Men see me as some woman who they think they can control. They want a 'pretty Hawaiian woman'—and a yoga teacher to boot.

And so they treat me like I am not real. I don't want to sound stereotypical, but they think I am some—trophy. And when they are bored they just—whatever."

"Whatever?"

"Well, they're like hunters. They think it's all about trapping me and getting their way." Noelani has inched too close to the cliff, and she is now precariously trying to balance herself on the edge. Her arms are flailing. Her body is wobbling.

Dr. Amos Adler watches this tightrope act. "Noelani, this is the next challenge for you. I don't want you to live a life of fear or a life alone. I think it is time we broached this and at least got it out. I think you know that your instincts are solid. I think you know a lot more about whom to trust, much more than you give yourself credit for. You will know who that person is when *your time* is right. Right now is not that time, but that time will come. I am confident. I want you to know that."

"So what you're saying is that I need to wait to find the right man. Well, I don't think I need the right man to complete me."

"*Exactly*. You do not. But you may want to find someone who will love you unconditionally and unequivocally."

"Well, I'm not holding my breath, Doctor."

"No, you shouldn't, Noelani. But you are '*on hold.*'"

"Well, that is one way of putting it, I guess. But I am not waiting around for a man to make me happy."

"Good. That's just what I'd hoped to hear from you." Dr. Adler's smile reappears. "Now, I need to tell you something about me. But first I need to speak to both you and Mr. Lewis Bennett."

* * *

Miss Goldfinger has taken her leave for the day. Lewis sits patiently, but then rises quickly as Dr. Amos Adler cracks open the door and pops his head through. "Lewis, come on back, okay?"

Lewis moves quickly, drops his cane, picks it up, and then remembers something. He grabs the bag Noelani has left behind. "On my way, Doc."

When he enters, Noelani smiles, seeing that he has her bag. She stands and again notices that she has to reach out for it. Lewis has placed it near her but has not given it to her. "Thank you, Lewis."

"No worries. It's hard to avoid—kinda jumbo sized." Lewis smiles.

Apologetically, Noelani replies, "Oh, I know. It's ridiculous, really."

This is Dr. Amos Adler's cue. "Please, could you both shift over to this small couch here? I want to be able to not have to keep looking back and forth at you." The doctor fusses a bit with his chair, glances at his clock, and then looks at the pictures of his grandchildren on his desk. He appears to be gathering himself. His patients slide over and sit next to each other. The doctor finally sits and smiles at them both. "Well, this is a first for me in all my decades of doing what I do…and this will also be my last."

Neither Noelani nor Lewis knows how to react to this foreshadowing.

"So, let me not waste any of your time. Noelani and Lewis, this has been a tough day for me. You know," he says with a grin as he smoothes out his goatee, "I'm the one always listening. Now I'm the one doing all the talking. Anyway, you two have probably guessed that this old man is probably way past his 'expiration date.' Yes, that's right. I am officially retiring as of today." He waits for a reaction. On the surface, both feign surprise and give him the *Oh, you're not that old!* look. They both throw out versions of "Well, congratulations! You deserve it! So happy for you!" But Dr. Amos Adler knows that inwardly, these two are less than enthusiastic and even a bit troubled. He imagines that they are thinking, *Oh, no. Now what do I do? Who will understand me like him?*

He marches forward. "My wife, May, bless her soul, has a hankering—that is her word, not mine—to visit relatives and travel *all over the world.* She has been pushing me to retire before I die face down on my desk while talking to one of you two fine folks." The smile returns to his face. "Of course, May is right. I am an old dog, and I better scurry along before I have no legs to travel with."

Both of the couch invitees nod and smile at his folksy way of breaking the news.

"I asked to see you both because—and I'm disregarding the 'shrink's code' here, you two—because I have a special place in my heart for you both—for different reasons. Noelani, I inherited you, and I feel like I have known you for a lifetime. Lewis, you epitomize what an honorable man is all about, and you have battled adversity these last four years. Well, obviously, you both have. But the thing is, you two are—and have been—my favorites. I have always looked forward to hearing about your progress—and it has been amazing. But at the same time, I know you have a ways to go. I am very confident in your spirit and your determination."

Noelani is the first to interrupt. "Doctor, you have been so wonderful. I am so happy for you. You don't have to worry about me."

Lewis concurs. "Doc, I agree with Noelani—totally. Your wife is absolutely right. If you don't retire today, I am personally going to carry you to that airport that Mrs. Adler, I'm sure, has made plans for." Both patients are smiling, but Noelani's hand reaches for her hair, and Lewis' knee starts to bounce uncontrollably, as if it is somehow electrified.

Dr. Adler notices. "Here's my deal for you both. First, Dr. Susan Locke, who has been my partner here for years, is willing to take you two on. I am asking my other patients to see another doctor, if they wish. Dr. Locke has agreed to keep me abreast of your developments—that is, if that is alright with you. Believe me, Dr. Locke is terrific. I will update her on your situations before I leave. Again, if that is what you would like?"

Lewis and Noelani glance at each other and then at him. They nod in the affirmative. Lewis starts to speak, but Dr. Adler cuts him off.

"Before you say anything, I have something for each of you." He hands them each an envelope. "This is a little note from me; it includes my contact information. This was the deal I made with my wife. She said, 'Pick those two—no more—and stay in contact with them, Amos, if that is what will get you to retire.' To be honest, I don't tell her *every-thing* about you two, but she knows I take you both—and your well-being—very personally." That last word causes his throat to catch, and Noelani's and Lewis' eyes start to swell with tears.

"Look, you two, I know this is very hard on all three of us. Of course, you two don't really know each other—except you both have to deal with my rather obnoxious secretary. So that is why I am speaking with you two together. That note I gave you also has the information—and I think I am doing the right thing here—I surely hope so—but that note has the information for each of you to contact *each other* in the event that you just need someone to talk to. You know what I mean? You both have called me from time to time with various questions and have been a little bit...worried. Well, you can of course call Dr. Locke, but you can also call each other. In my experience—and I have a lot of it—too much, probably—is that everyone can use a friend who has been through similar things and can relate to some of the same concerns. Use each other—or not. That is totally up to you. I just hope I didn't offend you or invade your privacy. Most doctors in my profession would never do what I am doing—talking to you both—but I am too damn old to worry about what they think, and I care too much about you two." With that, Dr. Amos Adler leans back in his chair. A look of relief washes across his face.

Noelani and Lewis are both speechless. Noelani reaches for her tissues. Then she looks at Lewis and realizes that he is in need of one, too. They both smile at each other, then at Dr. Amos Adler.

"Get along you two, before I need one of those. Besides, May is not going to be happy if I don't pick her up on time. She has a reservation at some fancy restaurant, and I'm afraid she has invited some of our friends." Dr. Amos Adler pretends to scowl.

Noelani and Lewis do leave—together.

Dr. Amos Adler blows his nose when the office door shuts. His grandchildren's photos stare back at him. He can only see them through glassy eyes.

Part Three

"No where
Now here
Be Present"

— *Yoga Proverb*

Chapter Thirty-One: 1995

3:00 p.m. Hope, Lotte, and Lewis in Encinitas.

Lewis sits at the kitchen table, staring at a picture of Hope sitting on a bench with him at the "Daddy and Me Dance" a year ago, when she was seven years old. Lotte sits on the couch in the living room, staring at her conference schedule in Los Angeles. *She isn't the woman he married. Maybe she never was that person? How could he not see that? Did I? Or did I unconsciously believe I could change her?*

Lewis knows that the moment Hope sees an unfamiliar car parked in front of the house, she will know that her mother is "home." He tries to predict how Hope will react to the news that her world has changed, at least formally. Perhaps more importantly, he wonders how he will make everything better. *Everything better. That's what dads and moms do, isn't it? How do we keep the monsters away from their bedroom? How do we make their future bright?*

How, indeed.

And how does a father tell his daughter the truth? Lewis knows for damn sure that Lotte will sugarcoat it. She has to. It's part of her saleswoman DNA. "I'm sure you'll just love our newest line of guilt erasing gizmos and gadgets. Oh, and here are the newest clothes and accessories that every girl needs to make them pretty and popular!"

Lewis glances up at his reflection in the kitchen window and is reminded who the fool is. The face staring back at him takes over: *Lotte was the sensual, spellbinding, but a damaged young woman you met on the porch steps. The one you tried to change. Neither of you would compromise. You knew the truth, Lewis. You knew she never wanted the baby. She would have had an abortion if you had shown any willingness to acquiesce to her fear. But you wouldn't let her go there. Why? Because you wanted the baby. Hope is your baby, Lewis. And now you have to clean up this mess. Good luck with that.*

Lewis rouses himself and tries to fend off the anxiety that is making his heart beat faster. He knows he cannot make *everything* better. Hope is already tainted by their phony marriage. She is suspicious, but like all children, she hopes for a storybook ending where mom, dad, and their only child live happily ever after, watching the glorious orange sun set at Moonlight Beach. Maybe there will even be a green flash.

* * *

Hope enters with a bang. The door slams open, and she takes two steps in—pauses to see where everyone is—and rushes to Lotte as she beams in words and deeds. "Mommy!"

Lewis hears the muffled exchanges of *Sweetheart / I missed you / Me, too / I love you / I love you, too.* He winces.

Once Hope has pulled back from Lotte's grasp, her baggy blue jeans and her orange Lion King t-shirt swirl toward the kitchen, where her father sits. She points out the obvious: "Dad, Mom's home! Wow, are we gonna go out to dinner?"

Lewis looks at Lotte. This is her show. Her script. But he does not have the heart to not reply to Hope. "Well, that depends on Mom's schedule, kiddo."

Lotte's turn. "Hope, I just ran down here from LA, where I am at a business conference. I wanted to see you for a while—

and dad and I want to talk to you about something. But first, um, how are you, honey?"

Lewis knows Hope well enough that she is not going to let that go. Hope turns back to her mother and says, "I'm fine, but what do you want to talk to me about?"

"Oh, well, first tell me how school is going. You are graduating to fourth grade in September. Are you excited?"

"Well, yeah, it's not that big a deal. I mean, I'm still at the same school and all, and there are only three teachers. Dad hopes I get Ms. Hughes. She's younger, and all the kids really like her. I mean, she's fun and not crazy strict like my second-grade teacher was. Remember Mrs. Raymond?"

Lotte nods. "Yes, your father and I had a few meetings with her. Anyway, I see you are wearing the Lion King shirt I sent you. Have you seen the movie?"

"Well, duh, mom. Only three times! Even Dad liked it, but not as much as he liked *Beauty and the Beast*." Hope looks at her father.

He smiles. "Yep, that's true. Hard to top that one." He wonders how long all this can hold out. "Want something to drink, you two?" He knows this may open the door for Lotte to start the rollercoaster ride's first big drop. "I even have Coke, Mom's favorite."

"Oh, really?" Hope knows it is not on the usual menu. "Okay." She looks at her mother, and Lotte nods.

The whispering begins. Lewis pours the soda. He knows that Lotte is trying to set the scene. He gives her a few minutes, and then returns. They sit on the couch with Hope between them. *Pull the trigger, Lotte. The longer you wait, the harder it gets.*

Lotte, always prepared, has already read the books about talking to your children about divorce. This Lewis assumes. She may have a secret life, but he knows the way Lotte's mind operates.

"Hope, we have something to tell you. And it is going to be sad. But Dad and I want to be honest with you. And you are a big girl, so I want to explain."

"What is it?"

"You know that I have been away so much—at work in Phoenix. And it has been going on for almost as long as you have been—"

Hope turns to her father. "Daddy, are you and Mom getting a divorce?"

Lewis freezes for a moment, then looks at Lotte. After all, it is she who wants a divorce, so it is she who needs to say the words.

Lotte softly places her hand on Hope's thigh, signaling that she wants her attention. "Hope, Mommy and Daddy have loved each other for a long time. But we no longer love each other in the same way that we used to. We have tried, but things are very different now. My life and Daddy's are going in opposite directions."

"What does that mean? Am I gonna live here, with Daddy?" Hope pleads. Lewis sees that her eyes are melting, her mouth sagging.

Lotte quickly engages. "Yes, Hope, of course, you are staying here with Daddy, and I want you to know—we both do—that we love *you* the same. It's just that we need to be truthful to each other. Honey, we cannot stay married to each other. It's not fair to Daddy or to me."

"Why not? You have been like—like the way you are for so long." Hope looks at her father.

Lewis again finds himself in the crosshairs. He does not want to tell his little girl what he knows to be true: that her mother has been seeing another man for years—and that he, too, has been disloyal to his own vows. Instead, he says, "Mommy is still your mom and will always be your mom. But she can't live here because we don't love each other the same way we did."

Lotte takes the final plunge. "Sweetheart, I've met another man who is very nice. We love each other very much. But nothing about that is going to change the way you and I feel about each other. Daddy and I will make sure of that."

A beat.

Hope's eyes are now glued to her sandals. She has held back her tears so far. She looks up at neither parent and divulges, "I know. I understand. My friends' parents are divorced. I talk to them about it. They think it sucks, but they know…they know…" And at that precise moment, she realizes she can no longer keep a tight grip on her world. With each teardrop, Lewis feels a sting. He is positive that Lotte feels it as well.

"It happened to my friend Jenny this year," Hope chokes out.

Lotte hands out tissues from her purse. Several for Hope and more for herself.

Lewis does what he always does. He touches his daughter's back. He rubs it softly, as if there is a stain, a blemish that will disappear with enough kindness and effort. He is surprised by Hope's next question.

"What if I don't like this other man, Mom? Do I have to meet him or even see him?" These questions are spoken into the tissues, as eye contact is impossible.

Lotte regroups and puts on the face that clients see. It does not fool Lewis for a minute. "Hope, you don't have to see anyone. You and Daddy don't have to change anything. It's just me. I have to change. You don't have to do anything you don't want to, okay?"

"Will you still visit me and Daddy?"

Lotte is still in sales mode, but Lewis knows the truth. "Of course. Of course. Honey, I will always be there."

That is a lie. Lewis knows that the moment Lotte leaves, he will have to do what must be done: *make everything better.*

* * *

That moment comes sooner rather than later. Lotte makes excuses about the complexities of the conference in LA, which is fine because her presence is like an open sore. The sooner she leaves, the sooner the scab can form. So Lotte tells a few more lies, makes a few more promises. The goodbyes are choked off quickly, lest the scene completely devolve into tears. The moment she leaves, Hope wants to go to her room and be by herself. Lewis knows to leave her be.

The grief that attends divorce, he realizes, is similar to the grief one feels after the death of a loved one. Denial. Resentment. Anger. Sadness. And a gradual acceptance. He has been preparing for this for years. A small part of him knows that Hope has, too. However, Lewis cannot fully grasp what the finality of this means to her.

* * *

At dinnertime, Lewis knocks softly on Hope's door and asks to come in. She accepts his request.

"Hungry?"

"Not really, Dad." Hope sits cross-legged on her bed with her back to him. Her head is down; her eyes are focused on something small.

"Hmm. I know. Me neither."

"What if I don't like this man Mom is with now?"

"You don't need to like him."

"But what if they invite me to Phoenix?"

"You don't have to go."

"Yeah, but that will hurt Mom's feelings, won't it?"

Lewis picks up Hope's chin. She has been pretending to read her favorite book, *Charlotte's Web*. He turns her face toward him; it is twisted into a confused expression. It breaks Lewis' heart. "Mom knows just how difficult this is for you. She will understand. Can I tell you something?"

"Yeah, what?"

Lewis musters what one can in a situation that has no simple answers. "I am the luckiest Dad around, kiddo, because I have a daughter who has been so kind and so thoughtful to others—and was so very, very brave today."

Hope twists her body so that she can embrace him, wrapping her arms around his neck.

At times like these, a father can only gauge the depth of his child's soul by the sounds he hears. All Lewis can make out in the silence of Hope's room are her tender sobs and one simple sentence:

"Oh, Daddy."

Chapter Thirty-Two: 1998

5:00 p.m. Lewis' home.

As she has done whenever she is excited with news of the day, Hope Bennett bursts through the front door. "Dad, my sixth-grade teacher, Ms. Montañez, told our class that we'll be doing yoga starting next week, and a yoga teacher—one of her friends—will be leading the class for the first week! Isn't that so cool, Dad? I mean, Carly's mom has been going to yoga for a while—I think it might be with this lady at her yoga place—"

"Studio, Hope. It's called a yoga studio." Lewis is preoccupied with trying to look at a proof of his school's newspaper.

"Oh, yeah, whatever. Anyway, doesn't that sound cool? I mean, it's free and all—and Carly and I have been talking about it, and since her mom likes it—she says that kids go to the yoga pl—studio—well, it really sounds like fun—don't ya think? Dad! Are you even listening?" Hope, flummoxed by her father's focus on the newspaper, takes his chin and turns it her way.

Lewis smiles. "Hope, of course I am listening." He flips the article over on the kitchen table, trying to disguise his frustration with his inability to see what he wants to see when he needs to see it. He is having one of his "cloudy days." He uses this euphemism when his vision impairment makes it seem as though he is looking through a shroud of black lace. At least this week one eye does not have that *damn black spot.* He is acutely aware that it has gotten worse despite all the meds. Of course, that is what his doctors have always told him would happen. Some days, however, are better than others. Some are downright horrific.

"Well, you didn't seem to be listening, and you're not acting like this is exciting." Hope releases his chin and heads to the cabinet where the granola bars are kept. It's time for a snack before she and her father prepare dinner later.

"Sorry, kiddo. I think it sounds like fun. So, Ms. Montañez is teaching yoga with whom?" Lewis grabs a granola bar for himself.

"With a yoga teacher—they're friends. I think she is volunteering to show us all the yoga moves they do."

"They are called *poses.*" Lewis bites off part of the granola bar, and pieces drop to the floor. Hope automatically scoops them up.

"Since when do you know anything about yoga?" Hope leans into her father, elbows on the table. Her hair is just as wild and dark as when she was in elementary school, but now she uses a straightening iron, much to her father's disappointment. He likes her curly hair.

"Well, it's common knowledge. A lot of the teachers at my school take yoga. The women, that is. I hear them talking about these poses—downward dog, warrior... whatever." He pauses. "So, Carly's mom goes to this teacher's studio?"

"I didn't say that. I just said she does yoga. But she likes it. Hey, anyway, what's for dinner?"

"Spaghetti and meatballs. You need to grate the cheese." Lewis pauses, lost in thought for a moment. Then his voice takes on a detective's tone: "What's the yoga teacher's name?"

"Dad, you are so weird! Why are you talking like that?" Hope stares at him, and then starts looking around the kitchen. "Where do we keep the cheese grater?" She starts opening drawers. She does not notice her father's stillness. "Ah ha, here it is. Oh, one more thing—this is really cool, Dad—the lady is a yoga teacher from *Hawaii*. Isn't that, like, really amazing? Dad. Dad! Are you even listening?"

"Yes. Yes, Hope. I'm listening."

"So, why do you want to know her name?"

"Just curious."

"Well, I think it was Kona or something. I dunno."

"Oh, I think I might have met her once," Lewis says non-chalantly.

"Where?" Hope begins to grate the cheese.

"Oh, um…hmm…I think my newspaper staff did a story on yoga and—"

Luckily, the phone rings, and Hope dashes to answer it. "Hello? Oh, hi, Carly. Yes, my dad said it was cool. Tell your mom, okay?" She pauses. "What are you talking about? No, I definitely do not like him…."

Lewis breathes a sigh of relief as the chatter continues. He takes up his post at the cheese grater but finds himself distracted, pondering the letter that Dr. Amos Adler gave him.

* * *

Lewis tosses the phone from hand to hand. He has already punched in the numbers. He just has not pushed *Call*. He decides for reasons beyond what is sensible to make this call from his garage. Hope's nosiness and her ability to bounce all over the house makes Lewis nervous. The garage is his sanctuary. *Besides, what kid wants their parent to call their teacher?* Lewis reminds himself.

He has thought about Noelani off and on. He knows that Dr. Amos Adler's intention is for them to support each other. Simple. Innocent. *So then why be so damn nervous?* With the letter in one hand and the phone in the other, he takes the plunge.

After a few rings, he hears her voice. "Hi. This is Noelani Kekoa at Karuna Yoga. I'm not available right now. Please leave a message, and I'll get back to you. *Namaloha.*" Lewis freezes, clears his throat, mumbles something, and then hangs up.

* * *

6:00 p.m. Karuna Yoga.

Noelani looks at the studio's answering machine. An unfamiliar number. A man coughs and issues a quick apology: "Sorry, wrong number." Then a click.

"Weird."

Lisa looks up from the schedule she is working on. "What's weird?"

"Oh, nothing. Just a man's voice. Wrong number." Noelani grabs her travel bag, now even larger than ever, and digs for her keys. She feels the envelope. It has remained unopened in the depths of her bag amidst all her indispensable "stuff." She stops. Pulls it out. Places it near the top of her bag. She then scoops her keys out and begins to leave. "Lisa, let me know if someone named Lewis leaves a message here, okay?"

Lisa spins in her chair. "Who is Lewis?" Her eyes dance with interest and surprise. Noelani has never mentioned anyone by that name before.

"Oh, just someone—no one, really. I mean, he is just a friend." Noelani heads to the door. "It's probably nothing. Bye—oh, and have a good class! Watch the heat. It's not running very hot lately." She's out the door.

When she gets into her car, she takes out the envelope that Dr. Adler gave her. She mutters to herself, "He doesn't fool me. He is trying to get us together." She smiles. She is going to miss seeing Dr. Adler. Things have been going so well that she is not sure that she will keep her upcoming appointment with this new doctor, Susan Locke. Besides, she has a lot on her plate with her mother. She is about to turn the ignition but is distracted by something gnawing at her. *What if it was Lewis? What if he is having trouble? Maybe he is afraid to call me? I should at least open the letter.*

She pulls the key out of the ignition and uses it to slide open the letter.

Dear Noelani,

I hope you are doing well. If I was a betting man (which I am not), I would imagine that you will not open this letter for quite a while—maybe never, who knows? I have a lot of confidence in you, but don't be stubborn and try to ignore your symptoms. Below is the information on Dr. Susan Locke. Please keep at least the first two appointments with her. She is wonderful.

One more thing—Lewis will probably not reach out to you. He can be just as stubborn as you. I think he may be a little hesitant to be the first to call. That's my guess. So, do me a favor, please? Give him a quick ring, just to let him know that it is okay to call you if he needs to talk. Lewis is a teacher at Encinitas High School. Do you think you can do that for me, please?

All my best to you.
Sincerely,
Dr. A

Now Noelani feels guilty. *Maybe that* was *him?* She puts the key back in the ignition and heads home. She will call him later, after she speaks with her mother.

Chapter Thirty-Three: 1998

7:00 p.m. Noelani's condo in Encinitas.

"Mom, that's great! Really. Yes. Of course I will. I'm so glad you and Dee will come down. We can all look together." Noelani's phone is tucked under her ear; she is adding sundried tomatoes to her salad. Her kitchen's island is the center of all conversations, with stools on two sides and a breeze blowing in from the west through the wide-paned windows. Noelani tastes the balsamic vinaigrette with her fingertip, then sprinkles the dressing across the salad as her mother repeats the plan that she has already told Noelani twice. It is Kalani's way: she repeats to assure herself that she is doing the right thing.

"Okay, Mom. I understand. You will be down in two weeks with Dee to look at condos near me. Meanwhile, I will book the hotel for you for three nights. Right…don't worry about that. I have the real estate agent already looking, Mom." Noelani picks up a tomato and pops it into her mouth. "And we can talk about the boutique attached to my studio then. Yes…and remember, Dee has already been here twice, so… yes…and she showed you the pictures…okay, okay, Mom. Yes, I'm excited. Very. Me, too. Gotta go, Mom…love you…bye."

Noelani drops the phone from her ear and catches it with her hand. Her shoulders sag, and her body goes limp with the release of tension. She has been on the phone for forty-five minutes. She carries her bowl of salad into the living room and collapses onto the couch. She is starving and tries to make herself slow down—not just the eating, but also the thinking. Thinking of her mother's plans of selling her business. Thinking of her obligation to make sure that her mother will be happy living in San Diego. Thinking about whether she can deal with her mother being within an arm's length of her condo. Thinking about the implications of her mother opening a mini boutique in her yoga studio. Thinking of Lisa's reaction to that. All the "monkey chatter" that she encourages her students to quiet now pings around her brain. *God, I need to just breathe!*

Just as she finishes her last bite of cucumber, her phone rings. It is Lisa. She has just finished her class. "Hey, I tried calling you, but the line was busy forever. Then I realized you were probably talking to your mom. How are you? *Was* that your mom?"

With a sigh, Noelani rescues her worn-out throat, overused from back-to-back classes and mother-daughter pep talks. "Yes. Lisa, you are not going to believe it, but she is planning on moving here."

Lisa's voice drops an octave. "No way."

Noelani's raises an octave. "Yes way. She sold her business—or most of it. Look, I am just wiped. I'll explain when I see you tomorrow, okay? It is a long story that I've heard so many times I am numb. I have to shower and just chill out."

Noelani knows her voice implies a mixture of exasperation and exhaustion, but she senses that Lisa seems to have something else on her mind. They both go quiet for a moment, and then Lisa softly places the new item on the floor for discussion, "Okay. I hear you. You should go relax, but I just wanted to tell you something…"

Noelani defeatedly asks, "What?"

"This is probably the last thing you need to hear right now. You mentioned a man named Lewis, right? Well, um, I answered the phone here about twenty minutes ago, and this guy asked if this was the studio where Noelani Kekoa works. And I said, 'Yes, I'm her business partner, Lisa.' And then he paused and seemed like he didn't know what to say next. But then he asked me to just let you know he called—and that you didn't have to call him back—but that you knew his number. And he told me his name was Lewis—Lewis Bennett. I wrote it down. So, um, I just thought…you should know."

A beat.

"Noelani? Noelani, are you there?" Lisa pleads.

"Yes…yes." A breath and then a long sigh. "Okay. Thanks, Lisa. I am glad you told me."

"Noelani, is this bad? Or is he, like, I dunno—someone you *want* to talk to? I mean, do you even *know* this guy?"

"Yes. No worries, Lisa. I sort of know him. He is just a—" she hesitates at the word *friend* "—a person I met through a—a mutual friend. Did he seem upset or anything?"

"No. Not at all. He just sounded nervous. You know, like someone calling for a *date,* maybe?"

"Well, it is definitely not that, Lisa. He is just—oh, never mind. I'll give him a call tomorrow."

"Oh, you have his number? He said you did," Lisa rattles off.

"I do. I gotta go, Lisa. Thanks for calling. See you tomorrow. Say hi to Phillip." She hits the *End* button and tosses the phone on the couch. She throws her head forward, letting her long, raven black hair spill over like a waterfall at midnight. Then with equal force, she reverses the flow, tossing all her hair back. She swivels sideways on the couch. She positions her legs on the arm of the couch so that her calves can rest and her feet can dangle. She rotates her feet, trying to spin the day's tension out, as if her ankles are two knobs of a machine that can decompress her. Her hair now looks like a dark cloud hovering around her head; it contrasts with the cream-colored cushion of her well-worn couch. She gazes up at the ceiling, closes her eyes, and falls asleep.

* * *

The dream's plot remains the same; only the colors and the circumstances change. She demands answers from him. He gets progressively angrier, slamming drawers. She is backpedaling. He is on the attack. He grabs her by the hair and drags her to her bedroom. Then he pushes her back on the bed until she can retreat no further. He is yelling at her. All she can see is his fist. His finger points directly at her. Suddenly, she curls into a ball, holding her legs up against her chest tightly. She hears his voice as if it is in an echo chamber. "This is bullshit!" She bows her head. He is spitting out, "Bullshit! You don't trust me, right? You listen to your friends, right? God damn it!" She braces when she hears a thud. Looking up for a split second, she sees the same hole in the wall that she always sees. It is in the spot—one foot above her head. The white powder of the drywall is on his fist. It falls like flour drifting down to her face. That same fist now grabs her by the neck. She screams, and then words are a glob of guttural, beastly sounds. She tries to understand what he is yelling about, but the sounds are indecipherable. She jolts awake, sweating, always at the same moment: just as her head is about to be slammed into the bed's headboard.

Chapter Thirty-Four: 1998

8:00 a.m. Noelani's condo in Encinitas.

"Hi, Lewis. It's Noelani Kekoa. I'm sorry I didn't call you back yesterday. It was a crazy afternoon—long story. But I was happy to hear you left a message at my studio. This is my home number. Anyway, I was wondering if we could get coffee sometime? Or we could just talk—whatever. So, um, when you have a chance, give me a call, and we can set something up—hopefully. Thanks. Bye." Noelani is relieved that she could just leave a message.

She drops the phone into her purse and takes a deep breath. She knows she looks awful. Her eyes are slightly puffy and have dark circles underneath them. She feels an ache in her lower back that she knows is a result of stress. She feels anxious because *that dream* has not occurred for several weeks. She has no idea how many times it has repeated itself since the actual event happened. She stopped counting. Noelani looks around her apartment. She feels discombobulated as she stuffs even more items into her oversized bag, which has become analogous to Linus' blanket. He always was her favorite *Peanuts* character. Linus is the one sane character who can quell Charlie Brown's irrational, gloomy fears. She loves the Christmas episode when he puts everything into perspective. *Perspective. Good Lord, that is what I need right now.*

She wanders to the bathroom to do *something* with her face, and then realizes that her phone is chiming away in the living room. She looks down at the phone. *Breathe.*

"This is Noelani. Lewis, hello! I just left a message for you. Oh, you did? Great. Okay, well—wait. Oh, my God—it's Saturday. Lewis, I must be losing it. I thought it was Friday! Yes, I can meet for coffee or lunch. Sure. Okay. The Pannikin? Okay. Good, I'll see you at noon." She realizes that they were both abrupt and uncomfortable, maybe because the entire situation is so awkward. But for an uncanny reason, her anxiety level just dropped a notch.

Noelani looks at her watch and decides that her face will just have to wait. She has a 9:30 yoga class, and she needs to talk to Lisa first. She will bring clothes to change in to at the studio. She heads to her closet and grabs a sundress to go with her leggings. She looks around the kitchen. No time to clean up. No reason to. *Breathe.*

* * *

Lisa can tell that Noelani has had another nightmare. Over time, she has learned to read her friend's face. Lisa and Phillip are the only ones who know about John's violent assault that night nearly three years ago.

Lisa and Noelani were inseparable back when they began training to become yoga teachers. Lisa was a few years younger, but Noelani admired the fact that Lisa, a willowy blonde, had graduated from college and had pursued various interests in business before discovering her passion for yoga instruction. The two dreamed of owning their own yoga studio in LA.

When Lisa and Phillip married two years ago, Noelani was the maid of honor. Shortly thereafter, John proposed to Noelani, and a quick wedding was planned. Lisa had her doubts about their relationship, but she held her tongue. Lisa observed that John was cavalier with money; he spent loads on expensive cars, clothes, and vacations. He appeared to have no serious plans for the future, and he took no interest in Noelani's. Lisa also sensed that Noelani at that time seemed to need the security of a man, his affection, his charm. She was never quite sure Noelani could see warning signs. The adage "you see what you want to see, hear what you want to hear" became Noelani's excuse. And besides all that, Lisa knew that Noelani felt her biological clock ticking.

But that wasn't all that concerned Lisa. She knew John was a hothead. Noelani confided in her several times about her husband's temper, and she at times appeared anxious. But in the end, Noelani brushed off Lisa's concerns and said that John just needed to blow off steam sometimes. Lisa mentioned her concerns to Phillip, and soon he learned at a conference they both attended in Las Vegas that John was known to have had affairs with several women. Phillip revealed this to both his wife and Noelani.

When John attacked Noelani that night, Lisa and Phillip came to her rescue. Lisa now shudders at the memory of how she held her battered friend in Noelani's bedroom. She knows that the wounds Noelani incurred will take more time to heal and may never be forgotten.

Lisa is the only person Noelani confides in about her nightmares. Lisa had urged her to tell Dr. Adler once she began seeing him; then she even insisted. But Noelani has resisted. Each time Lisa has asked her why, Noelani has said that she is sure the nightmares will go away over time. From the exhausted look on Noelani's face, Lisa can tell that time has not yet come.

"Another nightmare? Did you get any sleep?" Immediately, Lisa hugs her.

Noelani drops her bag and falls into Lisa. She allows her

head to rotate from side to side. They embrace for several minutes. The morning yoga class will let out soon, and the teacher—a young, energetic, twenty-two-year-old woman—will be bopping out in a few minutes. They can't be seen like this.

Lisa can predict how Noelani will cope. She will pull back and wipe her tears away. Noelani, she knows, is a contradiction in so many ways. Her ambitions are bold, but her personal world is a small knot of people whom she trusts. With others, she is like a Swiss bank; all is locked away in her private vault. She is sometimes gregarious with men when they show interest in yoga, but she turns aloof when they show interest in *her*. Lisa wonders if that is why she has never told Dr. Adler about her nightmares and the physical attack that precipitated it all. Lisa's talks with Phillip often come to a similar conclusion: men have done great damage to Noelani. What concerns Lisa the most is that despite Noelani's esteem for Dr. Adler, she cannot tell him about the beastly attack she faced. How will she ever begin to recover if she cannot acknowledge what happened to her when she is seeking help to overcome it?

And now there is a mysterious caller named Lewis. What secret is Noelani keeping now? Does this Lewis character have anything to do with her being so upset and flashing back to her terror from three years ago?

* * *

When Noelani finishes her class, she and Lisa have time to talk about her mother's plans to move to Encinitas and perhaps become involved in their studio. Lisa listens intently. Noelani seems to have settled herself and keeps to certain talking points. Her mother has a buyer for her clothing boutique in LA. Kalani will retain twenty percent ownership of her business, with more details to follow. Dee will help Kalani find a place to live, something not too close but not too far away, either. Despite some misgivings, Noelani explains to Lisa that this is a good move for both of them. However, any involvement with their yoga studio is something Lisa must fully agree to without feeling any obligation to Noelani.

The conversation is a one-way street. Noelani catches Lisa up and asks her to think about all this. Right now, though, Noelani needs to shower, change, and meet Lewis.

This prompts Lisa to be blunt. "Noelani, who is this guy? Are you okay with meeting him? I mean, like, is he in any way connected with you being so upset when you got here? Because if he is—"

Noelani cuts in. "Lisa, this man has nothing to do with any of that. Lewis is an acquaintance. Dr. Adler asked us to check in on each other. He seemed to think we had similar…issues, I guess. Anyway, I'll just be down the street, and I'll be back in time to cover the desk for the 1:00 class. No worries."

Lisa has a puzzled look on her face.

Noelani grabs her towel and heads to the women's locker room. From inside, her voice echoes, "Besides, he's kinda blind."

Lisa mutters to herself, "Oh great. That makes perfect sense. Blind leading the blind."

* * *

Noelani does not see Lewis when she arrives. She checks upstairs and looks down at the outdoor seating. This seems odd to her; he seems like the type who would be on time. Then she notices him crossing the alley from Lou's Record Store, one of the few that still exist. He is using his cane.

As he reaches the entrance, he turns and very slowly starts up the steps. Noelani feels the need to rush forward and grab him by the arm to steady him. She hurries to him and touches his forearm. She notices he is startled. She perceives that he did not see her coming. She calmly says, "Lewis, it's me, Noelani. I saw you coming. Saturdays are always busy, so I got here early."

"Oh, hi, Noelani. Yes, this place is hopping. It always is on weekends." He turns his head a bit to the left, and she realizes that he can now see her more clearly. "Ah, there you are," Lewis says with a laugh. "Sometimes my vision is blurry, but if I look around, I can see fine. Weird, I know."

Noelani sees his smile, and her hand, still on his forearm, feels his muscles relax a bit. "I see a couple of tables out here. If you want, I can snag one." She quickly realizes her mistake.

"No, then how would I know what you want to order? We are almost up to the front of the line. I'm sure there will be a place to sit and talk." He removes her hand from his arm, but not without squeezing it slightly. "I can't thank you enough for meeting me."

"No, Lewis. I can't thank *you* enough for reaching out. Actually, your timing was perfect."

They are quiet as they approach the counter. Delicious pastries are on display, and the smell of freshly brewed coffee indulges the senses. Lewis asks, "Did you want—well, I mean, how hungry are you?"

"A little hungry. You feel like splitting something?" She is fighting the need to help him.

"You know, that would be fine. Have you ever had their omelets?"

"Yes. Would you go for a veggie omelet, or are you a meat and potatoes man?"

Lewis turns and smiles at her. "I swing both ways, but veggie sounds fine." He looks up, and the woman behind the counter asks them for their order. He responds, finishing the order with two coffees. He insists on paying. She insists on splitting. "But we are already splitting the omelet," Lewis protests. "How about you take care of the tip? I promise this will be the only time I treat, okay?"

Noelani nods. "Deal." She watches as Lewis carefully takes out his wallet, feels for a credit card, and hands it to the voice of the cashier. He waves off a receipt. Noelani takes a few singles out of her own wallet and drops them into the tip jar. Lewis carefully replaces his credit card in the same slot, which he feels with his fingertips. "Lewis, if you don't mind, I'll take our coffees. Here's the order number. You lead, and I'll follow. I think there are a few tables down at the far end—to your right. Oh, do you take cream?"

"Just a splash." Lewis moves gingerly, using his feet to feel for the steps that he knows are very small. He walks along the wall toward the tables. The sky is overcast with a typical stubborn marine layer, so he is unconcerned about a table with an umbrella. Noelani is fascinated by how he navigates the space—and how other café patrons watch him with curiosity. After all, he appears to be blind but can apparently see well enough to secure an empty table.

"We made it!" Lewis exclaims with a smile.

Noelani finds herself in the unusual position of being with a man who is behaving in the opposite manner that she is used to. Instead of being the object of the male gaze, Noelani finds herself checking *him* out.

Until now, he was just a nice, kind man. A rather handsome man, perhaps a bit older than her but with distinguishing features. His sandy brown hair, parted on the side and covering half his ears, seems soft. There is gray forming around his temples, but not nearly as much as in his beard, which is neatly trimmed. His grayish brown hair reminds her of the color of Lisa's Australian shepherd.

She wants him to take his dark sunglasses off so she can see his eyes, but she knows it would be rude to ask. Besides, he may need those glasses. He looks somewhat trim, not hyper-fit like many of her clients. She figures that he probably had to adjust to working out without the full use of his sight. The tan on his arms and legs matches that on his face, and when he smiles, the wrinkles around his eyes suggest to her that this is a man who laughs a great deal. She likes that. She glances at his ring finger and notices that there is a indentation there and the skin seems to be a shade lighter. *That's odd. He always wore a wedding ring.*

She also likes the fact that Lewis gives off an entirely different vibe than the men she has dated in the past. Instead of being preoccupied with looking at her or mentioning her figure, he is welcoming. He seems to really *want* to talk with her. She wants to know what his vision is really like because he is looking straight ahead, not at her. He does turn to her to speak but oddly turns away to listen. Nevertheless, Noelani relaxes at the thought that Lewis is not looking her up and down. On this afternoon, after that terrible night, she knows she does not look her best.

He doesn't seem to be trying to impress her, but he is also fighting to make it clear that he is not some invalid who needs to be pitied. She wonders if Lewis has the same stubborn streak in him that she has developed. *I'll own my own yoga studio. I don't need a husband.* Lewis projects, *I'll find us a table. You don't need to hold my hand.*

Chapter Thirty-Five: 1998

12:15 p.m. Noelani and Lewis at Pannikin Coffee and Tea in Encinitas.

After chitchat about what their lunch is like and how much they love the Pannikin, the two begin to nibble the heart of what matters. Lewis senses that Noelani will be more reserved, so he begins. "You know, what prompted me to call you was my daughter, Hope. She came home yesterday all excited about her new yoga program. She mentioned a Hawaiian guest instructor—Ms. Kona, or something like that—and I realized she was probably referring to you. And, of course, that got me thinking about everything that happened with Dr. Adler and how he gave us envelopes and such and asked if we would stay in contact if we needed to just, you know, talk."

Lewis measures the effect of this opening on Noelani. He realizes that she probably has no idea that he is watching her carefully, since he appears to be looking away. Noelani nods and seems receptive. The train roars by, and her hair blows with the breeze. She tosses it back, finds the ends, and twists them a bit.

Once the train's engine passes, Noelani confirms, "Yes, Lewis. I'm excited to be at the school helping Ms. Montañez introduce the kids to yoga. I'm so happy your daughter will be a part of the class."

Lewis agrees. Then he hopes to quell some of the awkwardness of this meeting by explaining, "Okay, well, two things
I feel I should tell you—actually, three. First, I did read Dr.
Adler's letter, and he told me the name of your studio. But
not the phone number. I had to look it up. I think I called
the wrong number at first. But then I called back and—well,
anyway, I just want you to know that I wasn't stalking you or
anything."

"I know that, Lewis. No worries." Noelani assures him,
lightly brushing his forearm.

"Good. Second, I want you to not feel obligated to 'return
the favor,' so to speak. I mean, if this is the only time we
meet—or talk for that matter—then that's fine. I mean, Dr.
Adler was kinda going rogue when he brought us into the
same room and said—I guess, *revealed*—personal information
about us. You know what I mean?"

Noelani smiles at him, then lets out a small laugh. "Lewis,
again, I understand, and I agree. We are just having a moment.
We don't need to continue talking or contacting each other if
you or I feel uncomfortable. But just so you know, I was very
happy to hear from you. Your timing was perfect—but let's
not go there. That's another story. Anyway, what is the third
thing you wanted to tell me?"

Lewis looks embarrassed. "Shoot. Did I have three things?
Oh, God. I'm losing it." He chuckles at his own foolishness.
He was so engrossed in watching Noelani that he forgot the
most important thing he needed to say. "Sorry, I remember. Okay, here is the deal with my vision. I know it is really
strange, but right now, I can see you clearly with my peripheral vision, even though it looks like I am not looking at you
at all." Then he smiles broadly. "So don't think you can stick
your tongue out at me or make funny faces at the kinda blind
guy—'cause I see you, Ms. Kekoa."

They both laugh. A genuine laugh, one that makes them

lean into each other, then lean back to catch their breath. Noelani pokes his shoulder and teases, "Oh, good. This whole time I thought you were more interested in those ladies over there."

"Over where?" Lewis pretends to have no idea where, bobbing his head around à la Stevie Wonder.

They laugh again. Then in a serious tone, Noelani questions him: "So, what is the issue with your vision? Is it correctable?"

"Well, I have this rare eye condition called *serpiginous choroiditis*. I won't bore you with all the details; however, this condition comes on later in life—for me, about four or five years ago. It started with lots of fuzzy, white spots, then some darker ones. I thought, no way can I be having cataracts. It was scary. After God knows how many tests, they told me my 'disorder' is a recurring inflammation of the retina. I am trying different treatments, and they seem to be at least keeping it in check—for now. At least, I think so. But as you say, 'let's not go there.' As for a cure, I am less optimistic, and so is my doctor. I just hope to stay like I am. Some days are better than others."

Noelani takes all this in. There is a pause. Sips of coffee. Cups replaced.

Lewis sighs. "So that's my scoop. It's part of why I am—or was—seeing Dr. Adler. I am still a little freaked out."

Noelani jumps in. "Of course you are, Lewis. You could see perfectly your whole life—and now this. So how do you work? Oh wait—my letter said you are a teacher at Encinitas High School? That's all the info Dr. Adler gave me. What do you teach?" Noelani hears a muted musical note and reaches into her purse to silence her phone. She does this without breaking whatever eye contact she thinks Lewis has with her.

"Don't laugh, Noelani. Journalism and English."

"Really?"

"Yeah, I read papers and news columns—sideways. Actually, my principal is very supportive. We used to be in the same English department before he went into administration. Anyway, I've run the newspaper for thirteen years, and just recently, she and I talked about me taking over a student services program. Long story short, it is a counseling program for kids who have all sorts of issues—drugs, divorce, smoking, you name it. She thinks I am a perfect fit. It would mean I would not teach English classes anymore, just two periods of journalism." He stops abruptly. "Listen to me, I am doing all the talking. Honestly, I am usually a pretty quiet guy. I guess maybe not talking to Dr. A has me chatting you up. Sorry. So…"

"No. No. No. Lewis, I don't think that at all. As a matter of fact, I'm very reserved, too. When I see—saw—'Dr. A,' as you call him, there were times he had to pull things out of me. I tend to keep things—well, kind of—*closed off*, I guess." She allows the last words to linger in the air like a leaf that refuses to fall to the earth with the pull of gravity. Finally, she releases her admission. "Yeah—that's me."

Lewis feels he should wait her out and find out why she agreed to see him.

"Hmm. I guess it's my turn, huh?" Noelani begins. "Well, as you can guess, I have problems that require me to see a psychiatrist. Mostly stress and anxiety." She stops and takes a breath. "Lewis, I don't want to make you think—God, I am so bad at this!"

Lewis remains silent.

Again, she tries to make herself speak. "Okay. I'm a yoga teacher because I love—I want to say—"

Lewis steps in. "Whatever you are trying to tell me that is so difficult, please don't feel obligated, okay?" He sees Noelani nodding, but he also sees her internal struggle. He's been there. He notices that she has been twisting her hair, which drapes over her shoulder.

"No. I don't want to bullshit you—or myself, for that matter. I do that too often. Look, Lewis, I've been struggling for years. Ever since I came to the mainland from Hawaii as a teenager, I have struggled. Emotionally, that is. But then some bad things happened to me physically, and I have really struggled to recover from them. Yoga has been my sanctuary."

Lewis tilts his head and moves a bit closer in an attempt to make her know for sure that she has his complete attention.

Noelani captures oxygen, and it fills her lungs with a surge of honesty, letting one tragedy see the light of day. "See, I was in a terrible skiing accident years ago, and just like that," she says with a snap of her fingers, "my dance career was over. It's a long story that doesn't need to be told. And then I just flailed around. I guess I lost my confidence. And that led to other... problems."

"I get that in a big way, Noelani."

"I bet you do."

"You have no idea. Try raising a daughter by yourself—and then having to do it out of the corner of your eye." Lewis feels self-pity washing over him and gets irritated with himself. "Sorry, I hate it when I feel *Oh, woe is me.*" He resets. "My daughter, Hope, is a great girl—really mature for her age. She helps me keep calm." He turns his head in the opposite direction to get a clearer view of Noelani's reaction.

Noelani is the one who smiles, having had some of the pressure of her confession absolved. "What's the expression, Lewis? 'Keep calm and carry on,' right?" Noelani looks at her watch.

Lewis knows the clock is ticking. "Noelani—or is it Noel?"

"Always Noelani, except when my business partner, Lisa, gets frustrated with me. Then she just yells, 'No!'"

Lewis appreciates the play on words. "Okay, Noelani. You know, I did see you glance at your watch. I have really enjoyed talking with you, but I know you have to go."

"Yeah, I'm sorry, but I do have to get back to the studio. It has been really nice talking with you, Lewis." Noelani leans down for her purse. "I know it sounds—well, I don't know how it sounds—but you have made me smile. And that has not been easy lately. So thanks, Lewis."

"Okay—well, good." He rises. "If you ever need anything or just want to smile, give me a call."

Noelani navigates them both to the sidewalk. "If I need cheering up, you definitely are the person I'll call." Then, just as he is about to pivot away, she reaches for his left hand, squeezes it, and says, "You are a very sweet, Lewis."

Lewis smiles and walks back to Lou's Records. His buddy will still be there. He only wishes he could have told Noelani the other reason he had called.

Chapter Thirty-Six: 1998

8:30 a.m. Karuna Yoga.

"What are you going to do?" Lisa has dropped the clean towels into the bin and her face takes the shape of one who's just been pulled over for a speeding ticket.

Noelani's face is flushed. Then she stammers out, "I...I said *okay*."

"Yeah, I know you said that, but why on earth would you agree to meet with him? I mean this is *Michael*! Michael, the guy from years ago, the guy who took you skiing and was a cokehead and responsible for...."

Noelani stops the verbal avalanche of criticism with at least one defense. "He wasn't a 'total cokehead,' Lisa. And remember, it wasn't his fault that I got in the accident...and, you know, I told you he felt terrible. Remember, his parents helped with some of my medical bills...."

People are just starting to come into the studio for the next class with yoga mats in hand. The customers stop as it seems the conversation between Lisa and Noelani warrants them to freeze, put their hands up, and not say a word.

Lisa turns and realizes *this is not the time*. Noelani rearranges the defensive look on her face to the smiling, warm tropical charm that Karuna Yoga projects to all who come to find an escape from the world's pressures. Lisa scuttles off to the yoga studio to check the temperature as Noelani greets each person. The last look Lisa throws at her partner is striking: *we are talking about this later!*

* * *

"So you are telling me that you *want* to have dinner with Michael? Noelani, just tell me why, okay?" Lisa and Noelani are sipping on smoothies during lunch in their small office. Noelani reaches for her enormous bag and pulls out a notebook she uses for various inspirational messages in her classes. She takes the rubber band off and reaches for the last page. There, taped to the cardboard back cover is Michael's picture.

"He calls this 'his head shot,'" She explains of the black and white picture of a young Michael Krauss, taken ten years ago.

Lisa can't help herself. She inhales, raises her fingers to her lips. "Oh my god. He is gorgeous." She looks up at Noelani. "This is, I mean, he is…."

"I know, Lisa. Drop dead Hollywood material. But that is *not why* I said I would have dinner with him."

"Okay, I'm listening." Lisa's eyes still rest to the photo, so Noelani closes the notebook.

"Here is the deal." Noelani begins. "Haven't you ever wondered what may have happened to an old flame? I mean, where did life take them? It's not like you are really interested in getting back together—because I'm not—but I just want to know what happened to *that Michael.* Did he make it in acting? And if not, why? Why is he working with his father now as a talent agent? Why? Did he give up? Did he ever marry? Is he…happy? You have to have had someone in your past that you wondered about?"

Lisa's head rocks sideways as she seems to ponder her own past lovers. "Well, I can understand, I guess. But I really can't relate. Phillip and I just clicked right from the get-go and I didn't have a *serious* guy before him. Certainly no one who looked like *him*."

"And that's not all. Yes, I am curious, but let's face it, what happened on the ski slopes was terrifying for us both. We have that in common." Noelani pauses. "The truth is Michael is like most actors, probably—super self-centered. And on top of that he was spoiled. But deep down he wasn't a villain, Lisa. He cared about me. Look, I'm not that woman that he knew or the one who was married to John."

Noelani feels confident and that radiates across the counter to Lisa, who replies, "Okay, but here are some things I think you really need to get your head around before you meet Mr. Hollywood…."

6 pm. Alfonso's of La Jolla

Michael Krauss sits across from Noelani and exudes the same powerful, sexual energy that made him a potential leading man. His emerald eyes still seem to glow as they did on the stage of *Romeo and Juliet*. But Noelani knows his affect and she is prepared. Her conversation with Lisa laid out all the parameters for the evening's encounter: dinner at a very public place that's well lit, preferably outside, *check*. Don't have more than one drink, *check*. Don't agree to another *date*, *check*. And don't, under any circumstances, go to his hotel, *double check*. Noelani knows to keep this in mind, but the reality of Michael's charm and disarming honesty are formidable. Besides, her curiosity about whatever happened to her long lost Romeo intrigues her.

Sipping a margarita and munching on warm tortilla chips and semi-spicy salsa, Michael's new costume shows he's playing a different role. His light blue button down shirt and black dress jeans are accented with a beige jacket. His expensive aviator sunglasses are nestled in his still blond hair. Although wisps of gray have begun to creep into the margins. He sprinkles salt on the chips and continues his saga, "So, after the years in New York where I was mostly in some way-off-off Broadway shows playing pretty boy parts of no consequence, I started looking at TV roles. I made a few spot appearances in pilots, all of which were dropped." He stops to see the impact he has made on her thus far. "Made a few commercials, and, Noel, the funny thing is, those spots paid so much better." He stops, dips a chip in salsa. "But none of it mattered. It was just a paycheck. Sure, I met some 'stars' but that wore off quickly, and frankly, I was pretty invisible to them anyway. So I eventually went back to LA where there were more opportunities." Michael's soliloquy of a post-Noelani life comes to an end.

Noelani politely listens and purposely doesn't show interest in the names he drops or the venues he mentions. Her interest lies elsewhere. "So now you work with your father, right? At least you mentioned that on the phone. And you are here on a conference?"

Michael speaks behind the rather large menu that suddenly engrosses him. "Yes, to the first part, but it's not really a conference." Then he peers over the top and places the menu down. "I'm here scouting talent at the Old Globe and the other local theaters like the La Jolla Playhouse. We are interested in signing some actors who we feel are underappreciated nationally or unenthusiastically represented by their agents—if they even have a serious agent yet. You know my dad," Michael raises his hands to the dark sky above them on the patio of Alfonso's, "He's always the 'Agent to the Stars'!" They both smile at the silliness of it all. Noelani thinks *at least he knows his lines.*

She asks, "So your parents are well?"

"Um, sort of. Noel, my parents have strange lives. Separate but equal, you know. They stay together because that is what they have always done. But my mother has had back surgery and my father has had triple bi-pass surgery and a pacemaker. I guess they're happy. I don't know. My dad is such a bullshitter that I never *really* know—and I guess I'm not sure I want to. Anyway, he's on the verge of retirement, and I'm carrying on with the show, so to speak."

Plates arrive. Carne Asada burrito for him, chicken enchiladas for her. Noelani waves off the offer of another margarita. Michael does not.

"Noel, how's your mother, Kalani, right?"

Noelani gives him the facts. Nothing more. Instead she asks the questions. "So you told me on the phone that you decided to track me down, and you went to my old yoga studio. What did the people there tell you?"

"Well, after I explained who I was, they told me that you and another gal, Lisa, decided to open your own studio in San Diego. One of them, I forget her name, said this all happened after your divorce—or while it was happening after you split with your ex. They told me he was a jerk, which surprised me because, I mean, Noel, look at you. You are beautiful. Jesus, you could have the pick of the litter and...wait, I'm not saying that you were not smart marrying this guy...."

"John. His name is...was John."

"Oh, right. John."

"Don't worry, Michael. No one's fault but my own." Noelani decides to try to cut Michael off. She really doesn't want her ex husband to be the subject of the evening. Nevertheless, Michael pursues one more point.

"Well, rumor has it he was, let's just say, not a nice person," Michael winces as he says this, trying to be diplomatic, "and the girls there said he was...."

"An ass. That's right. Let's leave it at that, okay." Noelani dabs her lips with her napkin, readjusting it on her lap.

Michael looks at her and they both nod. Message delivered. "I'm very sorry."

They decide to let things settle and enjoy their dinners. The conversation bounces from the wonderful ambiance of the restaurant, the charm of La Jolla, and eventually to Noelani's business.

"So, Noel, the yoga business is going well I take it. I'm very happy for you."

"Definitely. And thanks. Yes, Lisa and I have found our groove." She again turns the course of the conversation, "Wait, I'm still curious. How did you find me with all the yoga places here?"

"Ah, you don't realize the power of the 'New Agent to the Stars'," Michael laughs. Noelani doesn't. "Actually, one of the girls tipped me off that you're in Encinitas. I guess that's north of here, and then I saw the name of your place. It sounded Hawaiian and I took a guess."

"Ah, well, that makes sense. You always were smart… and resourceful when you wanted to be. Now if you could just remember your lines," Noelani decides to rib her former Romeo.

"Ah, yes. Discipline. I'm learning. Really I am." He pauses. "Noel, how is your leg…I mean, really. I still feel terrible. I mean your career in dance…I know it was ruined."

"It was tough, Michael. The rehab. The mental part of it. It still is. But yoga saved me. And the doctors were great. My mother and I still appreciate what your parents did to help us through it all. I'm at peace with it, and you should be, too."

Michael orders bourbon on the rocks and asks if Noelani wants anything. Again she waves it off but looks concerned at his drinking. "Don't worry, Noel. I took a cab here and I'll take one back." He smiles, "Unless you can drive me back to my hotel. Anyway, I'm not driving." He looks at her for a reaction.

"We'll see." She replies.

Michael moves into the present. "So marriage isn't in either of our spheres, huh? I may end up being a confirmed bachelor, unless I find the right woman." His drink arrives and he takes a sip. "Are you seeing anyone?" Placing the drink down, he reaches for her hand. "You know, I still care for you."

Noelani rolls her eyes and taps the back of his hand before pulling it back.

Michael admits, "Yeah, I know, the years of 'No News Michael'…but it seemed that that's what we both wanted. Wasn't it?"

Noelani's poker face reveals little except a hint of acceptance. A beat.

"Yeah, the rehab must've been a bitch. Well, it turned you on to yoga and, babe; you are ahead of the wave. In LA, yoga is the next big thing. I go to a studio myself." Noelani knows Michael is trying hard to get her to open up. Lisa's advice is still girding her against his frivolous charm.

Noelani rebuffs him, "I bet you enjoy seeing all those lovely, young *girls* at yoga."

"Ah, she cuts me to the quick," Michael's flamboyant Shakespearean accent appears. He smiles. "But, Noel, they are *too* young *or too* married. You know, most of them are looking for a young stud or a rich Sugar Daddy." Then he whispers, "Or they have one who can't get it up anymore." He sniggers.

Noelani straightens up and flatly says, "Or, these *women* are looking for a good workout at a *safe* place to practice yoga." Her eyes convey the message that she would slap him if they were on stage.

Michael knows a dagger has been placed on the table. "Of course, Noel. I know. It's just the LA scene can be a pick-up. Anyway, that's not what I'm about. But I do want to make sure that you know how amazing you look and how much I admire you and all you've accomplished."

The waiter brings the bill before Noelani can reply, and Michael insists on paying, tossing cash down and saying it's part of his expense account. Noelani acquiesces.

"Do you mind driving me back to my hotel? I'm at the Torrey Pines Sheraton. It's on your way home, I think?"

"Okay." Noelani's alarm goes off.

"We could have a drink in the bar."

"And then what?" Her face heats up. She gathers her purse.

Michael leans in closer, "We'll talk. And…look, I'm not trying to hit on you, but we are both adults…"

Noelani's posture is rigid. She must decide. "Are *we*, really? And, yes, you *are* trying to hit on me, Michael. So you can stop right there. I'm not who I was…then."

She leans forward, "Listen to me. I have learned the hard way what heartbreak and abuse can do to my soul, and I am not going to be the *object* of a man's temporary desires." Then Noelani pushes her chair back, "Trust must be earned, Michael. You still don't get it." She looks around making sure she is out of earshot of the other diners. "This isn't about the accident. I *never* blamed you for that. But I know what you did the night before. You snorted *all that cocaine* and then tried to sleep it off."

Michael tries to interrupt her, but she persists, "I don't care about how you wasted your acting chances. I was a missed opportunity for you and you are *not* getting that chance again. I came tonight because I wanted to thank you, and I was curious about how you were doing." She stands. He rises, too. Noelani steps closer to him. "Some things don't change about you, Michael. I wish you could see that. I really do." She grabs her jacket and reconsiders her closing lines. "Look, I don't want to end on bad terms, so if you'll excuse me, I am sure you can catch a cab." She slips on her jacket. "Thank you for dinner, but I have to work tomorrow."

Michael tries to apologize, "Noel, I didn't mean…."

"And one more thing—my name is *Noelani*."

Chapter Thirty-Seven: 1998

5:30 p.m. Karuna Yoga.

After the first five days working with Ms. Montañez's class, Noelani sits alone at the front desk pondering several things. Lisa is teaching the advanced class inside the studio. Noelani has picked up her phone on three occasions and then put it down. She twirls her hair. The more unsure she is, the tighter the knot. The tighter the knot of hair, the more it pulls on her scalp. Eventually, Noelani comes to a decision.

She dials Lewis' number.

"Hi, this is Lewis Bennett. I'm probably in class right now, but if you leave a message, I'll get—" Suddenly, there is a thud, like a phone hitting the floor. Then a "Hold on." Then a pause. Noelani wonders what is going on.

"Hello—is this Noelani?"

"Yes. Lewis?"

"Yes! Sorry, I dropped the phone. I do that from time to time."

"It's okay. Hey, I just wanted to give you a quick call." Noelani tries to stay on the script she has planned for this conversation. She lets go of her hair, and it slowly releases to its naturally straight form. "I hope I am not calling you at a bad time."

"No. Not at all. Hope is coming home from soccer practice soon, and I am just making dinner. What's up?" Noelani senses cautious excitement in his voice.

"Oh, well, she is active—that's great. Anyway, I wanted to ask you if she has mentioned how yoga is going at school. Ms. Montañez says the kids are enjoying it, but since I have an inside source, I thought I could get the scoop. Has she said anything?"

"Oh, gosh. Well, you should have seen her on Monday. She was so darn excited about it that I had to slow her down to understand what the heck she was saying. You know how fast teenage girls can get to talking. She went on about what you said before class—wait, I wrote it down. I thought I would tell my students, too. Hmm. Here it is: 'No where. Now here. Be present.' Very cool, Noelani. So anyway, she is loving the class."

Noelani tries to hide her broad smile as a woman walks past her looking at yoga mats. "Oh, Lewis. The kids are so cute. So energetic. I'd kinda forgotten what eleven-year-olds are like. They just want to please Ms. Montañez and me, and they are so funny, too. They are looking in the mirror and trying to have that tough warrior two pose, trying to look fierce! They crack me up, but I am so proud of them. I could go on and on."

Noelani knows the next move is hers. "Anyway, I'm so glad it is working out. And Hope is adorable, Lewis. She's not shy at all. She came right up to me and asked why I said *Namaloha* at the end of class. I told her that it's my own invention. We usually say *Namaste,* but being Hawaiian, I have blended it with *aloha.* She and the other kids all said *Namaloha* when they walked in on Tuesday. So, it has been very rewarding. Yeah." She starts twirling her hair again, fast this time.

"Well, teaching has its perks, doesn't it? Those are the great moments."

The twirling continues. Her hair is tight against her scalp.

"So, Lewis, I know you told me when we met that if we wanted to chat again, it would be up to me. So I called. And…well, I thought maybe you would— possibly—want to get together again…to talk, you know?" She freezes her wrist and makes one last pull on her hair.

"I thought you'd never ask. Why don't you meet me at Moonlight Beach?"

Noelani's hair falls down around her face as she smiles in relief. Never has she called a man and asked him if he wanted to see her.

* * *

As Lisa and her entourage of sweat-soaked clients emerge from the studio, Noelani jots down the time and place she will meet Lewis in her planner, then quickly closes it. She waves and asks the clients how class went as they move past her. Lisa, of course, follows suit and chats with various clients, all the while keeping one eye on Noelani. As soon as the group clears out, the two of them head into the studio to clean it up and wipe down the perspiration that soaks the glossy wooden floor and the mirrors from the heated class.

Lisa, while cleaning mirrors, looks indirectly at her partner. Curiosity oozes out of her as she calls across to Noelani, who is disinfecting the floor at the farthest corner of the room, "So, how is yoga going at the school?"

Noelani gives her the same pitch she gave Lewis.

Lisa prods about what she noticed during her class, "Well, I opened the door during my class to cool down the room and noticed you were having a fun time on the phone," Lisa says.

"Oh."

"Not to be nosey, but were you chatting with anyone interesting?" Lisa smirks.

Noelani does not look up from the floor of the studio

noticing it needs to be cleaned. "Oh, you know, just a friend."

"A friend? Lewis, perhaps?" Lisa has her hands on her hips as if to say, *What are you holding out on me?*

Noelani gives in. She knows she cannot fool Lisa and feels the need for advice. "Okay, yes, Lisa. Lewis is a very nice man. You remember, we met and had an honest talk about things we had in common...with Dr. Adler."

"Wait. I think I missed a chapter of this book, girl. So first, you tell me about the dinner with Michael, and that you finally, as you said—*Found your voice.* And you made it clear to Michael that you were not ever going to see him again."

Noelani reaches for the mop and the disinfectant. "Yes, exactly."

Lisa steps right up to her, "But as I recall, when you got back from the 'coffee talk' with this Lewis guy, you were as quiet as a mouse. I wasn't sure what to say to you. You seemed distracted. Then the Michael thing happened two days later, and that completely flipped the script...and wait..."

Noelani is nodding her head but can't get a word in edgewise. She starts mopping the floor before the next class.

Lisa stops only long enough to pull in enough air to blurt out. "Did you just say what I think you said: that you were both seeing the same psychiatrist? 'Cause if you did, then I'm blown away. *Who does that?* Who has coffee with someone who is seeing the same shrink?" Lisa walks toward Noelani and steps on the mop Noelani is using to clean the floor. "We have time for this. Tell me what's going on, please."

"Okay, but you're making way more out of this than it is." Noelani leans against the mop's handle. "First, he called me— you know that. Lewis, I mean. Then we met. He is dealing with an eyesight issue—"

"You told me he was blind."

"Well, he's not. He has this rare eye disorder. It causes blurry vision, and he only has clear vision in parts of his sight.

It's hard to explain, but he is not blind. Okay, well, he does use a cane, but he hates it and hates being pitied about it."

"Okay. Got that. Not blind."

"So, his daughter is in the class I'm teaching at the middle school. Her name is Hope. She is adorable, by the way. I called him to ask if she had said anything about the class and if she liked it."

"Uh huh, right. *Sure* you did. Anyway, then what?" Lisa finds a dry, clean spot on the floor and sits down cross-legged. Noelani follows. The mop drops to the floor, as well.

"Well, he told me she loves the class." Noelani knows that Lisa is not satisfied and that her partner's opinion matters a great deal. "So, wait, Lisa,—let me back up to our coffee meeting. At the Pannikin, we talked a little about my issues with, you know, panic and anxiety—which he must have known because why else would I be seeing Dr. Adler? Oh, and I told him a little about the skiing accident and how that ended my dance career. Just general stuff."

"Well, for you, that is like spilling your soul, Noelani. What else did you tell him? And more importantly—why?" Lisa's facial expression is a blend of cautious optimism and confusion.

"I didn't tell him the scary bad stuff, if you are wondering. Remember, only you and Phillip know about that." She hesitates. "I told him what I told him because…he is just so… God, I can't find the right words. He's so truthful, so trustworthy."

Lisa leans forward and grabs both of Noelani's hands. "Honey, you just said *trustworthy.* Do you have any idea—*any idea*—how that word plays in your life? *Trust.* You have not trusted a man other than Phillip and Henry in—in I don't know how long. You were afraid of John six months after you married him, when he started shouting at you and lying and doing all the crazy shit that followed. He is still responsible for your nightmares. So when you say this Lewis guy is trustworthy and *truthful*, I just gotta ask—how the hell do you know that? One meeting? A phone call?" Lisa stops and reconsiders. "I'm not trying to—"

"I know exactly what you're saying, Lisa. I get it. You want to make sure I don't do something stupid. And I love you for that. I do, Lisa. But let me tell you something. In ten minutes, I felt more honesty from Lewis than I have from Michael or any of these surfer dudes I have dated lately. I don't tell those guys anything about me, Lisa. It is all small talk with them. It's all about sex for them, and I'm just not interested in that with them. So then they figure I must be some kind of tease, and we go our separate ways. I don't care what they think."

Noelani glances around the studio and sees yoga blocks that need to be stacked. As she stands to do this, she gathers her thoughts about how to explain what makes Lewis special. As she does this, she does not look directly at Lisa, but rather glances at Lisa's reflection in the mirror. Lisa is still sitting on the floor.

"But Lewis…he's so careful with me. I think he gets me in a way that maybe only someone who has been wrecked can. I hope you can understand. It's like…it's like we were both damaged goods."

Lisa stands and moves to Noelani and wraps her arms around her shoulders. "I'm glad that you feel this way, really, I am. He must be nice, huh?"

Noelani nods and turns to face her, "Yes. He seems to be a great dad. But he is so humble. He's on his own with his daughter. He used to always wear his wedding ring, like when we first starting chatting at the doctor's office. I noticed it, even then. But not anymore. At least , when we met for coffee for the first time I realized it. And—and one more thing, Lisa. *I called him.* He told me he would not pursue me. It is up to me. I am the one in control. Until my dinner with Michael,

I've never been in control before. So I called him. I asked him to go out to lunch with me." Noelani descends again as Lisa follows. They sit so close their foreheads almost touch.

Lisa barely blinks, frozen like the Buddha statue in the foyer.

"Lisa, I have no idea where this is going." Noelani begins to tear up. "But I wanna…try. That's all, Lisa. 'Cause I'm so lonely." Noelani's throat tightens so much that just swallowing is painful.

Lisa uncrosses her legs and hugs Noelani so hard that they roll onto their sides. "Noelani. Noelani. I just want you to be happy," she whispers. They both nod their heads.

A minute ticks by. The roar of the train breaks the trance. When they pull apart and sit up, Lisa scoots across the room for a tissue to dab her eyes. Noelani grabs her mop and, like Cinderella, starts scrubbing the floor. But Lisa grabs the handle and makes her take another tissue and compose herself.

When they both take deep breaths and look each other in the eye, they grin. Only then does Lisa ask the old-fashioned question, "Is he handsome?"

Noelani nods and smiles. "He's a doll."

They burst into full-throated laughter.

Chapter Thirty-Eight: 1998

10:00 a.m. Lewis' home in Encinitas.

Days after talking on the phone with Noelani, Lewis can't contain his excitement and wonder about seeing her again. He has dutifully followed his promise to keep the ball in her court, but he can't get her out of his mind.

What is worse—or better, depending on his daily attitude—is that he has been slowly but stealthily making Lotte's influence on his home less noticeable. Of course, what runs through his mind is the effect on Hope, whose efforts to be "mature" about losing her mother have not gone unnoticed. But in truth, Lotte is still exactly that—her mother. Lewis cannot make her invisible. But each room has evidence of their lost marriage, their life together. He now feels like a foolish curator at a museum that has far outlived its relevance.

He wonders, *Is this how a widower feels? What do I do with all these remnants of someone who is gone?*

He started the task by asking Lotte about her personal effects. She brushed him off at the time; he had interrupted an important call about a business deal. Then two days later, she emailed him with a list of what to keep and what to send to her. "Of course, I'll pay for the shipping, Lewis." Then she listed what to toss. As a postscript, she indicated that he should run things past Hope because, in her words, "There are things—mother-daughter things—that she may want, like jewelry." Of course, none of these objects had sentimental value to Lotte, nor did it really matter what Hope picked. Lotte flippantly closed with, "But let's leave it up to her."

Lewis cringes as he recalls Lotte's aside. How could his eleven year-old daughter understand or appreciate any of these material things, when she hadn't had a strong relationship with her mother to begin with? For now, he puts what he views as sentimental into a small box marked *HOPE*. As for pictures of his ex-wife and other artwork that personifies her, Lewis finds replacements. He knows his home is a work in progress, but he thinks it is important to change *what was* into *what is*.

But doing it is harder than he thought. *How do I live in a house in which she remains a ghost? How can our bedroom become mine and mine alone?*

Some of the first items to be dusted off and returned to life are Lewis' record player and some of his favorite albums. Hope is intrigued by the "antique," as she calls it, but the album covers truly fascinate her. "Gee, Dad, these guys look so young. Check out Billy Joel," she says, pointing to the *Stranger* album cover. "I saw him on TV, and he's, like, balding. And his beard is kinda gray. Gosh!"

"Yeah, well, honey, I'm a little bit older now too, you know."

"But you don't seem that much older to me. I guess 'cause I see you every day." With that, she heads off to her room.

Lewis ponders all the disguises he has worn in their masquerade. *Who am I now to Hope, besides her father and a lonely, soon-to-be forty-year-old guy?*

Lewis flips through other albums and stops at John Cougar Mellencamp's *Scarecrow*. He puts the record on the turntable and drops the needle on the fifth song. "Lonely Ol' Night" plays. Lewis closes his eyes and sees Noelani. He knows they are two scared and lonely ol' people. For a while, he loses himself in the drums and guitars.

Does Noelani feel this way? I hardly know her.

Hope interrupts and asks her father to help her reach something in the closet. "Dad, my English teacher has this project. It's really cool. You know that song I was telling you about by Jewel?"

"Who?"

"Jewel. You know, it's called 'Hands.' We just heard it on the radio yesterday." She frowns. "Gee, Dad, you even said you liked it."

"I don't remember, honey. What about it?"

"Well, our teacher played the song in class. My teacher's like you—always talking about the *meaning* of a song. Anyway, the song is about how everyone's hands are different, but mostly the same, you know? So, the project is to figure out what each of our fingers represents. We're supposed to write about our hand on a poster board, then draw or have a picture of it—something that symbolizes our hand. Dad, are you paying attention?" Hope's hands are on her hips.

Lewis awakens from his thoughts about Noelani's hands. "I am. So what is it you need in the closet?"

"The old photo albums. Like, the really old ones—you know, like, from when I was born."

"Oh." Lewis is still befuddled.

"See, I need a picture for my *ring finger*. My teacher says that's the finger that represents love or heartbreak. That's what Jewel says in the song. So I need a picture of you and mom—maybe with me, like when I was a baby."

Lewis tries to blandly say, "Oh. Let me reach up and get the right photo album." Meanwhile, he is wondering what Hope will write about. *Should I talk to her about what is appropriate to share with her class—or just trust her?*

He picks the right volume, opens it, sees the pictures of

another lifetime, and braces himself for what is to come when his daughter begins her journey back in time. "Here you go, honey."

"Thanks, Dad." Hope sits cross-legged and drifts through the pages. Lewis putters around, trying to decide what to do, what to say. Finally, Hope settles on a particular photo and calls out, "Hey, Dad! Can you come here? I gotta ask you something." As Lewis turns the corner, he sees that Hope is holding two things, one he expects and one he has long ago forgotten.

"I think this is a good picture, see?" Hope waits for Lewis to settle next to her on the floor. It is a picture of Lewis and Lotte, dressed up—perhaps at some party—holding Hope in a cute little dress between them. "Mom looks so pretty, Dad. I love her dress. And you—look at you wearing a bow tie and jacket! No beard, by the way, either." She inspects the picture as if it is under a microscope. "Do you remember where this was taken?"

"Um, yeah. We were going to your grandparents' house for their anniversary—up in the Bay Area."

"Oh. Well, that makes sense. Of course, I don't remember that." She laughs, but then her mood changes. "But Dad, what is this? I found it in the back of the photo album." She holds a single sheet of paper. On it appears a poem. Typed. "Did you write this?" Wonder waves across her face.

Lewis smiles slightly and sighs. "Yes, I did. A long time ago. It was the first thing I ever wrote that got published— some sort of poetry contest."

"Can you read it to me? Poems are always better when the writer reads it aloud. That's what my teacher said last year." Hope's innocence is on full display.

"Well, it's really old. I wrote it the year you were born." He pauses. "You really want me to read it?"

She nods.

Lewis clears his throat.

"La Petite Café at Midnight, New Year's Eve"

I used to plan out our evenings,
then present you with choices
on an elegant menu, next to a single red rose:
Stefano's and the Upstart Crow in Hillcrest,
Alfonso's and a stroll to the Cove Theater in La Jolla,
La Petite Café and the Pannikin in the Gaslamp.
Your choice.

And now we are hostage to busy babysitters,
limited to a couple of hours
—maybe three—
nodding off at films,
tired of dining at banal restaurants near our home.
And sometimes we even do the unimaginable,
finding ourselves in, of all things, grocery stores
—with coupons—
paying for the freedom to do
the mundane chores that life assigns.
Then home again
to kiss the forehead and pull the blankets under a chin
—drive babysitter home—
only to return to a house softly slumbering,
tucking your blanket under your chin.
Our choice.

Maybe someday we will stay up late again,
planning evenings until midnight
on a New Year's Eve
all dressed up with someplace to go,
but still worrying where you are
with no one to tuck her in.

—Lewis Bennett

"Dad, that is beautiful." Hope looks at her father with astonishment. Then she uncrosses her legs and kneels to hug her father.

"Thanks, Honey. Thanks. It was a long time ago." He takes her chin. "But sometimes I still check to make sure you are tucked in."

Hope buries her head into her father's shoulder. He hears a muffled, "I love you, Daddy." Lewis doesn't hear the word *Daddy* much anymore; it is an anachronism in the house now. Their embrace is broken by Hope's need to wipe her eyes.

"Dad, do you still love Mom?"

"I will always love your mother, Hope. But our relationship is not what it was, and it can never be the same again. I love her for what we had. For you. For our past. But love is much more than that. It is unconditional. I no longer have that kind of love for her, and I'm sure she no longer has that kind of love for me. I think—I imagine—she loves another man like that now." He pauses. "I do know one thing for sure, though."

"What?"

"She has that kind of love for you."

"Dad, I'm not a kid anymore. I know Mom. She loves me, but like you say—it is not unconditional." Hope looks certain and determined, like she does when she battles on a sports field or works through a homework assignment. Lewis pushes back and studies her face. She has aged right before his eyes. He makes a decision.

"Hope, can I tell you something personal? It's about me and someone else." He tilts his head, and on cue, she saddles up next to him. They lean back against the wall.

"Really? Okay. What is it? Wait, is it about someone else you know?"

"Yes, it is. I have not wanted to say anything for a lot of reasons."

"Like what?"

"Well, for one, she is someone you know and—"

"Someone I know?" Hope's eyes widen, but she looks straight ahead, not making eye contact with her father.

"Yes, but it is someone I have just met, so I can't say I know her all that well."

"Wait. It's a woman? And I know her?"

"Yes. Her name is Noelani. But to you, she is Ms. Kekoa—your yoga teacher."

"No way!" Hope turns to her father, her face a mixture of emotions. She looks both confused and shocked.

"Honey," Lewis begins as he desperately tries to read his daughter's thoughts. "We are just friends. We have a lot in common. We enjoy talking to each other. That may be all that comes of this, but I want you to know because—well, because I want you to understand that I'm just—I'm sometimes—"

"You don't need to tell me, Dad. I know what you are trying to say. It's cool. I mean, it's okay." Hope looks at her father and smiles.

They both pause to let their world catch up with their words.

Hope and Lewis hold hands. Hope starts, "I'm really glad you told me, Dad. Ms. Kekoa is really nice."

Lewis' smiles, "I'm really glad I told you, too. And she *is* really nice."

Hope stands, holding both the photo and the poem. "But you still have to tuck me in sometimes, okay?"

Lewis grins at his daughter's sweetness. "Deal."

Chapter Thirty-Nine: 1998

4:30 p.m. Las Olas Mexican Restaurant. Cardiff-by-the-Sea.

Noelani explains to Lewis that the studio closes at 4:00 on Sunday. They decide to meet on the benches that overlook Moonlight Beach, which is just a short drive from Noelani's studio. Lewis is on the bench closest to the lifeguard station. Each of the four benches have some letters that indicate how previous young loves have etched their names into the brown oak. Moonlight Beach is dotted with a rainbow of umbrellas and the smoke from the numerous fire pits begins to lift into the sea breeze. The aroma floats higher into the blue gray sky. The sand volleyball courts are dotted with competitors, each exuding the joy of sport blended with the rollicking, effortless power of young knees and tanned, toned bodies. Lewis tries to see all that he hears and knows exactly how the rhythms of Moonlight Beach will drum on as night falls: umbrellas will give way to the fire pit's flames, laughter will ring out from those who form its circle, twilight surfers will catch one last wave, and the aroma of various cooked meats will indulge the senses and spur the appetite. Lewis is a veteran of the twilight beach scene.

Noelani appears, calling out to Lewis and for a while they sit together quietly taking in the spectacle that is Moonlight Beach. Noelani touches Lewis' shoulder signaling him that she is ready to move on. Lewis asks if Noelani has ever been to Las Olas Mexican Cantina. Noelani admits that she has heard of it but that she has never been. "Well, time to change that," Lewis replies.

* * *

They sit at a table under the outdoor canopy to watch the sunset as the ocean's breaking waves settle down for an evening's rest. Noelani tells Lewis the restaurant is charming. Lewis explains that Las Olas was built as a laid-back cantina back in 1981, when the beach community two miles south of Encinitas was just waking up to the idea that beachgoers needed a place to eat after surfing or playing along the long Cardiff shoreline. Noelani notices how the people at the tiny bar are laughing with the bartender, as if they have hung out there for years. Lewis remarks that the staff has worked at the restaurant for as long as he can remember. It is an unpretentious place. A surfboard hangs over the bar; colorful tiles glued to it spell out *Welcome.* The wooden chairs are all multicolored, and the tables show signs of use. The table tops are all tiled with yellows and blues. A Corona beer bottle has been repurposed as a salt shaker.

The fare is Baja Californian—tacos, enchiladas, chips, and salsa accompany the margaritas. Nothing fancy, just San Diegan comfort food. After ordering, Noelani sips her margarita from a thin straw, then licks the salt off the rim. Lewis smiles whimsically.

"Yum, delicious. Lewis, this place is awesome. Bet you've been here lots of times over the years."

Lewis nods. "Hope and I call this our go-to place on the beach. Glad you like it."

"Love it." She winks, but she is unsure if he sees it.

Suddenly, the breeze kicks up, and the surf follows its lead.

Las Olas' windows are all opened so the ocean breeze drifts in. Smelling the ocean is a pleasure Noelani does not take for granted. It reminds her of Maui. The ribbons of thin clouds streak the western skyline and they glow pink.

Noelani slides her long hair off to the side so that it drapes around her shoulder and over her arm. She wears a purple, sleeveless, linen top with white capris and sandals. Lewis has a classic blue Hawaiian shirt on—untucked, of course—along with the obligatory shorts and sandals. Noelani again notices his tan and asks if he spends a lot of time outdoors.

"Well, up until recently, I rode my bike up the 101 to Oceanside and played a little golf—sometimes tennis. But I never picked up surfing. Guess I am a chicken. I am amazed at the surfers, because, I mean—the waves are so powerful, it just intimidates me. Now with my eyes, road biking is out, but I have this contraption that I can put on my bike's back wheel; so I can ride stationary in the backyard at least. Tennis is out. Golf—well, I play with guys who spot the ball for me. I try to hit straight, and we play the same two courses, so I kinda know where things are. But to be honest, I have gone from mediocre to terrible. I just play for fun now—and for a beer at the end. I can still putt!" He smiles.

Noelani listens carefully. She cannot imagine life without sight—or even life with partial sight. Suddenly, it dawns on her. "Hey, Lewis, why not try yoga? It's a great workout, and it is also about releasing tension. I mean, after all, you live in the yoga capitol of the West Coast—and I just happen to know a place." She smiles.

"I don't know about that. Isn't it a girls' thing? I don't mean to sound like I'm afraid of my masculinity or anything, but seriously—do *any* men do yoga?" Lewis looks toward the sun, which is moving closer to the horizon, causing a baby blue hue shadowing the pink clouds.

"Lewis, when I opened my studio three years ago that may

have been true, but you'd be surprised. More men are trying it. We have at least a dozen regulars at the studio, and that number is growing." She cannot contain her enthusiasm.

"Okay, but I bet they are young studs who are just there to check out the girls—or is that a dumb stereotype and I am being totally stupid?"

"You are not completely wrong," she says lightly, "but there are a few old-timers like you who are practicing."

"I deserved that."

"You did." She begins to slowly twirl her hair.

"Maybe I'll give it a try. So, um, where should I go? Just kidding. Would you at least teach me some basics?"

"Of course. Tell you what—after dinner, let's drive to the studio, and I'll show you the basics so that when you go to a beginner class, you will know what the teacher is saying, especially since—"

"I know, since I may not be able to see what's what." Lewis smirks.

"Yes. That's true. But you're in great shape, and I think you might like it. What do you think?" Noelani hopes she is not coming across as too pushy. She continues to twirl her hair.

"I'm game. Let's eat and see that sunset first." Just then, the plates arrive.

"Oh my, this looks delicious," Noelani says as she takes a bite of her carnitas taco. She looks out toward the horizon. "Darn, the marine layer has come in a bit but see—the sun is poking out underneath. The sky will be super pink when it sets, but I doubt we'll see a green flash." Noelani reaches across the table and touches Lewis' hand. "I sometimes feel strange saying things like that, Lewis, because I don't know what you *can* see. Sorry."

"Don't apologize, Noelani. Never. I see what I see, and I have been trying to embrace what is before me. And even if I miss the green flash, I see you and your lovely purple top."

Lewis says this in such a soft tone that to Noelani, it is like the sound of someone blowing into her ear. She lets her hair go, and it falls over her breast. Her eyes drop demurely.

"Thank you, Lewis." She turns from the compliment to his attitude. "That is a good—a positive—way of looking at what life brings with it." Noelani realizes she keeps using words like *looking*.

"So, is Hope alone this evening?"

"Well, no. She promised me that she and her friend Carly and another girl would work on a history project. Carly's parents are 'on call,' so to speak. I told Hope I wanted to see what they had done—not that I don't trust her, but you know how it can be."

Noelani ponders her answer for a second longer than one would expect. "To be honest, I don't, really. I don't have children, but I do know girls. I bet you two have a level of trust."

"If we are being honest, Noelani, I do trust her, and I have learned not to lie to her. I teach *To Kill a Mockingbird*, and in it, the father—Atticus—explains that children can always spot an evasion better than adults. There was too much of that going on for too long a time when she was younger—with my ex-wife. You've never directly asked me about that, but we've been divorced for three years now. We were separated for practically Hope's entire life, though." Lewis turns away from the setting sun to assess Noelani's reaction.

Noelani simply nods her head. They take a few bites and sip their margaritas.

Noelani decides to return to a more pleasant subject. "You know, Lewis, I *loved* that book. It was my favorite in school—and I loved the movie, too. I guess maybe because—like every girl—I wanted a father like Atticus." She pauses, puts down her fork, and takes a sip of her margarita. She looks right at Lewis. "I never had a father."

"Never?"

"No. Never knew him. I'd say it was a long story, but it isn't. He was a sailor—an American—and he had an affair with my mother. She got pregnant with me, and he sailed off—" Noelani looks out toward the ocean waves again; they are no longer rumbling but are merely coasting to the shore. "At least, that is all I can ever get my mother to tell me." Noelani realizes she has just told Lewis something she *never* tells men. She never even told her ex-husband, John. *Of course, he never asked.*

"It must have been very difficult for you and your mother."

"My mom's name is Kalani. Yes, it was. It was part of why we moved to the mainland when I was close to Hope's age." She shakes her head. "My mom did *not* trust me—and looking back, she was absolutely right." Again, Noelani's internal voice is alarmed at what she is revealing. *What am I saying to this man?*

Lewis puts his fork down and reaches for his margarita. "I'm not going to ask why she didn't trust you. At least you now accept that her intuition was probably right." Lewis' eyes seem to be pointed straight at her, but he is actually gazing at the ocean. "Look, the sun is setting. Isn't the sky beautiful? You were right. Whenever we have a thin marine layer, the sun peeks out under the clouds as it dips to the ocean to let us know it's still there."

Noelani gazes westward. She wants to stay focused on the sun in all its glory. *I've said enough.* "It reminds me of something I tell my students in yoga: 'Some people see the beauty of movement all around them, but they themselves refuse to move. Others can move beautifully in their lives, but sadly, do not know where they are going.' I read that somewhere."

"The moral?" Lewis shifts his gaze to her.

"Be present. Be brave. Own your truth," Noelani replies. "I wish I followed my own advice more often."

"I think you just did." Lewis takes off his sunglasses and tries to force his eyes to focus on her.

Noelani realizes that this man understands something she has buried, and he has signaled this comprehension to her not just in words, but in his own vulnerability. "Lewis, your eyes are so striking. Do I see flecks of light green in your light brown eyes?"

"That's what people tell me. I guess so. Sorry I am always wearing sunglasses. You probably think I am trying to hide my feelings."

"No, Lewis. I have never felt that. If anything, you are very perceptive and open. More than any man I have ever known."

They finish eating. The sun is halfway down. From this point on, neither speaks. They cannot pull their eyes away from the glowing sun as it is sliced horizontally by the ocean. Blue streaks now blend with the pink sky. Only the top of the sun is left. And then, like a stone falling to the ocean, it is gone. All the customers in the restaurant break into applause, as is the custom along the north shore. Smiles all around. Glasses clink—a toast to the sun and the twilight that beckons.

* * *

As Noelani unlocks the studio's front door, she turns to Lewis and says, "I still can't believe you had a friend drop you off at Moonlight Beach! What if we had a terrible time and I took off? How were you going to get home?"

"Ah, good question. First, I promised Hope I would not drive at night anymore. Of course, she is two years from getting her permit and can't wait to drive me around. Second, I know the bartender here." That smile that melts Noelani appears.

"Okay, well then I'll have to drop you off at your house. I'm happy to do it. I agree with your daughter—you probably shouldn't be driving at all." She glances back at him, expecting a stubborn rebuke. Instead, he only shrugs.

"I appreciate it. Wow. This studio is something. Love the Hawaiian décor. And the floor is fabulous." The refinished oak that Noelani and Lisa spent a fair sum of money on was well worth it. Lewis surveys the studio as best as he can while Noelani turns on the lights. She gives him a brief tour. "You and Lisa have done a terrific job here," he says. "You mentioned a man named Henry?"

"Oh, yeah. Henry is Dee's husband. Dee was my dance teacher for years and years. She and Henry came down when we were first checking out the place. Henry is a great handyman. He helped with the heating and plumbing. Well, I guess we need to get on with some pointers, huh?" Noelani begins to feel something unfamiliar in her yoga domain: anxiousness. Not the troubling type, just the nervous excitement that comes with being in a new situation.

"Okay, Lewis. Here are some yoga mats. Let's start with the basic poses." Noelani and Lewis face the mirror. "Let's start with child's pose. Kneel down. Spread your knees as much as comfortable—so they reach to the widest part of the mat. Big toes touch behind you. Mmm, good. Then bring your bottom to your heels, arms outstretched. Nice." Lewis follows her instructions. "Perfect," she says. Noelani touches his hips and gently pushes down a bit. "As your hips relax, you sink into the pose. I am just applying a little pressure. Great."

"So far, so good." Lewis' voice is muffled by the mat.

"Now we go into a plank pose. It is like a push-up, but your hips need to be parallel to your shoulders. Good. From here, we do what we call a *chaturanga*—again, like a push-up, but keep your arms tight to your ribs and only go halfway down to protect your shoulders. Now, from here we go into a modified cobra pose. Sort of a backbend, like this." She demonstrates, and he follows. "Perfect. Very strong."

They stand. "Now, this is mountain pose. Arms straight up, but shoulders released and down." She takes her hands and presses down on his tight shoulders. She senses he is nervous, perhaps for the reasons she is. "Then we bend, like a swan dive with your back straight, into a forward fold. Here, you relax your head; this helps your hamstrings stretch out." She runs her hand down his spine. He reacts and softens downward. "Mmm, great. Just two more things." She again demonstrates. "This is called downward dog—"

"Ah, I've heard about that." He looks carefully at her body's position: body in an upside-down V. Her hips up, head down. Noelani knows her body grabs his attention. "I'll give it a try. Your heels are down all the way. That seems impossible for me."

"That is not important. But get your hips up." She straddles his legs, spreading hers apart, and pulls his hips up toward her. "There. That is a good pose. Very strong."

"I hope so. Does every teacher reach around and help like you do?" he asks facetiously.

"No. You are getting special treatment."

"I certainly am."

"Okay. Last one. This is called warrior two." Again, she models, and he follows along. Noelani gets down on her knees and pulls his front leg more toward a right angle. Then she rises, purposefully close to him now, such that her breasts almost brush against his chest. They are face to face. She takes his arms and makes sure they are stretched out in opposite directions. "Keep them firm. Don't look at me—look forward."

"I am looking forward," he says with a laugh.

Noelani stays tight to him. "Okay. You're funny. But let me just turn your head to the mirror." She reaches for his temples; her fingers slide into his hair. Her palms brush against his well-trimmed beard. A slight twist causes him to lose his balance and tip forward into her. Whether it was her body pressed against his or his balance catching him, she does not know, but Noelani allows herself to hold him, her head resting next to his chest, as he is several inches taller. He repositions himself with her help. And then, without warning, she rotates his face directly toward hers and kisses him. Lightly. Softly.

Lewis brings his arms down and shortens his stance quickly for balance, putting his hands on her hips. She moves her hips upward so that she is on her tiptoes. She feels his lips pressing on hers with equal pressure. His hands move up her back, and he lifts her slightly off the oak floor. Her hands drop from his face, and she wraps her arms around his neck. The kiss consumes them.

Again, her inner voice keeps invading, warning. She ignores it as long as she can. She wants to toss herself into the romantic abyss and wrap herself around Lewis. But caution cannot be thrown to the wind. She begins to pull away. She notices his release is as gentle as her retreat. *Oh, how that matters.* She stands inches away from his face. *Oh, what have I started?*

"What pose was that, Noelani?" he whispers. His breath is sweet. His arms feel much more relaxed. His shoulders soften.

Noelani does not look up. She stares at his chest. "Um, that is a pose I have not been in for a long, long time, Lewis."

Lewis lets that comment settle for a few seconds. "It's all new to me. But I can see why yoga is catching on." Lewis' humor helps her regain her composure and slow her heart rate. *He is controlled. He knows what I want. But this is happening way too fast.*

"Lewis, we need to talk. I have to tell you something important. And I want you to know now, before things go— or get too complicated. Okay?" Noelani sits cross-legged on the floor. Lewis makes an attempt to do the same, but then decides to sit facing her, leaning against the mirrored wall for support.

"My life is pretty complicated, too, Noelani. So I agree we need to talk—and maybe not say everything, but at least know something more about why we both needed Dr. Adler's help." A look crosses his face that conveys sincerity.

Noelani has never seen this look on a man before.

He wants to tell me the truth. And he wants the truth from me.

Chapter Forty: 1998

7:00 p.m. Karuna Yoga.

They sit on the floor and look at each other for a few moments before Noelani starts the conversation. "Lewis, you're right. There are so many things about me that are," she sighs, "very private. And because of your kindness and honesty, I told you more about myself than I ever reveal to anyone except Lisa and her husband, Phillip. I want you to know that I'm very attracted to you. I like being with you. But I don't know you well enough, and you sure don't know me—yet—so I really need us both to slow things down. Maybe it was the margaritas or the sunset or whatever, but I kinda lost my head there. I'm not saying I didn't enjoy it, but right now, I don't trust myself."

Lewis picks up the thread. "Look, I'm a father of a teenage girl. I spend a lot of time at work. I'm losing my sight. And I won't lie, Noelani; you're probably hanging out with a guy who most likely will keep losing his eyesight. Man, that is a lot to deal with." He pauses. "But you are so lovely. I don't think you realize how much you've learned about living and coping with all you've faced. I think you are a strong person, but we should be patient."

Lewis remembers something else. "And, *obviously*, I'm very attracted to you—and not just because I am lonely—and I am, trust me. But I just want you to know that I am not some divorced guy trying to hit on you." Lewis looks right at her, and Noelani knows that this means he is not willing or able to look into her eyes. "I've denied myself the touch of a woman for so long that…that it's hard—very hard—to not hold you. But I want you to know that I will *not* move first. I worry about why we are in therapy. If you have the issues I deal with, then I gotta let you dictate the direction we go in."

Noelani leans closer to him. "Lewis, that is exactly what I need to know. You have *no idea* how much I don't trust people." Now she pauses. "Okay, men." She gains strength. "I have been used and hurt badly."

Lewis decides to start to give Noelani part of his back story, "How about if I tell you why I first saw Dr. A?" Lewis tilts his head to see her.

"Okay."

"All right. I'll keep it short. My ex-wife Lotte and I had a totally bizarre marriage. She is super ambitious, and, as I learned, she never wanted children because that would mess up her plan for us to be, I guess, wealthy and have the lifestyle that money provides. That's not priority one for me. It never has been."

"What you don't know is that Hope was an accident. For me, she's the best thing that ever happened in our marriage. For Lotte, she was the worst. So when she told me her job meant she would have to live in Phoenix, I thought…we thought it would be temporary. Eventually, after two years, we began…she began to realize that we did not see the world the same way. I guess on that point, I was naive. So despite her efforts to keep up the illusion of a happy family and a devoted mother, it was all just that—an illusion."

Noelani quietly asks, "Why didn't you move to Phoenix?"

"Good question. We fell in love *here*. We had a home *here*. The 'plan' was for her to come back. Besides, Phoenix holds no attraction for me—it's in the freakin' desert. Here, I'm a mile from the Pacific Ocean. She misled me to believe that she wanted to come back and be a mother to Hope. That was not the reality. I learned that she had another life—other men, other jobs—and she kept all that from me. We were just playing parts. Besides, I love my job, love the kids. Teaching isn't a job to me; it's a lifestyle. Her world is corporate America, making lots of money and just not at all what I am about." Lewis lets out a breath of regret. "Sorry for the long answer. I tried to keep it short."

"No, I'm glad you said it all. So why'd you see Dr. Adler?"

"Panic attacks. Sleeplessness. Totally worried about being alone. Raising Hope alone. My parents are in the Bay Area, and they are well along in age. I just felt like I was on my own island. But the kicker was—and I kept this from Dr. A for a while—was the diagnosis of my eyesight. That sent me over the edge."

"When did you—when did this—all happen?"

"Well, three years ago. But the whole marriage breakdown began long before."

"Oh." Noelani absorbs this and tries to cradle it because she knows this can't be easy for him. She certainly can't lay her cards on the table like Lewis. *No way.*

Lewis admits, "But I'm not going to bash my ex-wife. Lotte has been generous, and she worries about Hope and me."

"Does she know about your eyesight?"

"Well...probably not. Maybe Hope tells her things. I ask her not to. I just don't want her pity—or anyone's. So many people have it way worse. No, I'm good."

At times like this, Noelani feels that Lewis is putting up a good front. *We both do that.* She rises and asks Lewis if he wants to sit in the foyer. "I'm sure it's more comfortable there. I can make us coffee. It's nothing fancy, but would you like a cup?"

Lewis agrees to both. This buys time for Noelani to decide what, if anything, she wants to tell Lewis. Small talk fills the void. Coffee brews. They sip. She thinks about his ex-wife. She understands how ambitions and business can suck a person in and away from the people they love. Maybe that is what started John on the road to infidelity. Then she reminds herself, *but that can't excuse all the years of lying, all the humiliation…and then his brutality.*

Noelani tries to not twist her hair. She keeps her hands on her coffee cup. "Lewis, we have more in common than you realize. I saw a psychiatrist back in my teens, when we moved here. Long story, but I was depressed and angry. Thankfully, my mom and my family in LA got me help. I had a great doctor. The funny thing is that my doctor, Dr. Chan, started her career as an intern for Dr. Adler. So anyway, I saw her off and on in LA, and when I moved here, she recommended him. I remember when I first saw him, I thought to myself, 'This old guy? Seriously?'" They both chuckle. "I miss him. Do you?"

Lewis concedes, "Very much. But I also want to not be dependent on him or any psychiatrist. I think I am doing much better. I'll probably see the other doctor—um, Dr. Locke—at least once. You?"

"I suppose so. There are some things I still need to work out. I guess change makes me anxious." They both nod their heads, almost as if they are moving to the same beat of music.

Noelani takes a small leap of faith. "I divorced my husband—John. He cheated and was—" She stops. "He *is* a liar. And all that other bad—" She stops again. "Anyway, that's when I moved here. I had to get far away from LA and that whole world." She looks to see how this has registered on Lewis' face. He is nodding, as if he at least understands that it was not an amiable, "let's just call it quits" divorce. *Does he suspect?*

Noelani takes a breath. "So, Lisa helped me a lot. I owe her my sanity." Noelani puts her cup down, implying, *That's all for now.* "Gosh, Lewis, look at the time. Hope is going to wonder where you are. I should get you home."

Lewis nods. "Yeah, I suppose so. I don't want the girl's parents to think I am taking advantage of them."

Things are put away. Noelani wraps herself in a shawl. Lewis grabs his cane. They walk slowly to her car. Noelani leads him by the crook of his arm. Then she stops and softly says, "I want to kiss you goodnight now. I want you to know how special you are. And then let's let a little time pass before we see each other again. Is that all right?" She feels awkward leading this dance with him, as if the night has made it harder for *her* to see her way.

Lewis embraces her softly and kisses her. Again, the kiss is more passionate than they had planned. It takes Noelani's willpower to pull them apart.

They ride in silence, except for Lewis' directions.

After they say goodbye, she drives home, then sits in the driver's seat, lost in her thoughts. She closes her eyes and remembers how he lifted her up and how intensely they embraced. It is an image she cannot—and does not want to—shake.

Chapter Forty-One: 1998

4:00 p.m. Solana Beach Train Station.

Dee and Henry wave goodbye as they step onto the north-bound train to Los Angeles. They have spent the last two days helping Kalani move into her new condo, just a couple of miles away from Noelani's. Mother and daughter hold each other and wave, watching the train pull away from the station.

At last, they are alone. Walking back to her car with her mother, noticing her mother's slower pace, Noelani wonders aloud, "When was the last time we were by ourselves, Mom? It must have been when we moved into the LA house from Uncle's house, huh?"

Kalani nods. Her shoulders sag.

Noelani realizes that without Dee and Henry here, her mother is going to be both lonely and dependent on her. She knows Lisa will help, and meeting and greeting people at the yoga studio will hopefully give her mom a purpose and some-place to be, at least in the short term. However, this is not going to be easy…on either of them.

Time and distance have taken a toll. Their relationship has never been as equals; they are neither friends nor con-fidants in the way that Lisa's parents are to her. Kalani still wants to parent and tell Noelani what to do and how to do it. Noelani understands that her mother knows no other way.

She has always been the boss. Now, Noelani realizes, when her mother steps into *her studio,* she is the boss, and her mother is a guest. Fortunately, Dee helped pave the way regarding selling Kalani's Hawaiian designs at Noelani's studio, explaining to Kalani, "Now, your daughter and Lisa will run the show, honey. You'll get your share of sales, but you don't need the money, what with the income still coming in from your old store and all your investments. Wish Henry and I were as well off!" Noelani sees that her mother seems resigned to being a bit player in the business, at least for now.

They drive in silence. Kalani looks at the people walking the streets or heading to the local beaches. It is in her nature to carefully observe what they wear, which colors they choose, and how their clothes fit. She finally breaks the silence as they pull into her condo's parking space: "They wear clothes here like it makes no difference what matches. And they don't dress up at all, not like LA."

"Well, it's a beach town, Mom. Maui was the same, as I remember. We walked around in bathing suits a lot of the time, you know." Noelani wonders if her tone is too argumentative.

They walk to Kalani's front door and enter. There are still boxes to unpack and some household items to purchase, but for a few minutes, they sit and rest. Noelani makes her mother's favorite tea. Her mother's feet are swollen, so Noelani gets a footrest and insists that Kalani elevate her feet for a while.

"Mmm, tea's nice, Noelani. Oh, and a cookie, too." Kalani closes her eyes and just seems to soak in the entirety of what has transpired in the last few weeks.

Noelani watches her every move, trying to discover just how her fifty-eight-year-old mother has changed in the three years since Noelani left Los Angeles. She knows her mother did not have to make this dramatic change, selling most of her business and the duplex she lived in for so long, all to move closer to her only child. Noelani wants to believe that this is her mother's way of showing her love for her—or maybe she just desires to not be so alone. Kalani had her business and her employees, but they were teenaged girls. Noelani knows that her uncle is also busy with his family and caring for his wife, whose health is diminishing. In a way, she admires her mother's courage to start all over. And Noelani has come to appreciate what her mother did for her and how hard it must have been. Kalani has aged due to standing on her feet for long periods of time. Her English has improved over time; so has her business sense. Somewhere along the line, Kalani became "one smart cookie," as she likes to say of herself. Noelani looks up at her mother and says as much.

"You know, Mom, in a way, our lives have been the same: we've started over after someone left us and hurt us."

Kalani puts her teacup down on a coaster and sighs. She looks at Noelani and murmurs, "Your father did not leave me."

Noelani is peering into a small box, "What did you say, Mom? I couldn't hear you."

Again, Kalani sighs. This time, her voice is stronger. She is determined to tell her daughter a truth hidden so deeply in her heart that to reveal it requires greater strength than she could have anticipated. "Noelani, I want to tell you about your father."

"What? What are you saying?" Noelani leans forward, as if pulled out of a crowd by a stranger's hand.

"What you know about him, Noelani—it's not true."

She continues, "Your father was a soldier. That's true. I told you he left me, but that's not the truth. He went to Vietnam to fight. He died in the war. His name was George, but that's not his real name. It was different."

Noelani's shock cannot be disguised. "What? What do you mean 'not his real name?'?"

"My George, your father, was a Dakota Sioux Indian. He came from Wisconsin, far from here. Noelani, there he was called 'Tall Tree,' since he was a tall man. *Very* tall. Give me that box there. I will show you his pictures."

Noelani's trance breaks with her mother's request for the box. She shakes her head as if dazed by a boxer's punch, then wordlessly jumps from her chair, grabs the box, and places it on her mother's lap. "Mom—Mom—I don't know what to say. I'm trying to wrap my mind around this. Are you telling me my father was Native American?" Noelani feels like she is looking in a mirror, but someone else is staring back at her; there is an image that shadows her own but is not her own.

Kalani nods. Her eyes do not fall on her daughter. She is looking for something in the box. She pulls out a black moleskin notebook. It is tattered, with a red ribbon holding it together. Noelani has never seen this notebook. Kalani unwraps it and delicately removes two letters and two photos. The first photo is of a soldier: tall, handsome, and alone. His gun is over his right shoulder. He wears green fatigues. He has a brownish helmet that casts a shadow over his forehead. He stands in a field amidst wild, green grass. The hills in the distance seem unreal somehow. He is not smiling, but he does not look menacing either. Noelani stares at the picture, trying to see in his face what she sees in her own. The photo is faded, and the colors have a yellowish tint; nevertheless, his skin is clearly light brown. She flips it over. The words "Nam '63 on duty" are written in pencil.

She then devours the second picture. It is this one that breaks her.

Her mother, all of seventeen, holds hands with this soldier, George, still in uniform but without a helmet. What hair he has is black. His smile is both proud and warm. Her mother's face could easily be identified as hers when she was the same age. They stand next to a dock; behind them, out of focus, is a ship. "That picture is the day he left me, Noelani. He was stationed on Maui for three weeks. We met at a soldier's luau. I was a hula dancer there." She finally looks up at her daughter. "Just like you."

Noelani is hypnotized by the images and the narrative. Her hand covers her mouth. Again, she turns the picture over. The words, "I Love You, Kalani. George—Too Tall" are scrawled in black ink.

"These are his two letters to me, Noelani. This is all I have left of him."

"Your uncle helped me find out that George was KIA—killed in action. He died six month after we took this picture. I haven't looked at these…in so many years."

Noelani's muted voice finally emerges. "Oh, Mom. Why did you keep this from me? Why?"

Kalani waits. "Because it hurt so much. Because I loved him so much, Noelani. I thought, 'He can't be dead. He's so young, so strong…'" Kalani grips the armrest of the chair she has sunk into. "…our family said I was foolish for having his baby. For long time, I said nothing to you. And then when you got older, I wanted to, but we didn't get along. I got so angry with you, or you got so angry with me and—" Kalani takes a deep breath and seems to suck into her lungs all the unhappiness and guilt she has carried for forty years. Then she releases it, "I'm so guilty for not telling you. Then I got so busy, busy, busy with work—and now," Kalani looks at Noelani, "now, I'm not busy and there is no excuse. Besides, Noelani, you are a woman and lovely—and I am so proud of you, and…we are not angry anymore. I hope."

"Oh, Mom. Oh, Mom." Noelani kneels before her mother, and they melt into an embrace.

* * *

"Lewis, I didn't know what to say to her, or what to think. I mean, I feel like I was adopted and just met my biological parents. Like, my God, I have a different ancestry, a different view, a different attitude. I mean, I thought my father was a villain—a reckless, selfish bastard who got my mom pregnant and then *poof*—took off. And then I read his letters, and the whole story changed from a horror story to a romantic tragedy right before my eyes. I'm still in shock." Noelani can't sit; she paces around the kitchen, holding the phone in one hand and a glass of white wine in the other.

Lewis says little. When he speaks, his voice is calm and reassuring. "But isn't this better? I mean, Noelani, now you know the truth, and you have some idea why your mom did some of the things she did, right?"

"Yes. It's still…so much. So different than what I assumed. It's going to take time for me to…"

Lewis jumps into the breach of confusion she is feeling. "Look, the way I see it, your mother is hoping that the relationship you two have will change and that you will become much closer. I guess she couldn't be genuine with you until she told you about your father and what he meant to her. She loves you and felt she owed it to you to explain your father's true intentions. Just let that be for a while."

Noelani looks up at the ceiling and rolls her head left to right, releasing a tight knot at the base of her neck. "I know you're right. I do. Thanks. Okay, listen, I gotta go. I'm picking her up for dinner, and then we need to talk about getting her a used car."

"Your mom drives?"

"Duh, Lewis—she lived in LA."

"Oops, sorry. Me being stupid. Okay. Anyway, glad you called. Really." Noelani hears in Lewis' voice what she feels in her heart.

"Well, Lewis, of course I called. You are…someone I can

bounce things off." She pauses. "I called because you matter to me. Okay? Really."

"Good."

"Yeah, good. Talk to you tomorrow, okay?"

"No, I'm too busy."

"What?" she almost spits out her wine, of which she has just taken the last gulp.

"Noelani, I'm kidding."

"Don't mess with me, Lewis Bennett. I'm too damn confused right now. Bye." She hangs up and smiles. *Damn it. I go from lonely to loony.*

Chapter Forty-Two: 1998

6:00 p.m. Somewhere near Lewis' home in Encinitas.

"Lewis, I am totally lost!" After driving around his neighborhood for twenty minutes, Noelani gives up.

"Okay, relax. What street are you on?"

"I think…Requesa Street?" Noelani hates being late and being lost. She dropped Lewis off weeks ago, after their passionate heart-to-heart yoga session, but it was dark then—and besides, she was distracted.

"Okay, are you past the freeway? If so, turn back. I am the next left. I will be on the street looking for you—sort of." She hears Lewis' chuckle.

"Oh, okay. I am on my way." Noelani bears down, makes a left, and then sees him on the sidewalk. She bursts from her car, which is very unlike her, and leaves her purse on the front seat. "I'm so sorry I'm late, Lewis. My mom kept talking to me, and I was trying to get going and—" Noelani's nervousness has rattled her. She has never seriously dated any man with children. And even though she has taught Hope yoga for two weeks and remembers what she looks like, Noelani feels awkward about meeting her. That is not all that is on her mind. Twenty minutes ago, she and her mother finished talking about "Mister Lewis."

* * *

"Mom, I have go soon or I'm going to be late." Noelani is looking in the mirror in her mother's bathroom. Her eyes are fine. Her hair is boring—the same way she wore it last time they met. Her jade green sundress is loose fitting, and she knows her mother is going to make a comment about her black bra straps showing. No lipstick is applied yet. Kalani turns the corner.

"Noelani, come out here, please. I want to talk before you go." Kalani sits in the kitchen, and her voice is a tactical demand rather than a pleasant request. Once she sees Noelani, she assesses her and announces, "Noelani, you look...um...so nice. Well, your dress is too loose on top, Noelani. And I can see your bra straps."

"I know, Mom. You probably want to take it in, huh? It's fine. Look, Mom, I'm going to be late picking up Lewis, so if you want to talk, can you at least braid my hair?"

"Oh, okay. How you want it? French braid the best, yes?"

"Great, thanks." Noelani sits. Kalani fiddles with her bra straps to try to hide them as much as possible. She sighs at the futility of making her daughter look less risqué.

"Noelani, I'd like to ask about this *Mister* Lewis. You like him?" Kalani carefully starts the braid.

"Um...yes, I do. He is very nice. But we need to get to know each other better."

Kalani focuses on more than just the beginning of the French braid. "Ah. Noelani, he's not married, but has one *keiki*?" The braid's weave begins.

"Yes, but she is eleven, Mom—and very sweet. At least in my class she was." Noelani feels the tugging on her hair and wonders where this line of questioning is leading.

"Ah, not a small girl, then. Hmm. So you know her a little, yes." Kalani separates Noelani's silky hair and crosses one rope-like strand over the other.

A beat.

"Noelani, are you *serious* about this Mister Lewis?" The weave grows tighter.

"Well, like I said, we have a lot in common, but we are taking things very slowly, Mom." Noelani remembers how her mother can extract information delicately.

"Why do you like him? Is he nice looking—not too old?" The braid grows tighter still.

Noelani takes a breath and looks at her watch. "He's very handsome, and he is three years older than me, Mom. Are you almost finished?"

"Yes. Hum. I'd like to meet this Mister Lewis if it's okay with you." Kalani finishes the French braid and ties it off with a black elastic. "I can cook something—a nice, Hawaiian, *special* dinner." Kalani takes her hands and smoothes Noelani's hair back.

"Um, okay. I'll ask Lewis what he thinks." Noelani stands and kisses her mother. "Thanks, Mom. I'll see you tomorrow, and we'll go to the studio, okay? I'm going to be late."

"Oh, Noelani, invite his daughter. I like her name—Hope." Kalani smiles. Her mission is accomplished—for now.

* * *

"I hope you like Italian food, Noelani. I love this place." Lewis places his napkin on his lap and looks at the wine list. "I've never asked you what wine you like, either."

Noelani smiles. She loves his etiquette. She has also determined that "Mister Lewis," as her mother calls him, knows how to dress. Gone are the shorts and sandals; they have been replaced with a brown and gray tweed sport coat, dark blue jeans, and a cream-colored button-down shirt. To her surprise, Lewis slips on tortoise reading glasses. "I like all wine," she answers, "but with Italian, probably red."

She takes in the ambiance of Vigilucci's, a corner trattoria. With windows facing downtown Encinitas' main street, Vigilucci's sits a stone's throw from the landmark Encinitas sign that forms an overhead archway just as one approaches the heart of this beach town. She appreciates the traditional white linen tablecloths, waiters in classic black tie, and the owner, Roberto, greeting each patron at the door with his debonair Italian accent. The cherry-stained wooden chairs are comfortable, and the tables are close together in the European fashion, providing an intimate setting in which the diners feel they are part of a village, dining in a quaint, charming setting. Andrea Bocelli's *Viaggio Italiano* plays softly in the background. Nothing seems rushed. People are gregarious, but a single voice does not disturb the dining room; there is just a soft murmur of dialogue with splashes of laughter. Noelani looks back at Lewis. "This place is very romantic. I see why you love it."

"I'm glad. Should we order a bottle of wine? Or would you prefer just a glass?

"A glass will be fine." Again, she is aware of how considerate he is. *He knows I'm driving and that we are likely to meet Hope, so I need to be clear-headed.*

"Perfect. Hmm." Lewis glances at the wine list, then looks up at Noelani. "And if you think I haven't noticed, I have— you look very beautiful, Noelani." Lewis' eyes are directed at her, and Noelani knows that even if he cannot see her clearly in this manner, he wants her to know he is focused on her.

"Thank you. You look quite stylish yourself." Noelani touches his hand. "Yes, please order the wine, if you don't mind. I like merlot, but I don't know any of these wineries." She glances up to the ceiling. "Do you know this music?"

"Funny you should ask. Andrea Bocelli is a very popular opera star in Italy, and now he is crossing over the Atlantic and gaining popularity here."

"Oh, I think I have heard of him. Wait—I know about

him." Noelani's eyes widen. "Isn't he blind?"

"That's the guy." Lewis' head pops up from the wine list.

Noelani reaches across the table and touches Lewis' forearm. "He is also handsome, not unlike my dinner date." She sees Lewis smile and knows he has flashed a look over to her. He then orders the wine and places his hand on hers.

"Flattery will get you somewhere. We blind guys make up for what we can't see with our other senses." Lewis removes his glasses.

"Well, that is what I've heard. What do your senses tell you?" she counters coquettishly.

"Hmm. The food smells rich and delicious; you are not wearing perfume because you know you have no need for it; your voice is poised and delightful; and your hand is very warm." He turns her hand over to feel her palm. He runs a finger down from her wrist to the tip of her ring finger. "A slightly moist palm and no ring, hmm. Maybe you are a little nervous, perhaps?"

"Hmm. You are going to be a challenge for me, Lewis. I am usually 'mysterious' to some people. But I must say, you are pretty close to spot on...though I am not nervous about you. I'm more concerned about meeting Hope."

"Trust me, that should be the least of your worries. She can't wait to meet the famous yoga teacher, Ms. Kekoa. My concern is she'll talk your ear off." They both lean back and grin. Noelani feels a release of tension in her shoulders.

They discuss the appetizing choices for dinner. Noelani suggests they share a salad, and Lewis recommends some entrees that are on the lighter side. Roberto, the owner, comes to their table, offers a red rose to Noelani, and warmly chit-chats with the couple.

During dinner, current events and the daily routines of their lives are part of the light discourse. Finally, Noelani leans forward and makes the request. "Lewis, my mother would like to have you and Hope over to my house for a home-cooked Hawaiian dinner. You don't have to say yes—I understand your situation with Hope—still trying to deal with everything that has happened with her mother—and the fact that I'm teaching at her school—you know—all the awkwardness of meeting someone who is dating their father—"

"Let me stop you there. Of course, we would love to come over. You can tell her yourself."

"Oh, good. My mom will be very excited to meet you both. We actually discussed you today." Noelani wants to twirl her hair but realizes it's braided.

"Oh, really? My ears were burning, I think? By the way, I noticed your hair is in a French braid. It looks lovely on you."

"Ah, well, this is my mother's work. She used to braid my hair when I was a little girl. Do you do the same with Hope?"

"I'm afraid I'm not in your mother's league. Frankly, lately I've been banned from helping her with a great many things—except homework. Besides, she knows I would completely mess up her hair."

Noelani finishes her dinner. The plate disappears, and her water is refilled with a typical Italian flourish; the waiter pours from a silver pitcher hovering a foot over their glasses, not spilling a single droplet. "Well, your ears would not be burning—it was all good. My mother has a way of getting the information that she wants. You've piqued her curiosity. She asked the typical questions. I've been pretty tight-lipped about you until now. Does Hope ask about me?"

Lewis takes the last bite of his lobster ravioli, dabs his lips with his white napkin, and replies, "You know girls. She thinks I can't see how lovely you look, so she dutifully tells me every detail—how you do your hair, your different yoga outfits, and the calm, soft way you speak to the class. I must say, she did mention that you were so nice to all the girls at her school, particularly the ones who were self-conscious about their weight. That is very much how Hope sees the world. She roots for the people who are not the most popular or the most gifted."

"Perhaps she gets that from you." Noelani waits until she knows he is angled to see her, then nods to him. She sees him smile back; the message is delivered.

"Perhaps." Lewis repeats. He then asks if dessert is a possibility, but Noelani says the meal was more than enough. "Coffee, then?" Noelani tilts her head and surprises Lewis.

"I think it's your turn to make us coffee. Let's head back early and go to your house. You have not given me the tour— and besides, I'd like to talk to Hope. I have to admit, Lewis—I am a bit worried about meeting her as your *date*." Noelani pauses. "I have never been in this situation before."

"Really?" Lewis quickly follows this potentially awkward question with an offer to pay the bill. Noelani insists on splitting the check. After saying *arrivederci* to the proprietor, Roberto, they head out. Noelani leads them into the brisk evening arm in arm. There are just a few stars shining over the ocean.

As they approach Noelani's car, Lewis pivots and quickly but softly kisses her on her glossy pink lips. A kiss that implies sincerity rather than unabashed passion. Noelani is not disappointed; rather, she is enticed by Lewis' subtlety and tenderness.

Chapter Forty-Three: 1998

8:00 p.m. Lewis' home in Encinitas.

"Lewis, I've never spent much time with a pre-teen like Hope. I'm not sure how to talk to her."

"Noelani, my daughter is a talker. Not like me. You'll find she is also very curious about you." Lewis' voice has a lightness to it, knowing that Hope will be both surprised and pleased that she will get to meet Ms. Kekoa, since she was not sure that would really happen.

This morning, Lewis and Hope set to work putting the house together, making it clean and tidy for their anticipated guest. Lewis' home is one story, and when it was built in the early seventies, Encinitas was a fairly small community. In the last five years, it has significantly expanded. Lewis wonders how Noelani will react to his décor—beach casual, wood floors, simple taste, and a minimalistic feel. Most of the furniture is a variation of white or blue. Bookcases are jammed, and now albums have joined the party, sitting alongside the record player.

As Noelani enters, Hope quickly turns off the TV and leaps up excitedly. "Oh, hi, guys—I mean, hi, Ms. Kekoa. I hope you remember me—oops, I do that a lot. I say *hope* and then realize my name *is* Hope." Hope is wearing her flannel pajamas, as the autumn weather and the coastal cool-down have arrived. She extends her hand to Noelani, who takes it and touches Hope on the shoulder with a degree of affection.

"Of course I remember you, Hope. And I have to admit, it is kind of funny how your name can have a double meaning. That's not true of mine. Please call me Noelani."

"I'll try, but it is hard with teachers—you know, because, like, you only know them as Miss or Mister Whatever. But I'll try."

Lewis interjects, "I'll put on some coffee. Noelani, please make yourself comfortable. And Hope, please don't bombard Noelani with questions, okay?" Lewis shuffles over to the kitchen, which is open to the living room, his favorite aspect of his home. From there, he can keep track of the conversation.

Hope rolls her eyes at her father. "Okay, Dad. Can I at least ask Ms. Kekoa how she got her name—Noelani?" Then she turns to Noelani.

Noelani smiles back at Hope. "Of course you can. It's not really an interesting story—"

"But it's such a pretty name!"

"Thank you. As you know, I was born in Hawaii, and my last name is very common there. Hawaiian first names usually have a meaning. Mine means *heavenly mist*. I guess that is what my mother felt about me."

"I've never been to Hawaii, but I would like to go—someday." Hope's voice projects into the kitchen, and Lewis nods knowingly.

"Well, I have never been back," Noelani continues, "since I left for the mainland when I was a teenager."

"Oh, how come you left?"

Lewis' eyebrows rise as the coffee begins to brew. *This should be interesting.*

"Well, my mother felt it best to move us to LA for her business. She is a seamstress. Do you know what that is?"

Hope's face contorts so that one eye is open and the other is closed. She takes a good guess: "She *sews* dresses?"

"Yes, but she does much more than that, Hope. She also *designs* dresses, and she has a whole line of clothing that is inspired by Hawaii. And that is not all. She has—or had—her own shop, where she sold her clothing. But there is more—"

"Wait. You said she *had* a shop. Did she lose it?" Hope leans forward.

"No. She decided to sell most of the business to another person. She still has clothing there, and she still owns a small part of the business. But like I was saying, that is not all she did. She also made or mended costumes for the theater." Noelani finds herself filled with pride for her mother's accomplishments.

"Oh, wow. You mean like plays and stuff?"

"Exactly. When I was working with her years ago, I was a runner. I would run the costumes that needed alterations or mending back and forth to some of the biggest theaters. I even met some famous actors from musicals. But that was long ago, and you probably wouldn't know them—but your dad would."

Hope looks toward the kitchen, where Lewis is getting coffee cups and saucers out.

Noelani starts, "Hmm, if I recall, I saw *Cats* and *Phantom of the Opera*—"

Hope's jaw drops. "Oh, my God! No way. Really? My dad took me to see *Phantom of the Opera* when it was in San Diego. Wasn't it cool how the chandelier almost came crashing down on the audience? My dad didn't tell me that was gonna happen. Did you, Dad?"

Lewis looks up. "Nope. Not like me to ruin a surprise. Noelani, I suppose your mother worked on costumes for many of the shows. *Cats* must have been a challenge." Lewis brings coffee, milk, and sugar over on a tray.

Noelani thanks Lewis and takes a sip. "Mmm. Very good. Well, I did get to see a lot of the plays my mother worked on. The musicals were my favorite because I loved the dancers."

"Were you a dancer, Noelani? I mean, you look like a dancer." Hope is rocking her chair back and forth now; Lewis and Noelani share the couch.

Lewis realizes his daughter may uncover some of the mystery that clouds Noelani's past.

Noelani straightens up a bit and takes another—longer—sip of coffee. "Well, I was, Hope. I danced for a long time. I studied with a wonderful teacher in Los Angeles. We all called her Dee. I was even in a play I'm sure you know: *Romeo and Juliet*. I was one of the dancers."

"You weren't Juliet?" Hope is incredulous. "You would've been a perfect Juliet."

"Ah, well, maybe if I were an actress. But I was in the cast of dancers. I played Juliet's maid."

Hope then takes Noelani by surprise. "I bet the guy who played Romeo wished you were Juliet!"

Lewis senses something awkward in the long pause. Up until now, the dialogue has been fast paced. Hope's question gives Noelani pause. Lewis interjects, "Um, honey, that's not really what Ms. Kekoa was talking about."

Hope looks at her father and quickly back at Noelani. "Oh, I'm sorry. I sometimes ask too many questions."

Noelani pipes up. "Oh, it's okay, Hope. The play was fun, but the guy who played Romeo was not...a very good actor. But I still loved dancing. Unfortunately, I had to stop because I hurt my knee. And, well, now I'm too old to dance." She laughs.

Lewis wonders what Noelani has left out of this story. He files it in his memory for another time. Then he gives Hope a look they both understand.

"Oh, that's too bad. I am really glad to meet you, Ms. Ke—

Noelani," Hope says as she stands up. "I'm going to read before I go to bed, Dad. I am sure you would like a break from me."

Noelani grabs her hand. "Hope, I'm so glad we talked. My mother would like you and your dad to come over to my house sometime," she says as she glances toward Lewis for consent. "She wants to make you to a nice Hawaiian dinner. Would you like to come?"

Hope looks at her father, who looks at her. Lewis knows exactly what Hope is thinking. *This might be serious, Dad.* "Hope, I told Noelani that I would love to come but that I would ask you if—"

"Duh, Dad. Of course I wanna come!" Hope turns to Noelani. "I think it would be great. Oh, but can I say one more thing?" Her eleven-year-old tendencies bubble up despite her best attempt to act more mature. "Noelani, I love your hair. What kind of braid is that?"

Noelani turns her head so that Hope can see the back. "It's called a French braid. I'm glad you like it. And I am very glad you will come over for genuine Hawaiian food."

"Me too. Goodnight." Hope walks down the hall, but when out of Noelani's sight, she looks back at her father and mouths, *I love her.*

Once Lewis determines that Hope is out of hearing range, he is the first to speak. "I know what you're thinking: *she's too much.* Sorry for all the questions. I guess my journalistic tendencies rub off on her." He smiles, hoping to assuage any tension.

"Lewis, I have to tell you: you have done a terrific job raising her. She is lovely—and so sweet...and curious, too. And she absolutely adores you. You should be proud. Teenage girls can be very tough to deal with—I speak from personal experience." Noelani puts her coffee down on the table. She reaches out for his hand and gently pulls it toward her so that it rests on her lap.

"Well, thanks. But I haven't raised her alone."

"Oh, don't be modest, Lewis."

"Well, I had help. But thanks, though. Um, sorry about that question about Romeo." He pauses, considering what he is about to ask. "Was he one of the men who hurt you?" Lewis looks sideways at Noelani.

She squeezes his hand. "Yes and no—but that was a long time ago. I was injured in a skiing accident. It was my first time. I was twenty-one or so. The guy, Michael, who took me skiing was a crush, I guess. Anyway, I was blindsided by a reckless teenager. He was out of control on his snowboard. I broke my leg and ruptured my ACL. It was terrible. Michael took me to the hospital. He took responsibility, although it wasn't his fault. When I got out of the hospital and started physical therapy, he told me he was going to New York to pursue acting full time. And that was that. So…." Noelani pauses and begins to formulate her next sentence.

To Lewis, it seems odd. Almost as if she is carefully measuring her words. *Why? It was ten years ago?*

"But we really had nothing in common," she says with a shrug. "He was a pretty boy with rich parents." She says casually, "I really don't know if he made much of himself. I doubt it. We stayed in touch for a year…or less, then, I never heard from him again."

"Oh. Maybe that was for the best?"

"Yes, definitely." Noelani's smile reappears. "Lewis, this was a fantastic evening for so many reasons."

Noelani begins to prepare to stand up, but Lewis' hand presses her down, and he leans forward to kiss her. Noelani reluctantly inches forward but makes it clear that she is too self-conscious at his home.

They kiss quickly and pull back. She rises.

"Don't worry about the cups," Lewis says. They walk toward the front door. "I would walk you out to your car, but then you'd have to walk me back to my door, and—you get it." Lewis means to be funny, but he realizes his voice sounds bittersweet.

"I'm a big girl, *Mister Lewis*. I think I can manage. I'll call you and see when we can schedule dinner. But I hope—ha, there's that word again, *hope*—anyway, I really want to see you before then." She looks up and touches his face.

"I know, Noelani. Believe me, I know."

* * *

From her bedroom, Hope calls out, "Dad, did Noelani leave?"

From his rocking chair, Lewis responds, "Yes, honey."

"I *really* like her, Daddy."

"I know. I know."

"Goodnight, Daddy."

"Goodnight, sweetheart."

Lewis rocks back and forth, thinking about what his life will be like when she stops calling him *Daddy*.

Chapter Forty-Four: 1998

5:00 p.m. The Sunday before Thanksgiving at Noelani's home.

Noelani and Kalani finish the place settings as everything is warming in the oven. They look at each other as the doorbell rings and quickly appraise each other's appearance. Noelani brushes her hair back to one side and adjusts the straps of her purple hibiscus dress while Kalani smoothes out her plumeria floral muumuu. They smile at each other.

"Aloha!" announce Lewis and Hope as they are welcomed by Noelani.

"Aloha to you!" Noelani ushers them in, then pivots to her mother, who appears tranquil and welcoming. "Lewis and Hope, I want you to meet my mother, Kalani Kekoa."

Lewis is surprised by Kalani's diminutive size; she is petite like her daughter but clearly five inches shorter. "Mrs. Kekoa, my daughter and I are so happy to meet you." He takes her hand; it is surprisingly strong, and he feels calluses on her fingertips.

Hope jumps in. "Yes, Mrs. Kekoa, I'm Hope. Oh, but, you already know that. Anyway, I love your dress. It's beautiful."

Kalani takes Hope's hand and says, "Ah, Hope. You are very lovely. This dress is called a muumuu. It is a traditional dress—for many older women, yes. Ah, but you are very nice to notice."

Noelani explains that she and her mother have prepared a Hawaiian dinner. "I hope you like it. I know it is not a Thanksgiving dinner, but it is what many Hawaiians make for special occasions."

Lewis hands Noelani the wine for the evening, and they head toward the kitchen. Kalani sits on the couch in the living room and beckons Hope to sit in the matching beige chair adjacent to her. Kalani's experience with teenage girls working in her shop allows her to ease into Hope's storyline.

"The school you go to—it is a good one, yes? Tell me about it and if you like it."

From that one question, Hope's world blooms before Kalani like a rose, with each petal revealing another of Hope's interests. Hope tends to speak in full paragraphs, and Kalani waits patiently to ask another question—until she realizes Hope will get to that question and many others without much prompting. When Hope stops to catch a much-needed breath, Kalani interjects, "Hope, you are very lucky that your father is able to be so much help to you. He takes you to the sports you play, and it must be very good to have a teacher like your father to help with homework. Noelani says you are very good student, and I believe so. It's very important. Very important to get good education. I tell that to Noelani—and look at her now! Has her own yoga studio and very success-ful."

As the daughter of a journalism teacher, Hope's tendencies kick in. "Mrs. Kekoa, my dad says you are a super business-woman, too. He says you design your own line of Hawaiian clothing and that you worked in the theaters with the cos-tumes. That must have been so exciting."

"Ah, yes. But hard work, too," Kalani responds. "Seam-stress and designer is the hardest work, but very, very reward-ing. Noelani was a little girl when I started in Los Angeles. She helped in my store, and when she was older, she took the costumes to the theaters. This was tricky because they wanted me to fix them at the last minute. But I did—and I made good money, too." She winks at Hope and smiles broadly.

Meanwhile, Noelani and Lewis move quietly, as they are far more interested in the conversation in the living room than anything they might be doing. Noelani pokes Lewis and whispers, "My mother loves her."

Lewis retorts, "I hope my daughter doesn't talk her to death."

They both hold their laughter inside their throats and get back to business.

* * *

As Noelani and Kalani serve dinner, Noelani explains, "Now, I know you two have never been to Hawaii before, and you've never been to a traditional luau. So my mother and I want to give you a sample of some of the kinds of food prepared. So first, my mother is placing on your plate what you may think of as an appetizer."

Kalani serves a greenish delicacy. "This called *lau lau*," she explains. "It's salt butterfish with some pork and chicken—and I wrap in a layer of taro leaves, yes. Then we steam. So open the leaf and taste." Kalani is bursting with pride. This is her specialty.

A duet of *oohs* and *ahs* hums from the Bennett side of the table, followed by pronouncements of how wonderful all the flavors taste. Noelani explains that only certain shops in San Diego have native Hawaiian ingredients.

The main course is Kalua pig and rice. Noelani narrates the history behind this island staple, then explains, "It is traditionally roasted in a pit that the men oversee at a luau. Here's the trick—they roast it for sixteen hours! So it is tender and juicy."

Hope can't help herself. "You've been cooking for sixteen hours? Did you stay up all night?"

The adults burst into laughter, and Hope's cheeks turn pink. "No, Hope—my mother and I used a pressure cooker. It isn't the same as a luau, but it's way faster—and it's still yummy." Noelani smiles at Hope, and Hope takes note to ask her dad what a pressure cooker is.

Again, this main course with pineapple slices adorning the plates is a hit. Lewis has been very quiet except for various compliments to the chefs. He, too, watches the interplay between mother and daughter—and between his daughter and the Kekoas. He is also keenly aware of Kalani's assessment of him. He is thankful that this day has brought him slightly clearer vision.

All agree to take a break before dessert. Dishes need to be cleaned, and Kalani makes her move. "Hope, can you help my daughter in the kitchen, yes? She'll show you where things go, okay?"

Hope is happy to spend time with her yoga teacher and escape her father's appraisal of her manners.

Kalani wastes no time. "Mister Lewis, Noelani says that you teach English?"

Lewis is prepared. "Yes. I teach journalism. I run the school's newspaper."

"How long have you been a teacher?"

"Oh, gosh—seventeen years or so. I love teaching."

"Ah, yes. That is very important." Kalani moves to the crux of her issue and leans forward. "Mister Lewis, my daughter is *very special*—you know that, yes. She can be hurt very easy, you know that? Please, her heart was broken by some bad men—very bad. I don't want to say too much about that. But I worry about her. Do you understand me?"

Lewis lowers his voice. "Yes, Mrs. Kekoa, I do. Noelani has told me a little bit about her…troubles. I've told her that she needs to feel safe and decide on her own what she wants out of our relationship. I want her to trust me and take her time." He pauses to make sure Noelani and Hope are not listening. "I want *her* to be in control. I have waited a long time for someone like Noelani. I can wait until she is ready."

Kalani nods. She has looked at Lewis intensely. Something about his tone has given her the impression that he is very different from the other men in Noelani's life. Nevertheless, Kalani warns Lewis, "What you say is wise, Mister Lewis, but be *very careful* with her. You understand this?"

Lewis touches Kalani's hand, as Noelani often does to him when she is making a point. "Mrs. Kekoa, I know *exactly* what you mean, and I promise you that I will be kind and think of her needs before my own."

Kalani takes this in, then slowly leans closer to Lewis' face. "She acts strong, but she's like a flower—delicate." She waits a moment. "You know, we both have daughters and bring them up alone. I know how hard it is. You're doing very, very good job with Miss Hope. She's a lovely little girl—but she's getting older fast, yes?"

"You got that right. One day she needs me, and the next, she tells me, 'Dad, leave me alone. I got this.' And she's a girl—and sometimes—for me—well, you know what I'm saying?"

"Ah, yes. With a boy, I think it's easier. Girls, whew. Trouble!" Kalani looks toward the kitchen. She whispers, "Noelani was not easy for me. It was part of why we left Maui."

Noelani's voice emanates from the kitchen. "I hope you two are not talking about me."

"No, of course not," Lewis volleys back. "We're talking about Hope." He winks at Kalani.

"Dad, what are you saying?"

"Only kidding."

At her regular voice volume, Kalani says, "Mister Lewis,

your eyes do not see so well, but Noelani says you *can* see, yes? What will happen to your eyes?"

Lewis leans back. "To be honest, Mrs. Kekoa, the doctors are not sure. Some days are better than others, and there are treatments to help." Lewis tilts his head. "I see you better when I look to the side."

Kalani tilts *her* head. "Hmm. What you going to do if you do not see later—as a teacher that will be very very hard?"

"My principal has me on a special assignment. I meet with students who are troubled with divorced parents or drugs, you understand. It is a tough time for kids.

Kalani nods.

"So I am not teaching English now. This helps because reading so many papers is hard on my eyes. But I'll take things one year at a time. My school has made accommodations for me—things that make it easier for me to work."

"Yes, I understand. That's very good that the school helps you. Noelani says you are an excellent teacher. I think you have a kind face—that must make the students trust you, yes?"

"Well, that's nice of you to say—"

Just then, Hope pops in and exclaims, "Dad! *You are not gonna believe the desserts!*"

* * *

Noelani places two desserts before them. "Okay, we were not sure you would like one of them, but we *know* everyone loves chocolate. So, this one," she points to four 2-inch squares and explains, "is my mother's favorite. It is called *kulolo*. It is a coconut topping mixed with sugar and butter, filled with mashed kalo. I know it looks like a fig because of its reddish coloring, but it's very sweet. The other is traditional haupia pie made with chocolate and coconut. We hope you like them." Both women beam confidently as their guests take a bite.

"Dad, the pie is to *die for!*" Hope proclaims. Kalani laughs at the expression.

Tea is sipped. Dessert disappears, and all are content.

Lewis looks at his watch and reminds Hope that they should not stay much longer. "Ladies, we have been honored to be the special guests of this Hawaiian luau. We have enjoyed meeting you, Mrs. Kekoa and Hope and I would like to have you both over to our house for dinner soon. But for now, we need to say goodnight; we both have school tomorrow. Hope and I are flying up to see my parents in San Francisco the day after tomorrow for Thanksgiving, but we'll be back soon."

The appropriate hugs and kisses are accepted and received. Lewis whispers in Noelani's ear, "I'll call you later." Kalani notices. Hope carries away an extra piece of haupia pie.

Once inside, Kalani makes more tea and asks Noelani to sit at the table with her.

"I like him," Kalani announces. "He likes you—*very much*. He has kind eyes. I see that. He may not see with his eyes, but he sees with his heart. I do worry, Noelani, about what will it be like if later he cannot see. That will be very hard…for you." She sips her tea.

"I know, Mom." Noelani's own teacup hovers at her lips. Then she recites, "But I once was blind,… but now I see.'" She smiles at her mother.

They both quietly sip their tea, lost in thought. "Yes. Sometimes our eyes can fool us." Kalani shakes her head in a manner that implies her own mistakes in judgment. Kalani puts her teacup down and pats her daughter's knee. "And I like Miss Hope, too. He's good father, yes."

Noelani smiles as she pours more tea for them both.

Chapter Forty-Five: 1998

11:15 a.m. Noelani's home in Encinitas.

Noelani hears the doorbell. She has just finished her class, showered, and changed. Her hair is still moist. She is glad Lewis is a bit late. She has goose bumps—not because the heater has not warmed her on this cold December day, but because her adrenaline is at a fever pitch. She is wearing her dark blue, knee-length beach cover-up—and little else.

"Be right there!" One last look in the mirror. No makeup. None. Just as if she has come from the ocean's waves. *This is who I am.*

Noelani opens the door. Lewis has roses. He is wearing board shorts, a half-buttoned, white linen shirt—and little else.

The roses are placed in a vase. He stands in the living room while she places the vase on the dining room table. Little is spoken that is remarkable. *This isn't about talking. This is about being. Being here with someone who desperately wants to be with you.*

Then she steps into him, and their dance begins.

Their clothing never makes it to the bedroom.

* * *

Noelani slides off Lewis' chest, legs still tangled with his. Her hair cascades from his neck to her back as they embrace. Half of Noelani's body is draped over Lewis', and the other half is nestled against him on her side of the bed. Her face rests between his shoulder blade and his face. Her lips kiss his neck. Her nose cuddles a spot below his jaw line so that with a darting action, she can brush her cheek next to his and retreat back into the splendor of his being. Her arm is slung across his chest. Their hands touch and their fingers mesh together. They both squeeze tightly, then remain still, fully present in the moment.

For the first time in years, Noelani has allowed herself to follow her own advice.

In yoga, the final pose is called *savasana*. She has told her students hundreds of times that it is the most difficult pose in yoga because it requires you to completely let go, to totally unwind and melt into the mat, eyes closed, shoulders relaxed, legs spread evenly. Noelani and Lewis have reached their own *savasana*.

Gradually, their breathing slows. Both are reluctant to move, their bodies so intertwined that the effort to untangle them would be futile. She lies there with Lewis Bennett, a man she has decided is worthy of her trust.

* * *

She lies next to him, and he loves the feel of her black hair, like a light blanket spread across his chest. He feels her heart beating rapidly in cadence with his. He listens intently to her breathing, which blows warm, sweet air against his neck. His lips still taste of salty skin. He is enamored with the delicate way she plays with his hair and how she strokes his beard. The sensations seem magnified to him. For the first time in his life, Lewis appreciates his sense of touch to the fullest.

He has hidden from Noelani his concern for his diminishing vision. He has not told her about the injections. His frustration is harder to hide with each passing month. He refuses to allow this passionate embrace with Noelani to end. He has cast off to the open sea with her, under stars he can only assume are blinking.

As he lies there with her, he hopes this is not a dream.

* * *

Hours later, they walk along the beach. It is chilly. Their bare feet avoid the low tide, but the water's residue still makes them shiver. They are not really dressed for this, but Noelani insists this is where they need to be—on Moonlight Beach.

They hold hands and stop at one of the now empty lifeguard stations. They notice that there is not a soul on this side of the beach, only two lonely surfers far to the south of them, where the ocean gently responds to the late afternoon winter breeze.

Noelani's hand pulls him toward a rock outcropping, and down they sit.

"What can you see, Lewis? Really—I want the truth. Can you see those surfers?"

Lewis confesses to her, "No. I can see the ocean." He glances sideways at her. "I can see what matters."

Noelani is not satisfied. "Okay, but I want to know something. Honestly, please tell me if your vision gets worse. I *want* to know. I want you to know that no matter how bad it gets—and whatever happens—I will stay with you, okay?" Noelani squeezes his hand.

He is surprised. He kisses her cheek and whispers in her ear, "I will tell you. Things haven't been pretty lately. They are doing these injections now."

"What kind of injections?"

"It's a drug—it's supposed to stop the blood vessels in my eyes from bleeding."

"You mean—injections into your *eyes?*" Noelani looks at Lewis, aghast.

"Yeah. It's strange…and horrifying." Lewis pauses to consider how descriptive he should be. "They numb my eyes, I lean my head back—and here comes a syringe. I'm completely awake—no sedatives or anything. I just hope to God my eye is actually numb." Lewis shudders, momentarily lost in a terrifying thought. "I can see the liquid going into my eye. It's not as fast as you would hope. I just try to keep breathing—try to stay focused and not panic. Afterward, it feels like my eye socket has been stretched out and sore. Sandy and gritty. I can't drive, of course, so I have to get a ride home. I lay down in the dark at home and just wait for the dilation and pain to wear off. Try to meditate and breathe. The whole process is an exercise in mind over matter." Lewis takes a breath.

"Oh, my God, Lewis. I'm so sorry," Noelani says. "That sounds terrible. When is your next appointment?" Lewis waves off her concern, but Noelani persists. "Please—I want to go with you next time. I'll drive you. I'll be in the room with you."

"Oh, no, Noelani. I wouldn't ask that of you—or anyone. Nobody should have to watch this."

"I'm not asking you, Lewis. I'm *telling* you," Noelani insists. "I'll wait in the lobby if you insist, and drive you home." A thought occurs to her. "Meditation and yoga are intertwined, you know. I can help you with this." She squeezes his hand tightly.

Lewis looks down. Takes a deep breath. "Okay," he responds. "You can go with me. I would like that."

Noelani smiles a bit.

Lewis breaks the silence. "You've noticed I'm a little unsteady lately. It makes me crazy. But I don't want to lean on you. I want what you want—to be strong and independent. I lean on my other senses—and you have become my eyes from time to time."

He decides to plunge forward. "But tell me something. Why *me?* Why pick a guy with a teenager. I guy who can't see all that well? And why make this choice *now?* There must have been other men. What is it that makes you want me?"

Noelani shivers, not from the cold as much as from anxiety. It is a feeling she has always experienced in these situations when nerves cannot be stilled. He wraps his arm around her and waits her out. "Are you too cold? We can leave."

"No. Lewis, this is exactly where I need to tell you what you need to know about me." Noelani exhales and some tension releases. A deep breath and courage follows. "I want you here, on this beach, because we are castaways." Her voice drops an octave. "Lewis, I left my husband, and I have only told two people why—Lisa and Phillip. I told them because they were the people who rescued me that night."

Lewis' ears listen for every nuance—her tone, her volume, her breath—as she forces out words.

Noelani tilts her head back and closes her eyes, allowing the nightmare to bubble to the surface. "When Phillip told me that John had been sleeping with other women throughout our entire marriage, I was shocked. We argued sometimes, and I knew he had a terrible temper. To calm him down, I would usually back down. But that day, I finally stood up to him and told him I knew the truth. He lied, of course. Said whatever my so-called friends had told me was all lies because they don't like him. 'It's bullshit' he kept repeating. I told him I didn't believe him—and that I had called one of his sex partners. Phillip had snagged one of her business cards," Noelani explains.

"That pissed him off, and his temper flared up. I told him that this woman had told me the whole story. She said she felt sorry for me because he told her that I knew about all his women, so she wanted me to know what kind of man I was married to. When I told John that, he flew into a rage. He said she was lying—like he didn't know this woman. He finally admitted it, though. Said it's just what business people do. He yelled at me. Said I didn't complain about all the money he spent on me. Said he was sick of supporting my '*Namaste* bullshit' lifestyle."

Noelani pauses to take a breath. A strong breeze whips up from the north, causing a mist of salt water to drift up from the ocean. "I told him our marriage was over. I said he could sleep with all the women in LA he wanted, but he would never, ever touch me again." Noelani looks down at her hands. "That's what made him snap. He said I was a bitch. Then he yelled something I can't shake: 'I'll do whatever the fuck I want with you!' He pushed me onto the couch. That's when I realized—he really *could* do anything he wanted to me. I reached for my purse, you know, the one I carry with me, and I scrambled up and ran toward the front door. I wheeled around and slammed him in the face with my bag. That was all I could think to do. He grabbed me by the hair and dragged me to the bedroom."

Lewis sees the pain etched across her face, "Noelani, I…."

"No, Lewis, I have to say this. I have to."

A beat.

"He threw me on the bed," Noelani continues. "He let go of my neck and slammed his fist into the wall so hard that it went through the drywall. I screamed. I was so scared. Then he started to choke me, and I tried to breathe. He put his hand over my mouth and told me to shut up. He hit me, Lewis. He slammed my head against the wall."

Noelani's head falls forward like a drawbridge. "He was so enraged—and his eyes were so terrifying—I didn't know *what* he would do." For the first time, her eyes flood. The drops begin to slip through her fingertips. Her trembling hands cradle her face.

A minute passes in silence. A wave creeps up closer to them. The tide is rising slowly. Lewis tries to wrap himself around her.

Noelani continues her soliloquy, trapped in the haunting visions she has seen far too many times in her dreams. "I was sleeping with a man whose entire life was a lie, Lewis. And when his betrayal blew up in his face—when I confronted him with truth—he attacked me like an animal. I was trapped." Noelani looks up towards the ocean. "He must have seen my face get red as I gasped for air because suddenly—he stopped."

Noelani sniffs. "And then—then he just cursed at me and told me he had never loved me. Said he only cared about the sex. Said it wasn't that good, anyway. He told me if I told anyone about this, he would say I was a lying bitch. Said next time, he would put his fist through my face—and then no man would ever want to look at me again. He pushed away from me and stormed out of the house."

Beads of perspiration drip down Noelani's forehead. "I waited to make sure he was gone. Heard his car start. Then I called Lisa. I couldn't move. She and Phillip came over and took me to their house. And it was over."

Lewis absorbs all her pain—her fears, her doubts, her anger. His body envelops her like a comforter should. But he remains silent.

Noelani turns to Lewis and admits, "He broke me, Lewis. My bones have been broken before, but not my soul—not my heart. I felt I would never trust any man again." She gazes up at Lewis, who cradles her. He loosens his hold on her the moment he feels she has more to tell him. She attempts to read his reaction to her confession. She sees sorrow in his eyes, and she can feel sympathy rising in his whole being.

"Oh, Noelani." Lewis' voice carries from deep within, out to the ocean's rising tide.

When the wave slides back and foam from the water begins

to vanish, Lewis decides to ask Noelani, "Has he ever bothered you—ever contacted you again?" Lewis tamps down the anger in his voice.

"One phone call right after it happened. Then nothing. I don't exist. Maybe I never really did. He sees women as sexual conquests. Disposable. He is long gone." She looks to the south. The beach is deserted; even the surfers have fled. "Dr. Adler managed my symptoms, but I never told him this, though I just knew that he knew. He always wanted me to be brave enough to let it out. But I wasn't ready. I was—I don't know what I was. Ashamed? Humiliated? Scared of what would happen if I told anyone about what he did—about what he might do if he *found out* I told anyone. I don't know—maybe I was in denial that I was shattered. I only told Dr. Adler that John was cheating—and what a coward he was to lie to my face and that we had had a bad fight. But I stopped there."

Noelani rolls her head, trying to release the tension and the anguish. She wipes the tears away with her sleeve. The shaking has stopped. Her breathing has slowed.

A full minute of silence passes with only the sight of a formation of pelicans floating overhead, making the silent trip south on the coastal breeze. They both look up and follow their graceful trail.

Noelani is the first to turn away and face Lewis. A whisper pours serenely from her lips and descends warmly into his ear. "Until I met you, Lewis. You're concerned with what is inside of me. You somehow see without seeing. You love without controlling. You are devoted to Hope, and you value me. That's all I've ever wanted in life. So I choose you. I may lead you by the hand, but your vision helps me stay true to myself."

Both of them are quiet for a time. The tide grows higher and higher, until it is about to reach their toes. Lewis finally speaks. "You give me too much credit, Noelani. Maybe independence is overrated. I think mutual dependence is our ticket. What do you think?"

She rises from the rock and pulls him up. "I think we have plenty of time to figure that out. But for now, hold me and take me with you."

* * *

When they reach Noelani's house and finally warm up, they find themselves slumped on the couch in the living room. They warm their hands with steaming mugs of coffee.

"You know I love you, Noelani?" Lewis tilts his head to again make sure the message is received.

"I do. And you know I love you." Noelani leans into him. They place their coffee mugs on the table.

"I want to tell you something about why things went off the rails with Lotte." Lewis slowly drawls.

Noelani remains silent and intently focused on this next portion of his life's journey.

"Anyway, for two years, she was a 'drop-in' mother—mostly weekends. Then that faded. Being with us was an obligation. She never told me that she had met a man whom she had fallen in love with and that she had become a successful executive in his company along the way. The most deceitful part was that she didn't reveal to this other guy that she was married with a child!"

Noelani straightens up, "Oh, Lewis. How long did this go on?"

"I'm not sure...several years." He wags his head from side to side. "I know, I was stupid—or just so damn naive to believe that things would work out. I didn't want to know the truth. I was just living from month to month, focused on Hope and my work. So anyway, she finally told this guy who she made a life with in Phoenix that she had been lying to him—"

"Wait, wait, wait, Lewis. You are saying she kept everyone in the dark? What! Did this man accept her? Did he understand and…stay with her?" Noelani's voices rises with each question.

"Yes—to every part of what you are thinking." Lewis has to think about what he is about to say. He's angry, but he also knows that Lotte isn't a villain. "People crash into others, walk away from the accident, and hope the damage is not permanent—or, in Lotte's case, try to make amends as best she can. I want you to know that I'm not scarred for life—and that you aren't either. There is too much life ahead for us." He is fully aware of the parallel betrayals they have faced down.

Lewis reaches his conclusion. "This may sound odd—and I don't want to make it sound like I am a hero or anything remotely like that—but Lotte is not a bad person, Noelani. She was too young. I was too young. She finally told me the truth three years ago. And thank God she finally told Hope. After all this time, I think Hope has a better understanding of her mother. Hope is not bitter. I know it hasn't been easy for her, but she is resilient. Maybe she's the hero of my story, huh?"

Noelani looks up at him so she is sure he can see her face. "Lewis, I am so, so sorry. I agree with you. Hope *is* amazing—and you are *her* hero."

"Ah, but her hero falls from his pedestal. You see, in all those years, I never once had an affair. God, I didn't even date anyone. Nothing. I was…lonely and miserable. But for the longest time, I thought Lotte was still loyal to our marriage. Then about a year ago, I got caught up with a woman I knew—a friend—who had been through a rough divorce… and one thing led to another. I felt guilty. I guess because she saw me as the kind of man she wished her husband could be. I had a brief affair with her but, Jesus, I don't know what I was even thinking. I wasn't thinking, I was just, just needing affection. And she was hurting. But I was living my own lie.

She saw that in my eyes, in my whole attitude. She tried to be the bigger person and not make me feel like an jerk—which is how I felt. So we ended the relationship before I did even more damage."

"Lewis, it was *years* that you were basically alone—"

"Yeah, and here's the really crazy thing. When Lotte confessed to her affair, she told me that the whole time, she had assumed that I had been seeing other women. When I told her that I hadn't—until recently—she said she thought I was a fool!" Lewis shakes his head in disbelief.

Noelani stiffens. "Lewis, you had a moment of weakness—of being human, of caring for someone as hurt and abandoned as you were. Your ex-wife had years of indulging in her dream and never being straight with you and Hope. You know that!" Noelani's voice is strident.

They go back to the kitchen and refill their coffee mugs. When they sit on the couch, Noelani sits cross-legged facing Lewis and then she looks down and softly asks, "Whatever happened to the woman you were with?"

"Hmm. She transferred to another school after the year ended. I heard that she is seeing another man who lost his wife. One of her girlfriends set them up. I really hope she is happy…that it works out. I guess that makes me feel a little better about it."

Noelani nods. She averts his gaze. Her evening with Michael could have been a complete disaster if she had given in to Michael's invitation. *Should I tell him about seeing Michael?* She feels heat rising up—anxiety knows a close call.

She realizes the irony of Lewis' next statement: "In my head, I have to let it go."

Noelani slowly re-crosses her legs. She takes a breath, trying to slow her heart rate. She slides under his arm. "I have to let some things go, too. I'm not totally there yet, but I'm trying, Lewis. Really, I am." She reminds herself of what she tells her yoga students: *Turn down the volume that fearful thoughts breed. Breathe into the sensation that you have overcome fear so many times before.*

Lewis pivots to her, "Can I tell you a story I read a long time ago?"

"Does it have a happy ending?"

"I think so. It depends on which voice you hear."

He turns from her and recalls a story that he read once:

"It is a Zen Buddhist parable. I appreciate it now much more than when I first read it. There were two Zen monks hiking to their monastery. Passing by a popular village, they came across a lovely young woman wearing a dazzling white kimono. She was standing near a muddy stream, which would surely ruin her dress. One of the two monks offered to carry her across the stream. She was embarrassed, but he insisted. He gently put her down on the other side of the stream. The two monks walked back in silence, but when they finally reached the monastery, the second monk broke the silence and yelled, 'Why did you do that? You know we monks cannot touch a woman! You broke the rules!' The other monk laughed at him and merely replied, 'I put the girl down an hour ago. Are *you* still carrying her?'"

Lewis squeezes Noelani. "Our past was years ago. We have to live in the present. We can't let the past dictate our future."

Noelani nods. "I think I can try that now—with you. This reminds me of something I say before my yoga classes. Can I tell you?"

"Does it have a happy ending?" Lewis grins.

"As long as someone is willing to make one small change." She takes a napkin and reaches over for a pen on the table. She writes:

No Where

Now Here

Be Present

Chapter Forty-Six: 1999

10:00 a.m. July—eight months and a wedding later. Kapalua Bay, Maui.

Lewis spits out his snorkel just as Noelani appears in front of him, her face surrounded by her mask. He speaks just as she, too, lets her snorkel's mouthpiece drop from her lips. "Did you see it? Wasn't it amazing?"

Lewis pulls off his mask and stretches his arm out so Noelani can hold on and remain buoyant. "The turtle I was following just went to the surface, so I followed," he says excitedly. "And then when I surfaced—BOOM—it was staring right at me! And with my mask on, for some weird reason, I could see it better. I'm blown away!"

Noelani can only nod and squeeze his forearm. They dive back down into what the locals call "Turtle City." This particular spot off Kaanapali's shoreline is where the ocean's turtles feed.

After an hour, Lewis and Noelani reach their kayak and climb back on. The early morning shadows through which they paddled out have transitioned into Maui's sunrise. The view of Maui from perhaps a mile out is breathtaking, but the turtles are the main attraction. Lewis is stunned by what he can see, but also by what these images make him feel: whole and alive, with a soulmate who also embraces the beauty before him.

Noelani, who left the islands decades ago, has finally returned…to her roots.

They turn the kayak around and paddle back to the shore. Lewis is in the rear, providing acceleration, and Noelani is in the front, steering, as will often be the case as they traverse life's currents.

This vacation is their one wedding gift to each other. For Lewis, Maui is an exotic world, one that Noelani wants him to see as often as possible while he still can. She wants him to feel the warmth and clarity of the bluest of oceans; feel the trade winds that bend the banyan trees in the afternoon; smell the sweet fragrance of sugar cane fields; fly with reckless abandon across the valley on zip lines. She knows they will return as often as they can to be on "Maui time," when the pace of life slows and allows them to be on an island removed from the world's woes for a time, however brief.

* * *

Their hotel room is only a stone's throw from Kapalua Bay. At night, as they hold each other, they can hear the soft, gentle splashing of waves that creep up to the top of the horseshoed beach line. Maui's ceaseless tide brings each day's adventures to its dénouement. As on Moonlight Beach in Encinitas, the sun sets with a reddish glow. And on some nights, the green flash appears, too.

Mornings bring Kona coffee and toast to their lanai, which overlooks the bay. The tiniest of birds eagerly await the crumbs that Noelani places on the railing. Lewis and Noelani's plans for the day are confirmed. Their plans for their life together are a work in progress.

Lewis kisses Noelani. "Good morning, you."

"Good morning, you, too."

"I love Kona coffee."

"Me, too."

"So about now, my dad is sitting in his car, white knuckled, while he teaches Hope how to drive." Lewis chuckles at the thought. "Of course, he'll be much more patient with her than he was with me."

Lewis watches the bird to his left steal away a breadcrumb.

Noelani makes her decision, one that she and Lewis have discussed at length. "I know we have talked about whether we want to have our own child—" She starts twirling her hair rapidly. "I'm thirty-six." The twirling persists. "I think being Hope's stepmom may be more than enough."

He pauses. "Are you sure? Just because I'm good with just having Hope and you in my life, that doesn't mean I wouldn't want us to have another child."

"I know, Lewis. We will always have Hope...and each other. I'm *not* sure. I am only certain that now, right now, I don't feel the need to have a child. I suppose that may change, but if it does, and I feel differently, I know you will be happy, right?"

Lewis turns his head in such a manner that he is sure Noelani knows his eyes are meeting hers. "Absolutely. If we feel differently, we will know it. Of that I am sure."

"Me, too." Noelani's fingers loosen, and her hair tumbles down comfortably, resting on her richly tanned shoulders.

A breeze gusts up from the west, causing ripples of white water on the deepest parts of the bay.

Noelani puts her cup down. She pulls Lewis' hand, indicating that she wants him to stand next to her. She has learned how to communicate her thoughts and feelings to him through touch. "I almost lost myself many times after leaving Hawaii. I lost my father. I lost my home. I lost my chance to dance. I lost my faith in men. I found *some* peace in yoga and meditation, but I was alone and lonely."

"So was I."

Noelani smiles. "But all that changed when you said 'Meet Me at Moonlight Beach.'"

* * *

A week later, they stride past the lone palm tree that towers as a sentry welcoming the beachcombers of Encinitas. Lewis and Noelani, hand in hand, decide to wade into the surf on their Moonlight Beach. Their feet sink into the soft, wet sand. The ocean's waves break against their knees, then their torsos, and eventually they submerge.

Acknowledgements

All writers have a band behind them. The band adds the sweet melody, the pounding drums, the soaring strings and the sensual styling that makes a novel sing. Since the publication of my first novel *Meetings at the Metaphor Café*, I have been blessed with that great band behind me, and I would never have been able to write any of my novels without their guidance. My editor Christa Tiernan is the person who makes sure I stay on beat. Mark McWilliams, my longtime collaborator, sees to it that the characters and the themes are part of a memorable chorus, one that will resonate with my audience. Joyce Daubert, lent an ear to the earliest version of this newest 'album' and gave me the feminine perspective. Carol Cretella, my first yoga instructor, is a new addition to the band, and helped me to understand Hawaiian customs and the Island rhythms. Every band needs a backdrop to the stage, and Jeanie and Dave Gibbs' knowledge regarding the ski slopes at Mammoth Lakes set the perfect landscape. Of course, no band can be without its lawyer, and David Fares' opinion on legal issues was much appreciated. As always, Linda Englund's voice is right beside me encouraging me to remain undaunted despite the daunting task of leading a band. As he has done with all my work, Bob Bjorkquist's photography and cover design put my 'albums' in the best light. Peggy Singleton offered a key piece of advice early on that shaped the timing of this work right from the get go. I am inspired by my background singers (all my yoga teachers), notably Grace Na, Carmen Krause, and Xuyen Bowles. Another newcomer to the band is Michelle Lovi, who does the interior book design and makes my words flow from page to page. As always, I never take the stage without my ever so patient, loving wife Pam, who harmonizes with me and who is responsible for helping me find my voice, and lead our children, Anna and Nicholas to discover theirs.

A heartfelt thanks to the best band of friends any writer can have.

About the Author

Robert Pacilio was born to teach. He taught high school English for 32 years and was awarded San Diego County's "1998 Teacher of the Year." He is a regular presenter at educational conferences, including the California Teachers Association Conferences, and in various school districts. *Midnight Comes to the Metaphor Café* is the sequel to his debut young adult novel, *Meetings at the Metaphor Café,* which has been adopted in several school districts as part of the English curriculum. He enjoys visiting schools, where he reads portions of his novels with classes, answers questions, and turns classrooms into the "Metaphor Café" as he transforms into the fictional Mr. Buscotti.

His most recent adult fiction *The Restoration* was set on the island of Coronado in San Diego. The Coronado Historical Society, the Coronado Village Theater, and the Coronado *Eagle and Journal* have enthusiastically supported the novel.

Mr. Pacilio lives in Encinitas with his wife, Pam.

He can be reached at **robertpacilio@gmail.com**.

His website gives information on his speaking engagements. **www.robertpacilio.net**

Excerpt from: *The Restoration*

In 1947, the Village Theater on Coronado Island held a "by invitation only" Grand Opening. The islanders were excited to have the opportunity to see a movie without navigating their way across the bay to downtown San Diego. Gregory Larson's parents sat in the red plush seats of the Village Theater to see the Best Picture of the Year, *Gentleman's Agreement.* The film so moved them that their son, born months later, would be named for the film's lead actor—Gregory Peck.

World War II was over, and the Baby Boom Generation was born. In the decades to follow, Gregory Larson became enamored with UCLA co-ed Raquel Mendez. Meanwhile, on the Jersey shore, Abby DiFranco held hands with her boyfriend, Navy hero Jack Adams. All four lovers were destined to face the sexual and cultural revolution in America, headlined by the mayhem of the Vietnam War, the debilitating posttraumatic stress disorder that ensued, the corruption of America's political leaders, and the insidious breed of terrorism that originated in the Middle East, eventually spreading across the Atlantic Ocean.

To escape these tumultuous times, the two couples turned to the movies, often a source of inspiration, humor, and hope. But soon even their quaint Village Theater fell victim to the ravages of time and profit margins. Consequently, their favorite cinema was boarded up. Its Art Deco design became dilapidated, and its once spectacular murals of the San Diego skyline vanished into faded, grimy walls and torn curtains. The Village Theater's long-time projectionist mused, "Some awfully sad things that happen just change you, I guess."

When does someone find the courage to face his or her

tragic past and haunting loneliness? *The Restoration* begins with a gentleman's agreement that binds Jack Adams and Greg Larson. But it is the women in their lives, Abby DiFranco and Raquel Mendez, who understand that by restoring the Village Theater to its original grandeur, they are actually restoring themselves—heart and soul. In *The Restoration,* it becomes clear that "you have to break down walls to reconfigure, remodel, and renovate…you have to leave the best memories and create new ones."